Copyright © 2020 Olivia Hayle

All rights reserved. No part of this publication may be distributed or transmitted without the prior consent of the publisher, except in case of brief quotations embodied in articles or reviews.

All characters and events depicted in this book are entirely fictitious. Any similarity to actual events or persons, living or dead, is purely coincidental.

The following story contains mature themes, strong language and explicit scenes, and is intended for mature readers.

Edited by Stephanie Parent
www.oliviahayle.com

BILLION *Dollar* ENEMY

"Always forgive your enemies;
nothing annoys them as much."

- Oscar Wilde

1

SKYE

My life changed that night in the hotel bar. Little did I know I had entered a different world, one of money and wealth—

No, it's not working. It's clichéd and predictable.

I put my phone down with a sigh and reach for my Old-Fashioned. The drink screams refinement, but as I take another sip, I have to hide a grimace from the strength. I'd ordered it to fit in, too afraid to tell the snooty bartender that I wanted something fruity and sugary. Glancing morosely down at the overpriced drink, it is a decision I regret.

I'd come here to research the novel I was working on. To understand the setting, the rich decor, the throbbing beat of unintelligible jazz music. It's an environment I'm unfamiliar with, and as the English Literature graduate I am, I know all about the importance of immersion. Where better than the Legacy sky bar atop one of the fanciest hotels in Seattle? Floor-to-ceiling windows open up to a skyline, glittering like the diamond necklace the woman next to me is wearing. It's a place to see and be seen.

The bar is only half-full, but every single person is interesting. I've watched a beautiful blonde woman in sky-high heels eat an entire bowl of olives while staring blankly at her much older partner.

The olives were consumed in boredom, I write in the note-taking app on my phone, *like so much of her life—experiences to seek experience itself, an escape from the tediousness of reality.*

Then I read it back and delete the whole pretentious thing.

Maybe this had been a mistake. I've been sitting at the bar for nearly an hour alone, and it's gone from empowering to embarrassing real fast. I smooth a hand over my tightly fitted black cocktail dress, an impulse buy over a year ago that had come in handy tonight. The novel I'm working on covers class differences and touches on the American Dream. Research is key, which is why I'd ventured to the Legacy on a Thursday evening, in search of inspiration.

But so far, I'd come to only two major conclusions: you have to be *really* rich to pay the steep drink prices here, and a nice bar is not immune to creeps.

The man to my left shoots me another leering glance. He's nursing what must be his umpteenth scotch, his glazed eyes telling.

Isn't it funny how creepy men exist everywhere, in each and every layer of our society? A suit and a six-figure income makes no difference.

I don't delete that. It's too true.

The man moves a few chairs over, a sly smile on his lips. "Good evening, gorgeous."

"Evening," I say.

"What brings you here tonight?"

"I just wanted a quiet drink," I say, a slight emphasis on the word *quiet*.

His gaze drops from my eyes to my modest cleavage. "Same here. Let's have a drink together."

"Thank you, but I'm here more for the ambiance than for conversation."

"Now, nobody comes to a bar to be alone." He leans in closer and I'm hit by too strong cologne and far too much whiskey on his breath. This man is keeping it together outwardly, but judging by his bloodshot eyes, he is well past simple tipsiness.

"Well, I did, so if you'll excuse me…"

I try to slip off of the barstool, but his hand on my bare shoulder holds me back. "Don't be so quick to leave."

"Please take your hand off me."

"I don't see—"

A deep voice drowns out whatever protest he was offering. "The lady made herself very clear. Take your hand off her."

The drunken man looks up at the stranger by my side—we both do—and shrinks back. "Ah. I apologize."

"You've had too much to drink," the tall stranger says. "I suggest you retire for the evening, but if not, at least leave the lady alone."

The drunken man's eyes narrow, but he nods. "Didn't know she was taken. Sorry." He ambles off, and I gaze in a sort of dazed horror at the stranger in front of me.

He leans casually against the bar, the top of his expensive shirt unbuttoned, the look in his eyes somehow bored and interested *at the same time.*

"Are you all right?"

That stupid phrase comes to mind, *a jawline that could cut glass*. It never made any sense to me, but seeing him now, it finally does.

His features are precise, a five-o'clock shadow darkening his skin. Thick brown hair falls in waves across his forehead—the kind any woman would want to run her hands through. Broad shoulders and an expensive suit. He looks ruggedly wealthy, as opposed to polished rich, which strikes me as an important distinction.

I should write this down, I think weakly. *Or take a picture.*

His eyes grow concerned. "Miss? Are you sure you're all right?"

"Yes," I say. "Thank you."

"It was my pleasure."

An unpleasant thought hits me, and dazzled as I am, it spills right out. "He left because he thought we were a couple, and not because I said I wasn't interested."

"That's probably true."

"I don't know how I feel about that."

"Bad, I imagine," the demigod says. "He should've respected your no."

"He should've."

"What are you drinking?"

I blink down at my glass. "An Old-Fashioned."

"And you hate it," he says, quirking an eyebrow.

"No, I don't."

"Yes, you do. I've been sitting right there"—he points to a secluded area of the bar—"and you've frowned every time you've taken a sip."

"You've been watching me?"

"I like to people-watch." He tilts his head to the side, giving me a better view of the sharp cut of his cheekbones. "As do you, I think. That's what you've been doing here tonight, right?"

"Yes," I say weakly.

"So? What have you concluded?"

"About our fellow patrons?"

"Yes." He waves the bartender over. "I'll have a whiskey neat. And the lady would like…"

I'm given a second chance, and I'm not going to hesitate this time. "A porn star martini," I say. "With lots and lots of passionfruit."

The stranger shoots me a crooked grin. "Interesting choice."

"The drink tastes good," I say defensively, "despite the name."

"Hmm. Or perhaps because of it?"

To my mortification, a blush rises to my cheeks. I clear my throat and nod to the other side of the bar. "I've been thinking about the couple in the back… They're clearly here for a special occasion. Have you figured out what it is?"

He glances over to the couple. They're middle-aged, nicely dressed, but look a little out of place. The man shoots a nervous glance at the waiter.

"A proposal?"

My handsome stranger shakes his head and leans in closer.

The smell of cologne, faint and masculine, hits me. "It's his first time having an affair, I bet."

"Wow," I say. "If I was reprimanded for ordering a porn star martini, what does this say about you?"

His crooked smile is back. "Noted. Let's go with a proposal instead. When in doubt, hope for a happy ending."

I crane my neck. "I hope we'll get to see it, if it happens."

He turns to me fully, eyes narrowing, like he's trying to figure me out. "Now, I've been watching you, but you're harder to crack. From the way you've been frowning at your phone, you must be having the world's most frustrating text conversation. Are you waiting for someone?"

I smile at that. "No, I've been trying to write."

"You're a writer?"

"Yes," I say. *Or I'm trying to be.* But this man—older than me and probably wildly successful—doesn't need to know that I'm a lowly bookstore clerk with nothing but a half-finished manuscript to my name.

"Would I have read anything you've written?"

I smile into my drink. "Probably not, no."

Not unless he'd been an avid reader of my college newspaper when I'd attended. I'd written some thrilling pieces about the cafeteria's lack of vegetarian options.

Our drinks arrive and he nods a thank-you to the bartender. His, imposing and worldly. Mine, fruity and orange. I take a sip.

"Better?"

"Much. How come you've been watching me?"

"I told you. I like to people-watch."

The bartender brings over the bill, and the handsome stranger settles it with a wave of his hand. "It's on me," he says.

The bartender gives a deep nod. "Of course, sir."

I frown. "I'd like to pay for my drink."

"Of course not," he says. "You didn't like the first one, so you shouldn't have to pay for your replacement. It's rule one of good service."

"Yes, but that's for the bar to fix, not you. You're not the bar owner now, are you?"

Something glitters dangerously in his eyes. "No, I'm not."

"Exactly." I cross my legs, conscious of how the fabric rides up, and try to still the quick beating of my heart. Talking to ridiculously good-looking men at expensive bars is wildly unfamiliar to me. *This will make for such good writing material!* "Don't think I haven't noticed what you're doing, by the way."

"Oh?" His crooked smile is back. "And what am I doing?"

"You came over to stop a man from buying me a drink, to then insist *you* buy me a drink instead."

He runs a hand over his jaw. "It's that obvious, is it?"

"Fairly, yes."

"Subtlety has never been my strong suit, I'm afraid."

I raise an eyebrow. "Is that the true reason you're here tonight? Not to people-watch, but to pick someone up?"

He laughs then, and the sound is magnificent, rich and strong and alluring. It rolls over my skin like a warm breeze. "Wow, you don't pull any punches, do you?"

"I'm right?"

"Not exactly, no. I certainly wasn't planning to. But the more you talk, the more I feel like going down that route, yes."

Nerves dance in my stomach, but I'm not going to let this chance slip out of my fingers. So I hold out my hand. "In that case, I think a proper introduction is in order. My name is Skye."

"Skye?"

"Yes," I say, and have to stop from shuddering in pleasure when his warm hand closes around mine. He shakes it once, twice, three times… "My mom was in her bohemian phase when she had me. The phase ended, but I remained."

His smile is back. "It's unique, just like a woman sitting at a bar alone to write."

"Well, said woman would like to know your name."

His hand slips from mine with the soft caress of skin against skin. "Cole," he says. "And since you didn't add your last name, I'll skip mine."

I take another sip of my drink. *Liquid courage, Skye.* "Isn't that part of this kind of encounter? Anonymity?"

His eyebrows rise again. "I wouldn't know. I don't usually talk to women at hotel bars."

"Somehow, I doubt that."

He takes a sip of his drink, the knuckle-length whiskey decreasing by a third. "I had my ideas about you, just from watching you. Judging by your comment, I'm guessing you have some about me."

"Assumptions?"

"Yes. You're a self-described people-watcher, after all. So lay it on me." He leans back, crossing his arms over his chest. Broad shoulders stretch out his suit.

This conversation feels like a tightrope, where I need to place my feet just right to avoid tipping too far to one side or the other. "Well, judging from the cut of your suit and the watch at your wrist, I'd assume you're well-off. If you're here alone, like me, and nursing a whiskey... well, I'd guess you were brooding."

"*Brooding?*"

"Yes," I say, ignoring the amusement in his eyes. "Some old wound is eating at you."

"I wonder what it can be."

"Oh, it can be anything at all. You're not divorced, are you? A veteran? An orphan?"

"No, no, and no. But good guesses. I'm enjoying this game. It's not often I get the chance to hear what a beautiful woman thinks when she sees me."

Beautiful? I take another sip of my drink to gather my scattered wits, and watch as the amusement in his eyes grows. Oh, he knows what an effect he has on me.

"Go on," he prompts.

"Well... the bartender seemed to know you. So I guess you're a regular here."

He tips his head. "It's not my first time at this hotel, you're right."

"You're here on a business trip?"

"Of a sort."

I run my fingers along the edge of the bar. "See? You like the vagueness, just like I like the anonymity."

If I told him my last name, he could google me to find out just how big of a writer I was, and the only thing that would show up was my most widely circulated article, *college student finds hair in the cafeteria food*. If I could clear that from the Google archives, I would.

"I suppose I do, yes."

"And judging from your… well." I wave a hand over his features. "I'm guessing you're very used to chatting to women in places like this."

"Mmm. I'm not sure what you're referring to, but what I said was true. I don't often talk to women in hotel bars. If they're all like you, I've clearly been missing out, though."

That's the second compliment in only a few minutes. I take another sip of my drink. Is this happening? Am I being picked up?

"You're staying here?"

"I am."

I make a humming sound, thoughts in my head running wild with possibilities. It's already late. If he asks… what should I do?

"You're thinking too far ahead. I can see it." Cole nods at my drink. "Have another sip. We're just having a conversation."

"Trying to get me drunk?"

"No, but I think you need a bit of liquid courage after having asked me that." Something glitters in his eyes again, and it steadies me. He's enjoying this. I'm enjoying this, more than I have in a long, long time. I've so rarely been wild. The good daughter, the good sister, the good employee. Occasionally, the good girlfriend.

"Maybe I do," I say in a low voice. I feel like I've donned a different role here tonight. Playing a woman who's pursued and used to it. A woman who flirts effortlessly with handsome men at bars. A woman who dares.

We talk until the bar is near closing about anything and

everything, except ourselves, respecting the boundaries of anonymity and vagueness we've established. We debate the best drink on the menu. Whether the blonde woman with the olives is genuinely enjoying herself or merely pretending to. I make a game out of guessing what he works with, and it quickly turns flirtatious. He diverts all my suggestions with a crooked smile, with the exception of astronaut. That one he dismisses with a laugh.

Guest after guest leaves, and we watch as the middle-aged couple filter out hand-in-hand.

"No proposal," I say.

"No betrayal, either."

"I'm still wondering if it's concerning that your mind went straight there."

He laughs again and holds up ringless fingers. "I'm not married, and I'm not in a relationship."

"Phew," I say. "What a relief."

"And neither are you." He nods to my hand, and I glance down myself, to find my fingers familiarly empty.

"No. No, very much not."

He raises an eyebrow. "Very much not? How interesting."

"Oh?"

"Most people are either married or they're not. It's not really measured on a sliding scale." His smile turns teasing. "I take it you've been single for a while, then?"

I bury my face in my hands, giving an exaggerated groan, and he laughs again. A warm hand lands on my bare arm. "Come now, that's nothing to be ashamed of."

I peek up at him through my lashes. "I didn't think so either, but if you can tell by just a glance..."

"Hmm. Well, maybe I saw what I wanted to see." His thumb moves over my bare skin, sending little electric currents over my flesh. I feel too hot, like I've been running or tanning, caught in the depth of his gaze. And all the while his thumb keeps moving, rough skin smoothing over my arm.

"I get that," I murmur.

"You do?"

"I wanted you to be single too."

His breath is a hot exhale. "Well, look at that. We're both conveniently free of any attachments."

"And we're both in this big, nice hotel, too."

"Fancy that," he says, smiling crookedly again. Can I do this?

I'm saved from answering by the approaching bartender. He gives Cole an apologetic glance. "I'm sorry, sir, but…"

"I understand." Cole nods at the bartender and stands, knocking back the last of his whiskey. "Thanks for letting us stay later."

"Not a problem."

I stand on shaky legs myself, noticing for the first time how much taller Cole is than myself. And the cut of his suit, the lean physique, the powerful shoulders… What have I gotten myself into?

"What do we do now?" I ask.

He shoots me an amused glance. "Well, that depends on you."

"On me?"

"Yes. I have a room here. If you want to continue our conversation, I'd be happy to. Besides, I have a minibar. I could always mix you another Old-Fashioned if you're feeling thirsty."

It's a straightforward offer disguised as a joke. I laugh, averting my gaze, and use the pause as a chance to think. Do I dare?

His next words seal it for me. "I'm not the asshole you talked to earlier. If you want to leave at any point, you're very welcome to. If you want us to talk the night away, you say so." His lips curl into a smile that makes heat pool in my stomach. "Although, I have to say, you don't seem to have a problem with speaking your mind."

"I don't." I reach for his hand and it wraps strongly around mine. His skin is dry and warm and pleasantly rough. "Lead the way."

2
SKYE

Four weeks later...

"It's like we're on death row," Karli says. "We're just sitting here, waiting for it to happen. Soon we'll even have a date for the demolition."

I climb down the little stepladder and glance over at where she's standing by the till. Her shoulders are slumped, eyes downcast, looking the way I feel inside. Bleak and hopeless.

"I still can't accept it," I say.

"I appreciate your optimism, Skye, I really do... but the letters have made it pretty clear."

"Miracles happen."

She smiles at me, but it's the fond smile of someone indulging a child. "Maybe."

I move the stepladder from the H-L section to M-P. This bookstore is my life. It's where I spent most of my afternoons after school growing up, and it's where I had my first job. First sorting books, at sixteen, before I graduated to handling payment.

And it's being torn down so someone can build a *hotel*?

As if Seattle needs another sky-high development for the rich and mighty. This bookstore has been here for *decades*.

Karli and I had both cried when we received the first letter. The bookstore was on land rented from the city, and they'd sold the entire lot to Porter Development.

Then I'd gotten angry. In the storage room, I'd printed the logo of Porter Development and pinned it to an old dartboard. When I first handed Karli a handful of darts, she'd looked at me like I was crazy.

"You did this?"

"Yes. It's what people do in movies, so there must be some truth to it. Go ahead and throw." She'd shaken her head at me, but we'd both had our turn, and in the end we'd felt a tiny bit better to see the slick logo skewered by darts.

It's midday, and the bookstore is empty, like it is most days. And most evenings, if I'm being painfully honest with myself.

Karli calls out again. "Did you shelve the delivery of new contemporary romances?"

"Yes!" I call back. "And I saw your choice for *'recommended by the bookstore'*!"

She laughs. "Did you see how the story started? The main characters have a super-steamy one-night stand…"

"I can't hear you!"

"Liar!"

I roll my eyes and keep shelving the fantasy tomes. Ever since I told Karli about the night at the hotel with Cole, she's been finding ways to bring it up.

You end early tonight, she'll quip. *Maybe you should go back to the Legacy?*

I shouldn't have told her about him—but then, I hadn't been able to stop thinking about him, and eventually all the details spilled out of me on their own accord.

His strong hands. The crooked smile. The banter, the back-and-forth, the laughter. He'd been far, far out of my league, but for one night, we'd been equals.

The entire night felt like it belonged to someone else, to a girl in one of those romance books, rather than *me*, Skye Holland.

Aspiring (read: failed) writer. Bookstore clerk (read: soon unemployed). Twenty-five years old, renting a too-small apartment, and without a date in months.

The Skye I'd been with Cole was someone else. She was witty and brave. She said things like *you're hitting on me* without batting an eye. And she said yes when attractive, mysterious men invited her to their hotel rooms.

My cheeks flame as I think about it, but I don't stop the train of thought. Thinking about that night has been all that's kept me going since we heard about the bookstore's fate.

We'd talked for an hour on his bed before he even touched me, and when he did, to smooth my hair back behind my ear, I'd shivered from anticipation and excitement.

"You're unexpected," he'd said darkly. "I had no idea someone like you would be here tonight."

I'd smiled. "Are you ever going to kiss me?"

And then he did, and showed me exactly why I shouldn't have been nervous about this. It was sex, but with a capital S, the kind I'd always wanted but never really had. There was no fumbling or awkwardness. He told me exactly what he wanted from me, and asked me what I liked in return.

And then he gave it to me.

I pick up another stack of fantasy epics and shelve them on autopilot, my mind stuck on the several orgasms he gave me. How? I'd been in a two-year relationship in college and I'd only climaxed *twice* with the guy. Cole had managed it in one night.

It had been deep, and hard, and animalistic, his body moving over mine like he needed me more than life itself. *Three times* we did it, his body relentless, before both of us passed out cold in his giant hotel bed.

"You're fantastic," he'd murmured after the last time, his arm slung casually over my naked waist. "Am I going to be in one of your books now?"

"Maybe," I'd said, reaching out to tentatively run a hand through his thick brown hair. "Although I'm not sure I'd do you justice."

But he was already asleep, and I had followed him soon thereafter.

Perfection—it had been *perfection*.

And since I'd been unable to keep my excitement to myself and told Karli, she brought it up all the time. Nearly every day for four weeks I'd heard about it. Why would today be any different?

"I just can't believe you didn't give him your number," she says over lunch. We should take them in shifts, but there are no customers, so we eat our sushi by the checkout counter together.

"It would have spoiled it."

"No, it could have been the start of something."

"A man like that? No, he wouldn't have been interested in me long term. I basically just nipped it in the bud." I snap my chopsticks together to illustrate, defending my decision for the hundred-millionth time. It doesn't matter that I still wonder, at night, if I'd made the right call.

"You don't *know* that."

"No, but it's a pretty good wager. What if I gave him my number and he never called?" I can't explain it to Karli, but I know it would have crushed me. To spend a night like that with someone and then have them reject you, to say *thanks, but no thanks.*

"Remind me what you wrote on the napkin again?"

"Karli, you don't need reminding. You *know.*"

She laughs, in that high-pitched way of hers, and pushes her glasses back into place. "Yes, but I want to hear you say it. I'm living vicariously through you here. Would you deny me that? After eight long years of friendship?"

I roll my eyes at her extra-ness, but I oblige. "I wrote, *Thanks for last night, stud.* God, even just saying that makes me cringe!"

She chuckles. "It's *such* a cliché."

"Yes, well, that's me, a walking, talking cliché."

"And you left while he was still asleep. I wonder what he thought. Having someone wham-bam-and-thank-you-ma'am him."

"He's probably used to it. Trust me, with skills like his, he has *a lot* of sex."

She hands me her spare wasabi, knowing I love it. "Maybe. Or you could've had the hottest friends-with-benefits situation ever known to man. Imagine how much inspiration that would give to your book."

I grin at her. "It would be more like a distraction."

"What's your word count now?"

"Thirty-two thousand. But I think I'll have to rewrite the entire chapter I just finished. My main character's actions just don't make sense to me."

Karli picks up another piece of sushi, eyes expectant. "Tell me why. Let's brainstorm it out."

I love that she's so invested in my stories, that she always has been, ever since I started working here. Our love of books is one of many things we share in common. With only ten years between us, Karli and I are more like friends than co-workers. She inherited the bookstore after Eleanor died, and employed me full-time after I finished college. For that alone, I owe her everything.

I jump into my description and she listens, interjecting with comments and jokes. It's in moments like this that it's easy to forget this bookstore—with its nooks and crannies and dusty attic, with the mismatched bookshelves and little reading lights —won't be here in two months' time.

My life changes again after lunch. In one moment I'm sorting through modern American poetry, minding my own business, and in the next I'm a quivering mess of nerves.

Five minutes before it all goes down, I pick up a small book of short poems. "You're a brilliant little book," I tell it. "But you're very difficult to sell."

It doesn't say anything back, and I put it down with a sigh. We have over fifty of these. There's so much inventory to go through before we have to close.

The bell by the door jingles. A customer!

"Skye, I'm in the back!" Karli calls.

"I'm on it!" I call, already putting back the poetry book.

I love customers. I love guessing what book they might like, what they're here for, judging by their clothes, their accent, their reading preferences. Sometimes I'm spot-on, and sometimes they surprise me—a dignified old lady who wants to buy the latest horror novel. A man in a suit asking for a self-help book on happiness. Those are my favorite customers, the ones who teach me about the perils of jumping to conclusions.

I weave through the fantasy section and cut between the recipe shelves. A man is standing with his back to me, looking at the titles on our *Bookstore Recommends* shelf. Karli and I curate it monthly, often over a bottle of wine, and we have a lot of fun doing it.

He's tall. That's my first impression, swiftly followed by the fact that he's in a suit. Thick brown hair curls at the nape of his neck, just over his shirt collar. My instinct says that he's here to buy a book for someone else. A birthday gift, or to celebrate an anniversary.

"Hello," I say. "Are you looking for anything in particular? I'd be happy to help."

He turns.

And the ground feels like it's giving out beneath me.

Four weeks might have passed, and we're in a well-lit store and not a swanky hotel bar, but he's no less striking in daylight. The chiseled jaw, the same five-o'clock shadow. Thick hair and piercing eyes that don't look the least bit surprised.

"Skye," he says.

I open my mouth but close it again, my mind running empty. The ability to speak has left me altogether. He waits, eyes imploring, probably wondering if I've become mute.

"Umm. Hi," I finally manage.

Brilliant. Four years of studying English Literature, and that's my winning take.

"Do you work here?"

Can I play it off as if I don't? I'm supposed to be an award-winning writer in his mind, who sits at expensive hotel bars and writes clichéd goodbyes on napkins.

"I didn't think I'd see you again," I say stupidly. I'm in the same jeans as always, wearing a T-shirt with "Between the Pages" blazoned on the front. In comparison, he looks magnificent, the cut of his suit highlighting the width of his shoulders.

His voice is dry. "No, clearly, since you snuck out during the night."

"Yes. Erm, no hard feelings?"

He shakes his head, but it's more in resignation than negation. "I knew you were too good to be true."

Standing there in my shabby outfit and my low ponytail, I know I'm definitely confirming that fact. "Yes. Sorry."

He starts to walk down the aisle, glancing at shelves as we pass them. I follow him in a daze. The night we spent together was magical, and this is mundane. It's my place of work. The two don't mix, and my brain is trying and failing to handle this surprise visit.

"Tell me about this bookstore. Between the Pages, right?"

Of all the things to ask… "Yes. We cover all the major genres and stock newer releases. We stock all the major classics, too. You'll find them all here, Proust, Austen, Machiavelli." I wet my lips. "Homer."

"Hmm." He plucks a book from a shelf, flipping it over to read the back. I recognize it—it's a decent thriller, but I could recommend a better one. "So," he says. "What was your game, that night at the bar?"

"My game?"

He slides the book back into place. "Did you need a night like that for inspiration? To clear up some writer's block?"

My heart is firing at full speed in my chest. "You're asking if you were research?"

He smiles, a crooked thing that shows me just how devastatingly handsome he is. "If I was, I certainly don't mind. But I think I made that pretty clear at the time."

A flush creeps up my cheeks. Oh, he had. "You were unexpected."

"Likewise. And I have to say, I've never been referred to as a stud before."

My flush darkens. "Oh, that was… it seemed appropriate at the moment."

He nods. "But not now?"

"I don't… You're impossible."

His grin is back. "So I've been told."

I glance from him to the bookcase behind him, my suspicions returning. "Why are you here?"

"I came to buy a book."

"Really?"

"Yes. I am, in fact, literate."

I lean against the shelf and try to ignore the fact that he's seen me naked, that I know the groan he makes when he loses himself. "Well, in that case, I'm here to help. What are you looking for?"

He smiles knowingly, aware of the bluff I'm trying to call. "I want something that'll make my heart race."

"Horror?"

"No," he says. "Something else."

I clear my throat. "A thriller, perhaps? I have one I'm sure you'll love."

He sweeps out his arm. "After you, Skye."

He follows me to the other side of the store, footsteps echoing mine. He might have asked for a book that would set his heart aflame, but mine's the one that's racing.

"It should be here…" I murmur, running my finger along the length of spines until I find the one I need.

I hold it up to him.

His gaze flickers from the cover to me, wide and aware. Then he chuckles softly. "Well, well," he says, reaching out to take it from me.

"It's a thriller," I say.

"I can see that." His eyes scan the back, and I know what he's finding there. A description of a billionaire hero running rampant. Murders in penthouses, secrets hidden beneath silk and money, all to conceal a drug ring."

"Interesting," he says, voice thick with amusement. "Recommended to me, you say?"

"Well," I say, wondering if I took the joke too far, "it is a genuinely good book as well."

He tucks the book under his arm and looks around, eyes coasting across shelves of book, the little old armchair in the corner. "This is a nice place. Has a lot of old-world charm."

"I think so too," I say. "But it's closing."

"Oh?"

"Yes. A development firm is planning to build yet another hotel here, and the city agreed. We have two months to close shop."

"A hotel?"

"Yes, like the one we met in, I guess. The company who's developing it has that air, you know?"

"What air?"

"A hotel bar kind of air." My hands are gesturing, trying to paint a picture. It's hard to describe a feeling. "All swanky hotel music and beige furniture. Probably run by some old rich guy who has no need at all for more money, or more hotels, or more influence. So this place is going, lost forever to posterity." My tone is light, but the idea makes my throat clench. For years, this store was my solace, and Karli's grandmother—the original owner—was a light in the dark.

Cole's eyes are inscrutable. "That sounds complicated."

"Pretty straightforward actually. Out with the old and in with the new." I turn away from him before I make a complete fool of myself by tearing up. "Would you like your book gift-wrapped?"

"No."

"It's for you?"

He smiles at my surprise. "I wasn't joking earlier, you know. I *am* literate."

"I'm glad our school system didn't fail you. But you don't

strike me as... ah."

"The reading type?"

A blush creeps up my neck. "Well... yes, I suppose. I just wouldn't think you have a lot of free time on your hands."

"I don't. But sometimes you have to make time, especially for the things that matter."

It's the first serious thing he's said to me today, and I find myself nodding, unable to think of another witty comeback. What does he do for a living? He never mentioned that night at the hotel, and I never asked. We'd promised each other anonymity. "You're right," I say, my eyes dancing over his suit, his tie, the cuff links.

His voice is amused. "Are you trying to use your people-reading skills on me again?"

"It's a force of habit."

"Likewise," he says, "although I think I got you all wrong that first night."

"Oh?" My heart stutters in my chest at those final words. *First night.*

He leans against a bookshelf, too big for this store, for me, for this world. "Oh yes. I thought you did that sort of thing all the time."

"That sort of thing?"

"Hot sex with a complete stranger," he says. "Don't pretend to have forgotten that part."

My cheeks are on fire, but I force myself to keep his gaze. *Please, Karli, stay in the storage room.*

"I haven't forgotten," I say. "It would be difficult to, I admit."

"You enjoyed yourself?"

Okay, now I have to break eye contact. "You know I did."

"Good." His eyes darken. "After I saw that offensive note you left me on the dresser, I wondered if I had underperformed."

The idea that he could think what he did to me an *underperformance* feels ridiculous. There's nothing remotely vulnerable in his voice, nor his face, his jaw set confidently. I narrow my eyes at him.

"You know, fishing for praise is very unbecoming."

He laughs, and as he does, I catch a hint of a dimple in his left cheek. I hadn't seen that in the darkness when we first met.

"All right. You might be less confident than you pretended that night in the hotel bar, but you're just as quick to take me to task."

"You think it was a pretense?"

He shakes his head at me, still smiling. "I think you wanted to try on a different woman's clothing for the night. I'm glad I was available for your fantasy."

My throat feels desert-dry. "Me too," I say weakly. "And regarding the note…"

This is my chance. My chance to change things, to make amends, to *maybe* get another shot at seeing him. The things he could do… I haven't stopped thinking about him for weeks.

There's a smile on his lips. "Yes?"

"Maybe I was too quick in writing it."

"Mmm. Maybe you were." He ambles over to the counter, pushing the book and a twenty lazily over to the other side. "And if you'd had more time, what would you have added?"

Damn it, he's going to make me say it. "A few digits, perhaps."

"Ten, I hope."

"Yes," I breathe.

"Good." He leans in over the counter, his face so close to mine, a ghost of his hot breath against my skin. My body tenses, remembering his scent, the nearness, how his lips feel on mine. "I want you to remember that."

I blink my eyes open to see him smiling crookedly, standing straight once more. "What do you mean?"

"You'll find out." He steps back, toward the door, his book in hand. "And, Skye?"

"Yes?"

"I would have called you. I want you to remember that, too."

And then he's gone, as swiftly as he came, the handsome suit-clad stranger.

3

SKYE

"Tell me again where you guys talked," Karli demands.

I laugh. "All right, well, he came in through the front door. And then he walked down this aisle... before turning here. We stopped at this section for a bit—he took out *The Search for Elle*—and then we went to the counter, where he paid. Detailed enough?"

"Yes." She gives a dramatic sigh. "I can't *believe* I missed the chance to see Mystery Man."

"Bad luck," I say, though I'm secretly glad she was in the storage room, given our conversation.

"And I can't even search him, because you still don't know his last name. Honestly, Skye, do you know anything about getting a date?"

I hop up on the stool behind the counter. "You've been happily married to John for eleven years. The landscape has changed. The dating scene is a mess now."

She gives me a pointed look. "Exchanging last names is still customary. I don't need to keep up with the trends to know *that*."

"I don't know if I'll see him again. And look at this—he's already distracted us from our work! Again!" I pick up my pen and continue filling in the words on the little note. *Closing in two* months. *Twenty percent off your purchase if you buy three books or more!*

"Yes," Karli says dryly. "God forbid you're distracted while writing."

"My penmanship could be what saves us."

"God help us all if that's what it takes," she says, but her voice is amused. Since we got the news about demolition, Karli has handled it a lot better than me, despite the bookshop being hers. Growing up, I know it had been as much her salvation as it had been mine. But Karli has a husband now, two kids, and an interest in baking she dreams of one day transforming into a business.

"I got an email today," she says. "And before you go ballistic—don't look at me like that, I know you will, Skye—I didn't tell you right away because I wanted to think it through."

I put down my black sharpie. "What did it say?"

"It was from Porter Development. They've requested a meeting directly with me."

"*A meeting?*"

"Yes." She pushes her glasses back. "I don't know what they want. In the email, they only said they wanted to discuss 'our mutual future.'"

"Our *mutual* future? But ours is being sacrificed for theirs."

"It's odd." Karli leans against the register, a furrow in her brow. "I wanted to ask if you'll come with me to the meeting."

"Of course I will, if you'll have me. You don't even have to ask."

Her smile turns wry. "But we'll have to be civil."

I know she's saying we, but what she's really saying is that *I* have to be civil. "I will be on my very best behavior, I promise."

"Good. Now, these boxes won't unpack themselves. Why don't we get this done, and you can tell me what you did this past weekend. Did you babysit Timmy again? Eat dinner with Isla? Go out to a hotel bar and meet a handsome stranger? Tell me anything that's not related to diapers or books, please. I need to live vicariously through you."

I smile at her, my co-worker in name but so much more than that, and dive straight into the most entertaining re-telling of my boring weekend that I can manage.

I gloss over the fact that I spent nearly half a day on the internet, sorting through the search results of *Cole* and *Seattle*. He was like a needle in a haystack.

———

The day of the meeting with Porter Development, I put on my most professional blouse and a pencil skirt, hidden in the back of my closet. When I arrive at Between the Pages, Karli's dressed in a mirrored version.

She snorts. "Our armor, huh?"

"Anything to look like we know how to run a business." I reach for the *closed* sign and flip it in the window. It's just the two of us, and no one to watch the shop while we're out. Sadly, there's never been enough money to hire anyone else. Even sadder is my sneaky suspicion that we won't miss a single customer for the two hours or so we'll be gone. Business hasn't exactly been booming lately.

Karli reaches for the books behind the register. I know what they contain—all our financial information, our numbers, our nonexistent profit margin. She shoves it into her bag and shoots me a smile that's braver than I feel.

"Well, then. We're heading into the belly of the whale, aren't we?"

"We sure are," I say. "But we're a force to be reckoned with, too. I promised I would be civil—but I'll fight, Karli."

Her smile goes from brave to determined. "Why do you think I asked you to join?"

We drive in silence through Seattle, two-story buildings disappearing behind us in favor of brutal skyscrapers and harsh angles. Men in suits on the streets, women in heels, quaint coffee shops replaced by the big chains. Karli pulls into a parking garage close to Porter Development, at least according to the

GPS on my phone, but we still have to hurry the two-block walk.

Porter Development is located inside a massive building—tall, imposing, all glass. Someone pushes past us with an irritated sigh as we stand mid-sidewalk and stare.

"Well," Karli says faintly, "it's not so much a whale as a..."

"A giant monument to corporate greed?"

"Yes. That."

I thread my arm under hers and we head into the lobby. "We can do this. You're a business owner, Karli. And small business owners are the backbone of the American economy."

"Right."

"They can't intimidate us. We spend all our days surrounded by books! We're infinitely better than whatever lawyer or developer we're meeting with."

"Bryan Hoffman," she says. "And they spend their days surrounded by stacks of money. But you're right."

"Yes. Let's kick some ass."

"Civilly," she says with a smile.

"Of course. It'll be the politest of ass-kickings."

We sign in with the lobbyist, and not five minutes later we're escorted through security gates and a badge-required elevator.

Karli and I stand side-by-side as the elevator shoots up towards its fateful destination. An awful tune starts to play, and I make a show of shaking my head at Karli in disapproval behind the back of our escort. The elevator music is *terrible*.

She has to bite her lip to stop from chuckling. For a moment, at least, I've been silly enough to take her mind off our impending doom.

We're shown into an all-white meeting room. Light floods through the floor-to-ceiling windows, a view of the opposite skyscraper too close for comfort.

"Mr. Hoffman will be with you soon," the chirpy assistant tells us. "Would you like something to drink? A cup of tea or coffee?"

"Some water, please."

"Coming right up!"

He closes the glass door behind him and Karli and I are left in tense, expectant silence. "Well," she says. "At least they gave us a good tour of the building. Do you think the new hotel will look like this?"

I tap my pen against the notebook in agitation. "I hope not. Our area doesn't need this kind of showboating."

Voices sound in the corridor, steps approaching.

"Remember," she murmurs. "Be civil."

I nod. That's the third reminder, and I don't know if I should be offended that she thinks I can't control myself or grateful that she knows I care so deeply about the bookshop.

The door opens and a middle-aged man steps through, a small mustache on his upper lip. "Hello, ladies. I hope we didn't keep you waiting too long. I'm Bryan." Behind him steps a woman in heels, a notepad clutched at her side. "This is Tyra, our in-house lawyer."

"A pleasure," she says, shaking both of our hands.

A man appears in the doorway behind her and the world drops out from beneath my feet. Tall. Brown hair. Familiar eyes, now fixed on me, relentless and unyielding.

"Cole Porter, owner and CEO of Porter Development," Bryan says. "Now we're a full house."

My mouth is open. I don't know how to close it—or what to say. For the second time in a week, I've lost my tongue.

Cole reaches out and shakes Karli's hand. "Thank you for taking the time to meet with me, Mrs. Stiller."

"Thank you for inviting us," Karli says, pleasant and professional. Of course, the man in front of her is a stranger. "I'll admit that I'm more than a little curious as to the reason behind this meeting."

"Fully understandable. And this is your co-worker?" He turns to me, extending a large hand. I stare from it to him before reaching out to shake it in a daze. His skin is warm and dry and my traitorous body responds by shivering. "Cole."

"Skye," I say faintly. "I work with Karli in the bookstore."

"Of course." Amusement is faint in his eyes, but it's there. "Glad you could join us today."

Asshole.

The word rings clear as a bell in my head. Rich, arrogant, prick of a man. He'd known, when he was in the bookstore. He'd known who I was, what the place was, that he was going to tear it down.

And he'd kept all of that to himself.

"Well, shall we?" Bryan's voice is brisk, all business, a world away from the ire rising up through me. "As I'm sure we're all aware, Between the Pages will be closing on the fourteenth, two months from now. That's exactly two weeks before our building project goes into development. Now, the legal aspect is all settled. The land has been purchased and the city has approved the plans."

Something clenches inside me to hear the bookstore's fate discussed so cavalierly. A business deal like any other, just dollars and cents, but *it isn't,* because it's my life it concerns.

I glare at Cole across the table. It's a professional glare—one might even call it civil—but I know he understands what I'm trying to say. It's an accusation.

He'd known.

And worse than that is the knowledge that I'd slept with my worst enemy. The magical night in his hotel room, the one that occupied an almost mythical status in my mind, is now tainted.

Karli clears her throat. "I know all this already, Mr. Hoffman," she says dryly. "I'll admit that I've thought of little else since I received the news. It's not a business deal to me; it's the bookstore's death sentence."

Bryan has the tact to look contrite. *Go Karli!* "I'm sure. And we, uhh, that is, we're sorry for putting you in that position."

Cole leans forward, bracing his arms on the table and fixing his gaze on Karli. "Porter Development has never sought to push out small business owners or destroy people's livelihoods. That is not how this business operates, and I consistently try my best to avoid it. In this case, it proved unavoidable. I'm personally sorry about that, Mrs. Stiller."

Karli gives a stiff nod, staring at him. So am I. The hotel we'd met in must have been his. The hotel bar had been his. How had I missed just how much *power* he exuded? It's sucking all the air out of this room.

Karli doesn't back down, though her voice softens. "Thank you, sir. It's nice to hear, but all the good intentions in the world won't change the facts."

I have to resist the triumphant smile I want to send his way.

"Right you are," Cole says. "That's why we're proposing a compensation scheme. Tyra?"

The blonde opens her binder and pushes another binder across the table at us. "As the owner, Mrs. Stiller, we'll compensate you for the loss of income for six solid months after the bookstore closes. If you'd like to continue your business elsewhere, our realty team is at your disposal for finding a different locale. The agency fee is waived for life."

Karli reaches out to take a sip of her water, and I can tell it's to buy herself some time. These offers are generous—and entirely unexpected.

Cole's handsome features are straight-laced, impassive, professional. He's certainly managing to be civil. If the fact that I'm here bothers him, he's not letting on. Maybe he's used to having women stare at him with murder in their eyes.

"And I don't have to provide anything in return?" Karli asks, and I want to tell her no, that she's already giving up her business so they can build their multi-million-dollar project.

Tyra seems to agree, because she shakes her head. "No. This is part of Porter Development's corporate policy to all of those negatively affected by our developments."

Cole runs a hand over his square jaw. "As I understand it, the bookstore has been operating for decades. I'm sorry that it must come to an end."

The bastard. I was the one who told him that—*I did*. He'd let me stand there and flirt with him about our one-night stand, all the while knowing he was responsible for my soon-to-be unemployed state.

I see red. "Must it, though?"

Four heads turn to me, all wearing various expressions of incredulity.

"*Skye,*" Karli whispers, her face letting me know that my tone was neither civil nor professional.

I cross my arms over my chest and ignore her, my eyes locked on Cole. He leans back in his chair, his gaze daring me to continue. "Miss Holland?"

"The bookstore is old, as you pointed out yourself. We have a small but loyal customer base. It has... old-world charm." I use his own description and watch in satisfaction as his eyes narrow. "It could be incorporated into your hotel."

Bryan lets out a small chuckle. "I'm sorry, miss, but that's not possible. The plans for the new hotel are already drawn. We have apologized, but we—"

Cole raises a hand to cut him off. "We've looked over your financials," he says with infuriating calmness. "The bookstore is not profitable, Miss Holland. It hasn't been for a long while."

I can feel a flush rising in my cheeks. It's been a hard few months, that's true. "It brings in enough," I say. "It's been a staple of the community for decades. Give us these two months to turn things around."

Karli is staring at me, her horror evident in my peripheral view, but I can't look away from Cole. He's the only one I need to convince. Not Bryan, not Tyra, not the corporate entity we're sitting in. I just need him to agree to this.

Cole's eyes narrow. "You're pushing it," he says, and he's not just referencing the bookstore.

I spread my hands wide and try to soften my voice. "Look, if we're not financially sound in two months' time, feel free to tear the store down. You've run the numbers, and you're the captain of industry here. I'm sure you're right. But... on the off chance that we're right, we get to stay, incorporated into your new building."

Bryan is shaking his head at me, like he can't believe what I'm saying. Karli is a statue next to me. But Cole... he's staring at me with something unfathomable in his eyes, a challenge that reminds me of the night we'd spent together. *Do you like it when I touch you like this?*

"You want to make a bet, Skye? Is that it?"

"Yes." My mouth is dry. "What do you have to lose? Either you get a profitable new business as part of your new hotel, or your development goes ahead exactly as planned."

His lips twitch at the way I'd said *hotel*. Maybe I'd emphasized it a little bit too much. And in his eyes, there's depth and pride and arrogance. And something else, something buried deep. Dark amusement.

Bryan is the one who finally speaks. "Sir, this is highly unusual."

"It is. But then again, as Miss Holland and Mrs. Stiller have reminded us, their bookstore is as well." Cole's lips finally give, stretching into a smile just shy of being predatory. In the hotel bar we'd been on equal footing, two strangers meeting. Here, in the company he owns—the company seeking to ruin my life—he's legions above me. "We accept, Miss Holland. If you can prove that your bookstore is profitable in two months' time, we will reconsider."

"*Reconsider?*" Adrenaline is pumping through my veins. "I want your word."

He arches an eyebrow. "You want me to promise?"

"Yes."

His eyes flicker. "You have it. Is this acceptable to you as well, Mrs. Stiller?"

Karli gives a quick nod. "Yes. Yes, it is."

"Then I consider the matter settled." He shoots Bryan and Tyra a professional nod. "Draw up the appropriate paperwork and have it sent to Mrs. Stiller by the end of business tomorrow. Will that be sufficient?" The question is to Karli, but his body is angled towards me.

God. What have I done?

"It is."

"Then this meeting is concluded. I'll escort you out."

Cole stands, ignoring the looks of incredulity both of his employees shoot him. Karli and I pick up our papers and follow him in silence, down the hall, into the elevators. He strides easily through the office, a king in his kingdom, ignoring the daggers I stare into him. He doesn't seem remotely impacted, but I persist, hoping he might miraculously buckle under the pressure.

Cole might have agreed to my challenge, but I knew better than to think he'd honor it. Porter Development doesn't think we have a chance in hell of succeeding. He's gone from being my fun one-night stand, the perfect sexual memory, into a mistake. Worse than a mistake—an enemy.

"Well, ladies," he says, holding the elevator door open for us. "That was an interesting meeting."

Karli hums in agreement. "I appreciate you giving us this opportunity."

His eyes slide to mine, but I refuse to meet them. The anger in me is rising, and seeing the smugness on his handsome features would send it blasting. "Well," he says. "You two made a very convincing argument."

Karli's laughter is half embarrassment, half pride. "Yes. Skye and I practically spent our youths in that place."

"I understand."

Does he? Somehow I doubt it. *Asshole*, I think again, hopefully loud enough to send it across the airwaves in his direction.

Cole walks us through the lobby. He's more than a head taller than us both, his strides long and sure. The need to tell him off is burning under my skin, warring with embarrassment and anger, but there's no way I can admit to Karli that the one-night-stand guy I've told her so much about is *Cole damn Porter*. It already feels like a betrayal.

"Well, ladies," he says, voice deep and untroubled. "This is where I leave you."

I can't avoid his gaze any longer. It's heavy with meaning, referencing the things left unsaid between us—no doubt he can see the lashing waiting on the tip of my tongue. *I know you're angry*, his gaze says.

I meet it head-on. He might be used to intimidating employees, developers, servers. Not me, though. *For good reason,* my gaze replies. *Asshole.*

"Thank you for today." Karli shakes his hand, the picture of manners, and I'm forced to do the same.

His fingers curl around mine softly.

I squeeze his back as hard as I can.

"Yes," I say. "*Thank* you."

Cole doesn't flinch, though his hand has to be hurting. The only thing in his eyes is amusement. "It was my pleasure, Miss Holland."

4
COLE

"You're falling behind."

I scowl at Nick and reach for the towel. "I'll get you in the next set."

He rests his tennis racquet against the low bench and shoots me a wolfish grin. "That's what you said last time. Hell, man, this is *your* game."

"Thanks for reminding me." I wipe the sweat off my brow. Once a week, for as long as I can remember, Nick and I've played tennis in the mornings. And I haven't lost this badly in about as long.

"Your head is elsewhere."

I don't protest, because frankly, he's right. Focusing has been difficult since yesterday, when Skye Holland walked into my office and negotiated her way into a bet I should never have agreed to.

"It might be, yeah."

Nick frowns. "Business? The development on Fourth Street has been giving you a lot of shit, right?"

"It has, yeah, but that's not it. I've somehow managed to mix business and pleasure. *Again*."

Nick, who remembers the first time I did that, winces. "Ouch."

"Yeah."

He lobbies a tennis ball at me and I catch it easily, plucking it out of the air. "Does she work for you?"

"Not exactly. I'm planning to demolish the business she works in."

For a moment, Nick just stares at me, before he throws his head back and laughs. "You're not serious."

"Deadly," I say, tossing the ball back at him.

"Fucking hell." He lobbies it hard at my chest but I catch it easily, my skin smarting. "How can she stand to be in the same room as you?"

"At the moment, I doubt she can. We slept together weeks ago, before I knew who she was."

Nick runs a hand through his hair. "How'd you meet?"

"At Legacy."

"*You* had a one-night stand?"

I turn my back on him and fit my tennis racquet into the sleeve. My centrally located hotel has an indoor tennis court, conveniently close to work. Nick and I have a standing reservation.

"Yes," I say. I can practically hear what Nick isn't saying, the taunts we've both grown out of. Had this been five years ago, he would have flayed me verbally, and I would have given as good as I got. "And it was fucking *fantastic*. Best sex I've had in years. I was rather hoping to repeat it, but then… well."

"You became the devil," he says. I shoot him an evil look, and he grins again. "In her eyes, I mean."

"Yes, and with it, any hope of a repeat."

"If you want me to tell you to not tear down her building, I won't." His smile is gone now. "Business and pleasure don't mix."

"I know that," I say. Mixing them in the past had been the most expensive mistake I'd ever made.

"And if your team has run the numbers, drawn up the contracts, started planning… don't stop that. You bring business to Seattle. It's what you've done for years." He shrugs. "There are more women in the city."

I nod, thinking to myself that for so long, none of them had appealed to me, not until Skye.

Nick's advice is solid. But as I stand in the shower and warm water cascades around me, memories of her find me again. Her warm body against mine. How she'd tasted. The way she had been entirely herself—not afraid to tease me, to take the lead, but also oddly shy, like she was unsure of how I'd react. She'd whispered things in the dark, things I'm sure she regrets now, when my head had been between her thighs.

I've never come when a man did that before.

It hadn't been a lie, I'm sure of that, and I feel just the same as I did then, overcome with the desire to show her more of what I could do. To rise above her and fill her and make her come again and again.

I close my eyes against the tiles. She'd been seething yesterday. I could see it in her eyes. *Why didn't you tell me?*

And beneath it, a very different kind of anger. She'd had her impulsive one-night stand with a handsome stranger—a part I'd played willingly—and then I'd turned out to be the one person she despised more than any other.

Yeah. She was right to be fucking furious with me.

But I also know that what happened between us in that hotel bed hadn't just been a one-off or a fluke, either. Sex that good never is.

I'm going to have to convince her of that.

The car pulls up smoothly outside the little bookstore that evening.

"Should I wait here for you, sir?"

I straighten the collar of my jacket. "No. I'll call you when I'm done."

Charles doesn't comment. He's been with me for years, and

despite knowing the ins and outs of my life, he's never once crossed the line. Business and friendship, never mixing. The way it should be.

The way I'm ignoring at the moment.

It's a complete gamble that she's still here—I'll just as likely take Karli Stiller by surprise instead.

I stop outside the bookstore. Between the Pages has a certain charm, that's true, but most of it comes from being so clearly loved. The window displays are crafted with care, the sign by the door hand-painted.

The little bell announces my arrival gayly as I step inside. It might as well be a war drum, because the moment she sees me, there'll be hell to pay.

And I can't wait.

"I'll be right with you!" It's her voice, somewhere from the back. No Karli behind the register. *Perfect.* I pick up a book by the counter as I wait. Flipping it over, I see it's a romance novel, two people torn apart over and over again by life and fate. I put it down with a snort. If they're that good at miscommunication, they're clearly not soul mates.

Skye freezes in her tracks when she sees me. Her brown hair is in a ponytail, exposing her slim neck, a golden pendent resting at her throat.

"What are you doing here?"

"I need another book."

Her eyes narrow. "Bullshit."

"How would you know? Maybe I've already finished the one I bought last week."

"*Sure* you have." She puts her hands on her hips, a beautiful flush creeping up on her cheeks. The same thing happened in the meeting yesterday, but she hadn't backed down, not even when my employees tried to silence her. It's another piece of her puzzle. She's brave.

"You should have told me last week," she says. "Who you were."

"And interrupted our banter? Never." I lean in closer,

remembering the shyness she'd displayed when I'd come into the store last week. "You would have never told me all the things I wanted to know if I had."

Her color rises. "It wasn't fair. You let me talk about... *that*, and all the while you *knew* that I'd feel differently as soon as I found out. I even called you an asshole to your face!"

I have to stop myself from smiling. "You did. I haven't been called that in a long time. It was novel."

"I'm *so* happy to provide you with some entertainment."

"You're misremembering things," I point out. "You made it very clear that *I* was your entertainment that night, not the other way around."

Her brow furrows. "That's not fair."

"No? I kept the note you left me. Do you want me to find it? I think it's in my wallet, actually."

"No, thank you, and I actually don't think it's something we should talk about again. It's unprofessional." She takes a deep breath, crossing her arms over her chest, her slim waist and the curve of her breasts accentuated. Being this close to her—knowing what her body feels like against mine—and not being able to reach out is like the sweetest form of torture.

"You're right. We're now in a professional arrangement, thanks to you."

"You agreed."

"So I did." I deliberately look away from her, putting on my most contemptuous face, and sweep my gaze across the store. "Making this profitable is going to be quite a task."

"You don't think we'll succeed? People don't read as much these days, it's a dying industry, yada yada yada. I've heard it all before. But you know what? You'll thank me in the end."

"I will?"

"Yes, when you get a perfectly run, highly profitable bookstore to add to your development."

I pick up a book from the self-help section. *How to Face Your Demons*. "I'm not sure how I'd manage to incorporate a bookstore into the lobby of a hotel."

"You'd break your word?"

I look up at the clear fury in her voice. "No. If you manage it in two months, we'll manage the rest. Somehow."

She hums, like she's not convinced, but it's a start. I put the book back. "How are you planning on doing it?"

"Making the store profitable?"

"Yes."

She crosses her arms. She's wearing a T-shirt with the bookstore logo printed on it. *Between the Pages* is written right across her chest. "Why do you want to know? So you can sabotage us?"

"You are terribly paranoid."

Something in her shoulders loosens. "Maybe. But this bookstore is too important, and you're too annoying. I have to be on my guard."

My smile is back. "I'm annoying? That's not what I remember. I distinctly remember being called amazing. Great. Or, my personal favorite, the time you whispered that I was *the biggest—*"

"God, Cole!" She reaches over and hits my shoulder. For such a small woman, she's strong. "What part of let's-never-speak-of-it-again didn't you understand?"

"I didn't agree to that."

"You have to. What were you thinking, anyway? What if Karli was here?"

I look back at her calmly. "Then I'd be here to see the place in person."

Skye is looking at me like she has absolutely no idea what to do with me. If it wasn't for the fact that I feel the exact same way regarding her, I would have found it funny.

"That hotel bar was yours. You own it."

"I own that hotel, yes."

"The hotel room. Was it yours?"

I put my hands in my pockets. "Technically, they're all mine."

"You weren't there on business."

"I was, I just wasn't from out of town. That was your assumption."

"Why were you there?"

"I was waiting for someone at the Legacy. Someone who works in the building, but who was late."

"You blew them off?"

"Can you blame me? A gorgeous brunette by the bar kept me pretty occupied."

She fiddles with the hem of her T-shirt, as if she feels underdressed. Maybe I should have changed out of my suit. "You can quit with the compliments now. I've already climbed into bed with you once, and it's not going to happen again."

There's a pang of disappointment, but I don't let it show. I take a step closer. "Are you sure that's a promise you're willing to make?"

"Yes," Skye says, but her voice is a bit breathless. It's so quiet in the bookstore that I could hear a pin drop—not a customer, not background music, nothing.

"Are you here alone in the evenings?"

She puts a hand to her forehead, taking a step back. "Most of the time, yes."

I look at the flimsy front door, the cash register sitting right by the entrance. It doesn't seem like a particularly safe situation. Skye sees my gaze and raises her hackles immediately. "We have a panic button. There's never been any incidents, and I don't expect they'll start now."

"Mhm."

"That is *not* a strike against the bookshop." She puts her finger up, like she's scolding me, but the look in her eyes could kill. "I won't let you come here and snoop around and try to find reasons to shut us down. We made a bargain."

"I don't intend to—"

"Skye? I found another one!"

Her head snaps to the side, to the child's voice echoing from the back of the store. Then she looks back at me. Indecision is clear in her gaze.

"Look!" A boy wanders up through one of the aisles, holding

a newspaper. He can't be more than ten, dark brown hair, round glasses perched on his nose.

He stops when he sees me. "Oh. I'm sorry, I didn't mean to interrupt." Judging by the way his cheeks color, they have to be family.

"You're not interrupting, Timmy. What did you find?"

He sidles up to Skye, opening the newspaper while shooting me a furtive glance. He points at something—an article for a school project?—but I'm not listening.

Skye has a son?

I look at her again. The smooth skin, her thick hair, the natural curve to her lips, the pointy chin. She can't be much older than twenty-five. A son this age?

The boy is openly staring at me now. "Hello," I say, dazed from the realization. "I'm Cole."

"Timmy. It's nice to meet you."

Good manners on the kid, I'll give him that. Skye puts a hand on his shoulder. "Cole isn't a customer. He's... an acquaintance."

Her dry tone makes me want to smile. "That's right," I say. "Who are you?"

He looks at me blankly before turning to Skye. She smiles at him, a soft, genuine smile, nothing sardonic or mocking in it. "Timmy's my nephew. I think Cole was wondering if I was your mom there, buddy."

The kid laughs, like that's ridiculous. "She's *not*."

"Timmy is here in the evenings sometimes, when my sister has to work late. But I think—" Skye is interrupted by the shrill sound of the bookstore's phone, ringing behind the register. She shoots me a look that says *behave!* and heads off to answer it.

The kid is shooting me glances above his newspaper. I clear my throat. "What's your school project about?"

"We have to find three articles that are all about the same topic and compare them."

I nod at the newspaper in his hands. "What have you chosen?"

He turns it around and holds it up high so I can see. "The Mariners got a new coach."

"So they did." I run a hand over my jaw and skim the article. "Probably a mistake, if you ask me, but I look forward to seeing his style."

Timmy's face lights up. "You're a Mariners fan?"

"Course I am, kid. You are too?"

"Yeees." He draws out the syllables, eyes widening dramatically. "I saw one of their games a few years back. Skye took me."

A few years back? I grin at the kid. "How old are you?"

"Nine. Well, I'll be nine in a few months."

I glance over at Skye. She'll hate what I'm about to say next, but the eagerness in his tone makes it impossible. "I see a lot of their games."

"You do?"

"Yeah. Most of their home games, in fact." Correction: *all*. It's one of the things I do with Nick and Ethan, and sometimes with my sister. I have a VIP season pass. One of the many benefits that comes with money; you can invest in your passions.

Timmy's eyes are glowing. "Who's your favorite player?"

I pretend to deliberate. "I don't know. I have so many. Why don't you tell me yours?"

He grins and launches into a debate about the pitcher. Arms gesticulating, he's so invested that he has to put down the newspaper to fully execute a swing, just to show me how good his reach is. Any shyness is completely gone.

"Do you play?"

"Sometimes," he says, but he doesn't look at me when he says it. "Not that much, I guess."

"I bet you'd be good at it."

"You think?"

"With that swing? Heck yeah." I bend down and pick up the newspaper. "Do you do your homework here often?"

"Yes. Sometimes Skye lets me have fun, but only after I've finished my homework." He says this with a dramatic sigh, and I grin in response. We both look over to where Skye is on the phone, nodding along to something the person on the other side is saying. Her face is set in brisk professionalism, her mouth softened into a smile.

"How do you know my aunt?"

My attention snaps back to her nephew. "I'm a friend."

He gives a slow nod. "All right," he says. "A *friend*. Do you want to see my baseball cards?"

"I'd love—"

"Cole was just leaving." Skye is back, a hand placed on Timmy's shoulder. "I'm sorry for keeping you waiting."

"No worries."

"Go back upstairs, Timmy. There are more newspapers in the crate by the door—you can look in those as well."

He shoots her an exasperated look before waving goodbye to me. We both watch in silence as his small form trudges through the bookshop, past shelves after shelves of books.

"Good kid," I say.

"He is. Why are you really here, Cole?"

I run a hand across my jaw again. Her eyes are blazing, a challenge in them, and something that runs deeper. Embarrassment? Hurt?

"I should have told you who I was when I was here last week," I say.

"So you came to apologize?"

My grin is back, and I take a few steps back toward the front door. "Consider me accepting the two-month bet my apology," I say.

"Accepted. But I'll still remember, Cole."

"Good," I say, my hand on the front door. "As long as you remember what I told you last week. I would have called, Skye, if you had left me your number. And you would have picked up."

5

SKYE

"See? We could put these up around the neighborhood. The noticeboard by the grocery store, inside cafés, by bus stops…" I hold up one of the flyers I made for Karli to see.

"When did you make these?"

"Last night. I went to the copy shop this morning." I put it down, two cups of coffee and determination making my skin itch with excitement. "You know the author we featured last week? She's a Seattle native. Maybe we could organize a book reading and signing with her?"

Karli is laughing. "Did you get *any* sleep last night?"

"Yes. Well, a bit." I'd stayed up late, doing everything from brainstorming ideas to watching videos on YouTube by prominent businessmen. The latter hadn't helped at all—I wasn't planning on building a multi-billion-dollar empire here—but it had definitely given me motivation. Never give up, never surrender. My plans of finishing my manuscript before the year is out have all been scrapped. Between the Pages is more important.

"The posters are fantastic."

"And the mic night?"

"And the mic night." She nods. Karli reaches across and puts a hand on mine. "Skye, what came over you in the meeting yesterday?"

I meet her earnest gaze with one of my own. "I honestly don't know. I was so angry, and so... well. I couldn't let it go down without a fight. I still can't. I'm sorry if I embarrassed you."

"Embarrassed me? Skye, we were sinking, and you bartered your way to a lifeline."

"We can't just let him win, you know."

"Him?"

"Yeah, the titan of industry. Cole Porter. Big business. Corporate greed. *Them.*"

Karli shakes her head at me. "You're starting to sound like a conspiracy theorist, but I like it. Give me a stack of these posters and I'll hang some up during lunch?"

I grin. "This is just the beginning. I have so many ideas, Karli... This isn't the end of Between the Pages."

Her smile is excited, all signs of tiredness or resignation gone for the first time in weeks. "You know what? Even if it is, we gave it our all. Nana would have wanted nothing less."

I spend the rest of the day immersed in the store. I look at every shelf like it's the first time I've seen them. I stand outside for nearly thirty minutes and analyze our window displays, until Karli tells me to come back inside because I'm scaring away actual customers.

The bookstore can't fail. It can't. I walk through the second story, with the dark wood bookcases and the ratty old armchair in the corner, seeing it all like I'm twelve again. For years, this had been my safe place. My refuge from the world, from school and home.

I run my hand along the spiral staircase up to the attic. We never go up there, and the staircase is purely decorative now. A small sign hangs on it, the lettering artistic and flowing. *The staircase to book heaven. Unfortunately off-limits (at the moment).*

I'd put the sign there when I was fifteen, and Karli's grandmother Eleanor never took it down. This store has a place in the community. In the city. There is magic living between these dusty walls. It's a store that holds a thousand stories, a thousand characters, a thousand places just waiting to be explored. We just need to get the magic across more effectively.

And if I have anything to say on the matter, we will. Between the Pages will continue spreading its magic to tons of little girls and boys who need it.

"And you're okay with me leaving early?"

"Yes, of course I am."

"You're sure, sure?"

Karli laughs. "*Yes!* John is coming by soon anyway, and he'll keep me company before closing. Besides, it's not like you're going home and lying on the couch."

I lift the stack of posters high. "No, not exactly. I'm going to plaster the city with these. Between the Pages will be everywhere. Not a single Seattleite will be missed."

"Skye?"

"Yes?"

Her eyes soften. "I'm really happy to have you. I know you could do so much more than work here, with me... but I appreciate it."

The lump in my throat is sudden, and I have to swallow around it. "There's nowhere else I'd rather be. You know that."

"Even so. Thank you."

I walk up the street, as familiar to me as my own hand. There's a notice board by the old bakery, now turned into a laundromat. Ms. Janice is seated outside with her little dog at her side. *Yes!*

"Hi there," I say, putting up my poster.

She squints at it. "What are you doing there?"

"Protesting the new development."

She gives a croaky laugh. "No good can come of that."

"Oh, it might! If enough customers come to the store in the coming two months, we might be able to stay."

"Really?"

"Yes." I beam at her. "We're inviting everyone in the area to pop in, as often as possible. We're organizing a book reading, too."

"Really," she says again, softer this time. "Well, I'll have to swing by then."

"We'd be happy to have you."

I say bye to Ms. Janice and her little dog with a smile. She talks to everyone in this neighborhood—anyone at all who will listen. She's better than any noticeboard I could find.

I turn up Aven Street and continue on my poster quest. I ask cafés for permission to put them up. For the first time in weeks, there's purpose in what I do. *Save the bookshop.* It runs on a loop in my head, over and over and over again.

What had I said to Karli? Captain of industry. Big business. I use my phone to search the internet for Porter Development, but all I find is their generic website. I shake my head and try again. *What properties does Porter Development own?*

Jackpot. There's the Reese Hotel, with the Legacy bar, but I keep scrolling. I don't need to be reminded of the night I spent there.

Flitwick Apartments is another one—and it's nearby. I glance down at my remaining stack of posters. *Well, Cole Porter. Maybe it's time to show just how determined we are to keep Between the Pages running.*

The next day is calm. We get a few new customers—all of whom credit my poster—but other than that, business churns on as usual. That is to say, it's practically nonexistent.

By late afternoon, I'm alone again, working the evening shift. Karli has gone home to her husband and kids with a new cupcake recipe to try. I told her to save one for me tomorrow, and I'm already looking forward to it.

I turn up the radio and hum along as I scroll through Pinterest. Looking at bookstores and libraries around the world has given me a serious case of envy, but also a ton of ideas. Between the Pages has the same magical vibes—*old-world charm,* like Cole said—but we could definitely amp it up a bit.

I pause at a picture of a beautiful bookstore somewhere in Europe, a doorway between two adjoining rooms made entirely out of books.

I add it to the list next to me. *Doorway of books.* There are a ton of ideas there already. *Heart of books* is there, too. I saw that one on Instagram, with people traveling specifically to get a picture of themselves surrounded by books glued together in the shape of a heart.

Something like that would be perfect. Exactly what we need—a visual draw. A reason for people to come out to Between the Pages, to take their own pictures, to stay for a while and be enchanted. And, hopefully, to *buy* books.

I pause at another picture of little planters atop shelves, with green, flowing leaves hanging down. It looks gorgeous.

I copy it dutifully into my notebook. *Plants.* The list is half useful, half ridiculous. A picture of a beautiful old bookstore in Paris had a cat in it, so I had written *Cat* into my notebook. There was no way that was going to fly with Karli, but at least it was giving me something to do.

I'm interrupted by the jingle of the bell at the door. I drop my phone immediately, a welcoming smile spreading across my lips.

It dies the second I see who it is.

Cole is holding up one of my posters. Frustration has his jaw set into a hard line. "What the hell is this?"

I squint. "I'm not sure."

"You're damn sure, Skye. These were plastered to the outside of every single one of my buildings."

"Oh. *Those.*"

"Yes, those." He puts the poster down on the counter, anger in his eyes. A corresponding thrill runs through me.

"I'm trying to ensure we're profitable in two months. Encouraging community support is part of that."

"The Bluestone Hotel is halfway across the city, and its guests are from out of town. It's decidedly *not* part of your community."

I blink up at him. "I don't know what you're so angry about. We made a bet. I'm trying to win."

"What you *actually* did was informing every single one of my employees about it."

Shit. I hadn't thought about that. "Whoops?"

"Fucking hell, Skye…" He runs a hand through his hair, pushing it away from his forehead. "There have to be other things on your to-do-list besides ruining my reputation. Or is that number one?" He snatches the notebook from behind the counter, his movements too quick for me. "Is this it? Let's see, where is 'Destroy Cole Porter'…"

"Give that back."

He takes a step back, evading my arm, and I watch in horrified silence as his eyes rake through the list.

"Buy plants. Get a *cat*? This is your plan to save the store?"

A furious flush creeps up my neck. "They're just ideas."

"Your first idea was to plaster posters on all of my businesses, and your second idea was to *buy a cat?*"

I reach to snatch the notebook out of his hands, and this time, he lets me. The mirth on his face is only making my embarrassment worse.

"Look, I haven't asked you to contribute your *amazing* business sense to this, all right? Besides, you work with buildings, not bookstores."

"I work with people and profit," he says, and the implication is clear in his words. *And this is not going to make the cut.*

Looking at him standing there in his thousand-dollar suit and smug smile, I want to sink through the floor. My ideas had been fun. They'd been a way for us to create a more magical atmosphere, to draw in more customers. They'd been a silly distraction from the all-too-likely scenario—demolition.

"Look," I tell him. "People don't buy as many books anymore. It's sad, but it's true. We need to bring customers here for another reason. Some of the most successful bookstores in the world have people *queueing* outside, and it's because of their atmosphere and picture-worthy aesthetics. Instagram drives business these days."

He holds up his hands. "If you can pull that off, I'll be the first to admit that I'm wrong."

"There's a *but* in your tone."

Cole nods at my list, a strand of his thick hair falling across his forehead. It's silky to the touch—I remember.

"Going through your finances should be the first thing you do."

I tap my pen against the notepad. "Oh?"

"Yes. Cut down on all non-essential expenses and halt all new purchases of books. See if you can slash prices. Do you have an accountant?"

"Yes," I say, though in truth, I'm not sure. Karli always handles that part.

"Then meet with them as soon as possible," Cole says, shaking his head. "Why am I giving you advice? I received a call from my assistant today who said we had a *targeted attack* on the company."

"Wow. All because of my posters?"

"Yes. That's what you unleashed, you little demon."

"I'm not the one demolishing entire city blocks."

His eyes narrow. "Sometimes you have to make space for the new. Now, will you stop attacking my buildings?"

"I can't make any promises. And it was hardly an attack, Cole, I just put up some posters!"

"*Skye.*"

"Fine. Yes, I'll stop." I put my notebook back behind the counter and make a mental note to ask Karli about our accountant.

He raises a doubtful eyebrow. "You wanted to send a signal, and I don't think it was to any of my employees. Well, consider it received."

Cole's right about that. I run a hand over my ponytail—when he's around, I feel constantly underdressed. "I don't exactly have your number, so it was the only way I could think of."

"You could've had my phone number, you know. If that's what you wanted, all you had to do was ask, that night at the hotel." His voice has dropped an octave, smooth like crushed velvet and danger.

I produce an Oscar-worthy scoff. "I thought we agreed not to talk about that night."

"I never agreed to that. And I wonder... you act like it's all in the past. But I noticed something today."

"Oh?"

Cole steps closer, my eyes in line with the collar of his shirt. The top button is undone, a few dark hairs visible. I know it continues down his chest, darkening and deepening down his taut stomach and further still.

"You went to every single one of my properties," he says, "except Legacy. Was that another message, Skye?"

"No." My voice sounds faint, even to my own ears.

"Why didn't it get the same treatment, then?"

I wet my lips. "It has a pretty facade. I didn't want to ruin it."

"Of course. You're unaffected."

"Yes."

A rough finger tilts my head up slightly, until I'm forced to meet his burning gaze. Cole looks exactly like he did that night at the Legacy bar. Charming. Powerful. A bit dangerous.

He bends his head softly, until his breath ghosts across my lips. "Liar," he says. "I haven't been back to Legacy either, not since that night."

I'm like a rabbit, stuck in the headlights, unable to end this moment. My willpower is weakening. The part of my body that has been screaming for a repeat is roaring, preparing her arguments. His lips are so close.

"I hate you," I whisper. "So much."

He leans back with a sardonic smile. "Oh, Skye. I don't think that's true at all." He pushes the poster toward me. "Keep this. I have about a thousand more where that came from."

And then he's gone, striding out as quickly as he came in, and I'm left trying to clear my head. What had he been about to do?

And worse... what had *I* been about to do?

6

SKYE

I push the stool back further, gripping my phone tight. The angle needs to be perfect for this shot.

"Like this?" Karli asks, lifting the book a little bit higher.

"Yes, that's perfect. And turn it a little bit... yes!" I stand on the stool, maintaining my balance, and take about ten nearly identical pictures. With the beautiful dark bookcase in the background, and the spiral staircase, it's a great picture of this weeks 'staff favorites.'

"Can I lower it now?"

"Yes, we got it."

Karli shakes her arms out. "Wow. I had no clue I was this weak."

"Tell me about it. I had to run for the bus the other week and nearly fainted."

She laughs, bending to tuck the stool back into place. "How many pictures have you taken now? You must have a dozen."

"Nearly twenty." I favorite the picture I like the most and add it to the album on my phone titled *Instagram*. "We're going to become the most followed bookstore in Seattle."

Karli's voice is amused. "How many followers does the most followed have?"

"Well, technically speaking, they have fifteen thousand."

"Fifteen thousand?"

"Should be a piece of cake."

Karli pushes her glasses back. "I saw the poster you made for the book reading night, by the way."

"What did you think?"

"It's great. I've made a list with speakers I think would be interested in joining, as well as the author. I'll give them a call later this afternoon."

Relief floods through me. Karli has been on board with my ideas from the start, but having her active participation in these things is even better. She has tons of connections in this world, her grandmother's name opening doors, and it will mean a lot coming from Karli herself.

"That's perfect. I'll promote it on our new social media accounts too." I wave my phone at her, and she grins.

"What's our current follower count?"

I check. "Three hundred forty-eight. That's twelve higher than yesterday."

"Saving the bookstore, one like at a time."

"Exactly. About that, though… I've been thinking about something." I put my phone in my pocket and curse myself for following Cole's advice. "We should go over the finances as well, right? The only thing we need to show is that we're profitable. If we cut down on all expenses, and maybe have a sale on some of the more difficult inventory…"

Karli sits down in the old armchair in the corner with a sigh. "I know. It's exactly what we should do."

I take a seat on the stool opposite her. "It's a lot. I know."

"It is. And… Well, I haven't told you yet, but our accountant is quitting."

"What?"

"Yes. Terrible timing, I know. Greg's retiring, and I haven't figured out what to do. Honestly, before the meeting with Porter Development, I was so ready to throw in the towel on the whole thing."

I reach across and put my hand on hers. "You're not alone in this. I'll help you with anything and everything. I know it's not my place—"

But Karli just shakes her head. "It is. This is *our* store, Skye. We need as many of your ideas as we can get."

I squeeze her hand. "So now we need a new accountant."

"Yes. Someone who can start pretty much right away. Someone who's okay with only being guaranteed work for two months."

"Should be plenty of firms around here. I think I could—oh! I do know someone. Chloe. My old college roommate." I'm already fishing out my phone, scrolling through my contacts. "She's an accountant."

"Really?"

"Yes! I saw her just a few months ago at a mutual friend's wedding. We're not exactly close, but she was always good in school. Straight As. I could give her a call?"

Karli is smiling at me. "What would I do without you?"

"You'd be getting some peace and quiet, probably. This bookstore would be much calmer."

She chuckles. "But not nearly as entertaining. Come on, let's go downstairs and officially open for business today. Did you see what I brought? I put it in the storage room."

"No?"

"Cupcakes from yesterday. I tried a new recipe."

I'm already hurrying down the steps. "What kind?"

"Carrot cake."

My stomach grumbles at the sound of that. "Carrots are nutritious, so they count as breakfast, right?"

Karli laughs at me, already ducking behind the curtain into the storage room. "Absolutely!"

The day goes by without a hitch. I'm polishing some of our reading lights—golden, old-school, one of Eleanor's many touches—when the doorbell jingles again. We've had several customers already, and each jingle has buoyed my mood even more.

I might be a failed writer. An okay-ish sister. But I'm a good bookstore employee, and my posters are already paying dividends.

A voice reaches me. "Delivery for Miss Skye Holland."

"Oh. Wow. Yes, this is the right place. Skye!"

I peek around the corner. A courier is holding a massive box, filled to the brim with potted plants.

He nods when he sees me. "Miss Holland?"

"Yes."

Putting down the box, he hands me a small slip. "Sign at the bottom, please."

I sign my name on autopilot, still gazing at the delivery. There's at least ten plants, the green and leafy type. The kind that looks almost like ivy, spilling out of the rims of their pots.

"Well, have a nice day then, ladies."

"Bye," I murmur at the delivery guy.

Karli's voice is warmer. "You too. Thanks."

When he's gone, she turns to me with incredulous eyes. "You ordered this? For the store?"

Weakly, I nod.

"This must have cost a lot. But it'll look so good... like that picture you showed me the other day, of the old bookstore in Paris. Ours looks a little bit like that already. This will look amazing." She bends and pulls out a pot of Devil's Ivy. "We could have this on the spiral staircase. Look how long the tendrils are!"

"Yes. Fantastic." I bend and pick up the entire box, and as I do, I notice the small white envelope tucked inside one of the pots. "I'll put it in the back for now, all right?"

When I'm safely hidden by shelves, I pull out the note. There are ten digits written in a square, masculine hand. Below it, a single sentence. *For the next time you feel like sending me a message.*

I slip the note into my pocket, where it feels hot, like it's burning straight through the fabric of my jeans and searing my skin. I hate that he has this effect on me. That I can't seem to get over the amazing night we spent together, before I knew I was sleeping with the enemy.

Buy plants. He'd seen it on my list yesterday, the list he'd made fun of, before giving me "actual" business advice.

I smile down at the box of plants. I had gotten him to drive across town to confront me about the posters himself, and that meant I was succeeding in being a nuisance. Before these two months were up, the bookshop would be far more than just a nuisance. It would be a successful, thriving business, and he'd have to eat his bet and his smugness both.

Karli doesn't ask me about the decision to get the plants, not even as we put them up. She thinks it's a great idea. I nod, though guilt roils in my stomach at the credit. She still doesn't know that my one-night stand and the man bound to demolish our business are one and the same.

I should tell her, but as soon as it dances to the tip of my tongue, I swallow it back down again. It's a truth I'm having trouble wrapping my head around myself, to be honest.

Karli is in a great mood for the rest of the day, ever since I offered to call my accountant friend and the plants got delivered.

My phone rings late that afternoon, my sister's caller ID on the screen. I groan.

Karli looks at me sympathetically. "Isla?"

"Yes."

"Say you're busy. You're allowed to be, you know."

"I know." I step into the storage room and press answer. My older sister's voice, chirpy and high, rings out.

"Oh, Skye, I'm so happy to get a hold of you."

I always answer, I want to say. Getting a hold of me is never a problem. "What's up?"

"You know the car show Rodney is going to tonight?"

"A car show?"

"Yes. I told you about this last time we spoke, I'm sure."

I have to stop myself from sighing. Her new boyfriend seems nice—I've only met him twice—but he always has engagements out of town. "It's tonight?"

"Yes. And I was wondering… It's just no place for a kid, you know."

Translation—she wants to be alone with her new boyfriend. It was always the same story with Isla. She would be infatuated with a new guy, or with a new hobby, and I'd be expected to step in as the go-to babysitter or helper.

"You want me to watch Timmy?"

"Oh, would you? That would be so good of you. You're really helping me out here."

Yeah, which was what she had said just two days ago, when she dropped Timmy off without any advance warning.

"Bring him by whenever. When do you and Rodney plan on being home?"

"Oh, you know, it might run late."

"It's a school night."

Her tone sharpens slightly at the clear reproach in mine. "I'll pack all of his school stuff as well as his overnight stuff, don't worry. You still have that old pull-out couch in your living room."

Right. So that means cooking a nutritious dinner, driving him to school in the morning, and making sure he has everything he needs for the day.

My sister is a nice person. Most of the time, at least. But she doesn't *think*, and she never has, and somehow life had let her get away with it.

"Sounds good," I say, hating how much of a pushover I've always been around her.

"Perfect!" she chirps. "I'll bring him by around five. To the bookstore?"

"Yes."

She hangs up with a pearly laugh and I'm left staring at the phone in my hand. I love my nephew, and I really enjoy all the time we get to spend together. And the fact that she springs things like this on me—I can handle it, even if I don't like the lack of warning. But I don't like that she does this to Timmy every time a new guy comes on the scene.

I last two more hours before the phone number blossoms into an inferno in my pocket and I have to put out the fire. I add

Cole's phone number into my contacts, and under contact name, I write the first thing I think of. *Demolisher.* And then I send him a quick text.

Skye Holland: *The plants are nice. But please don't send me a cat next.*

My heart pounding, I slip my phone back into my pocket and tell myself to ignore it, and Cole, entirely. This entire thing is uncharted territory for me. It always had been, even back in that hotel room, despite my pretend-confidence.

And now, with him as the owner of Porter Development, the rules are muddled even further. We're not friends. We're enemies who've happened to see each other naked. And that made things a hell of a lot more confusing.

My phone buzzes nearly immediately.

Cole Porter: *Too bad. I already had a kitten picked out. She's really fluffy.*

I chuckle, despite myself.

Skye Holland*: Keep her for yourself. I'm sure she'll fit right in in your thousand-square-foot penthouse.*

His answer is immediate again.

Cole Porter: *You're making assumptions again.*

Skye Holland: *Isn't that what we do best, as people-watchers?*

Cole Porter: *Oh, but I'm not a stranger. Haven't we established that already?*

My cheeks are burning, my stomach tightening. It's playing

with fire, this conversation. Him. The bet. All of it, and still, I keep putting my hand to the flame.

Skye Holland: *Thanks for the plants.*

He doesn't respond for a long time after that, so long that I assume he agreed with me. But then my pocket buzzes again.

Cole Porter: *Is that the closest I'll get to an apology for vandalizing my properties?*

I can't help but smile. Oh, he had another thing coming if he thought I'd cave this easily.

Skye Holland: *I'll never apologize for that.*

7

SKYE

It's over a week before I see him again. And yes, I hate that that's the way I've started calculating time. The man is single-handedly responsible for the bookstore's potential destruction, and still, my traitorous body and my even-more-traitorous eyes love the sight of him.

Keeping busy helped, though. Karli and I hired Chloe, my old college roommate, to look into our books. More customers are coming in by the day, and the time we have in between them, Karli and I spend planning the book reading. Things are changing, and I feel like Karli and I can turn this around, even if it's with our own optimism as currency.

Life is busy. *And yet,* my mind finds ways to circle back around to the memory of Cole Porter. It hits me one evening, alone in Between the Pages, just before closing. Thoughts of his smug smile and the silken growl of his voice.

"No," I say. "No, no, no. Go away." I turn up the volume on the radio and sing along to a peppy tune, heading to the storage room instead. I grab the box of books I'd bought from the consignment store and I carry it out to the reading room table, my glue gun stacked on top. This should keep both mind and hands busy.

But then the doorbell jingles, and there he is, as if summoned by my imagination.

He's not in a suit today. That's my first observation, as Cole Porter stands in the doorframe in a button-down and slacks. Hands in his pockets, the picture of casual male power. A slow smile spreads across his face as he sees me with my pile of trinkets.

"An arts and crafts project, Skye?"

I put the box down on the counter. "Why are you here?"

"I wanted to look at my investment." His voice is infuriatingly calm. "I did agree to allow this business to continue, incorporated into my building, if you succeed."

I huff a sigh and start piling up the books I'd purchased. They're pretty, with old spines, but they'd only cost me pennies.

"If you're here for a financial checkup, I can't help you. I can give you the number to our new accountant, though."

"You took my advice?"

"Yes," I say primly. "I suppose something good comes from having a ruthless CEO as our overlord."

He chuckles and reaches for the glue gun. "I haven't seen one of these in forever."

My project feels a bit silly now with him standing here. He's a business tycoon, and I'm trying to create something that *might* be Instagram-worthy for our customers.

"We're doing great," I say. "We've had a ton of new customers. I think the posters are really working."

He arches an eyebrow in an infuriating move, hands still in his pockets. "Oh?"

"Yes." I grab a stack of the books and the glue gun, carrying them to the reading table in one of the adjoining rooms.

"Do you want the rest of this, too?" Cole follows me in, the heavy box lifted high in his arms.

"On the table."

He puts it down and starts to sort through the books. "*Gulliver's Travels?*"

"A classic."

He picks up another. *"How to Cook with Lavender, a Step-by-Step Guide.* These books look…"

"Old? Dated?"

"Completely unsellable."

I search through the photos in my phone, trying to find the inspiration picture I'd chosen. "I know," I say. "They're not for sale."

"They're part of your personal collection?" He opens the cookbook, eyes scanning with a doubtful look on his face. "Tell me, how does lavender quiche taste?"

I hold up my phone for him to see. "*This* is what I'm going to make."

"You're going to glue books together in the shape of a heart?"

"Yes. We have a small wall in between the Sci-Fi room and Contemporary Fiction, and right now, it's just a bunch of shelves. But by putting this there instead, people could look in between the two rooms in the shape of a heart. A bookheart."

Cole is quiet for a long moment, flipping through another book. I wait for the reproach, the tone of voice that will tell me it's ridiculous. Like thinking plants or cats will save a failing business.

I know it's a long shot. I know things like this are nothing more than fun little quirks. But if I keep pushing, maybe I can make this bookstore as magical for all customers as it is for me. Maybe I can make it a *destination*, a place people come to take pictures. A place for book lovers and dreamers.

But Cole doesn't say anything disparaging. Instead, I'm treated to the marvelous view of him carefully rolling up his sleeves, one inch at a time, methodical and calm. "Well," he says. "I think you'll need some help with that, no?"

"You want to help?"

"I know how to use a glue gun." He reaches for it and turns it back and forth. "Well, I think I do. Point and shoot. How hard can it be?"

I should tell him to leave. He's in the store he's planning to tear down, looking like a million bucks, and I'm letting him.

Consistency is key, Skye, and you're not displaying it.

I choke back my inner logic. "We need to stack them first, I think." I grab a few of the books and start arranging them in a formation. In my head, I know exactly how I want it to look, but actually getting there proves harder.

Cole feeds me books, one after another, and helps me prop them up on the sides. "Like this?"

"Yes." I glance at him under my side-swept bangs. He looks collected, like he does this all the time. "Why do you want to help? We're practically enemies," I point out.

He doesn't answer, just hands me another book.

"Well," I say, "maybe I'm giving myself more significance than I deserve. You're my enemy, but maybe we're more like a small obstacle in the way. An annoying mosquito, you know."

Cole's lips are twitching again. "You're not a mosquito."

"But we *are* throwing a wrench into your plan of world domination."

"Hmm. Yes, you are certainly doing that." He hands me another book.

"So why help us?"

"Maybe I don't like winning without a bit of fight," he points out. "Maybe I like winning fair and square. That's part of the joy of betting."

I inspect the heart we've constructed. It'll look good surrounded by yet more books, as if the shelf itself opened up into a heart-shaped window, a glance into a different world.

"So this is like entertainment for you."

He plugs the glue gun in. "Sure, if you want to see it that way."

That makes it easier to understand, then. I lean over and pretend to inspect his forearms. Cole glances down and then back at me, a frown on his forehead.

"What?"

"Just looking for scratches."

His face clears into a grin. "My new cat and I get along very well, I'll have you know."

I roll my eyes. "Of course. She probably has a butler and two valets."

"You seem to have a very skewed idea of my life."

I cock my head and look at him. Cole looks back at me, the picture of smugness itself. This might not be the right time to admit that I've been stalking him on the internet. Simply write in *Cole Porter* and a wealth of information appears. Nearly everything about him is available at your fingertips.

How much he's worth (in the billions). The building influence he's amassed at such a young age (thirty-four). The lack of a serious partner for years (at least four).

"I know you have a driver who takes you everywhere."

"You've been paying attention."

"I saw you arrive here once. You climbed out of the backseat."

"It's more efficient. I can work while I travel." He hands me another book. "The glue gun is hot."

I reach for it. "Thanks." Time to make permanent decisions.

"Do you want me to hold the books still?"

"Yes, please…" We both fall silent in concentration as I glue the base of the book-shaped heart into place. He helps hold it down, big hands spread across the covers of two discarded books. He has long fingers, tan across the back, with a smattering of hair faint across his knuckles. Those hands had been on my skin. Caressing, smacking, gripping. And his fingers had been inside me.

I glance away quickly, only to see amusement on his face. He might not be able to read my thoughts, but the flush on my cheeks is clear. "You're wearing your hair down today," he comments. "You normally don't."

"It gets in the way when I work. And you shouldn't be noticing that."

"I shouldn't?"

"No."

"In the way that you're *not* noticing my non-existing scratches?"

He's got me there, and my eyes drift down to the opening in his shirt, where skin beckons. "All right. So I'm not exactly consistent. I think we've established that where you're concerned."

His grin is back. "I disagree. You're consistently difficult."

I reach for another book and glue it, his hands moving effortlessly to help pin it in place. "You're a consistent nuisance, too."

"I haven't been told that in a very long time."

"Because you're surrounded by ass-kissing sycophants? I've heard that's a problem among the powerful. My sympathies."

Cole laughs, and it's warm and true. I'd meant to poke fun at him, but he'd taken it in stride, and the sound unsettles me. I like it too much. "Yes," he says. "I'm coddled from morning to evening, with no one daring to tell me the truth. It's how I've built a booming business."

"Really?"

"No. You have to handle critique, or you'll get nowhere in life." He reaches across and holds the next set of books effortlessly in place. "Also, excellent use of the word sycophants."

"I have a degree in English Literature."

"It shows. Now glue these."

I follow his advice. We don't know anything about each other, despite the fact that we've seen each other naked. "How did you build yours?"

"My business?"

"Yes."

He smiles, shaking his head. "Are you trying to get more advice out of me to win this bet? You know I'll give it to you, but it's a dirty tactic."

"Maybe." I reach for another book, stacking it on top. "Or maybe I just realized that we actually know very little about one another."

He runs a hand through his hair, pushing it back, and nods at the heart. "It's looking good."

"You're deflecting."

A sigh. "Well, I started with small business lots. They were old office buildings that no one wanted."

"Except you."

"Except me," he agrees, handing me another book to glue in place.

"And then you flipped them?"

He snorts, perhaps at my layman term. "Yes. We renovated them, timed it right with the market, and sold for a profit."

"You make it sound easy," I say. "Did it all fall in line perfectly for you?"

"No. It was a lot of work. We weren't many working together in the beginning, so it was a lot of long hours."

I wonder if he still works long hours. He must, to maintain the empire, but he still makes time to sit here and glue books with me. It makes me... well. There must be an ulterior motive somewhere.

"And then business took off. Going from office buildings to the Reese hotel..."

His eyes flash with the memory, but I don't look away from him, despite my own flushing cheeks. "Yes," he says. "It was a leap. Not everyone believed I could do it."

"But you did."

He inclines his head. "Your belief in yourself is all that really matters. Careful, there. It's toppling to the right."

He's right. I straighten the heart and lean back, inspecting it. Nearly done, and I only have a handful of books left. This couldn't have worked out better if I'd counted them.

"Your nephew isn't around tonight," he says. "He'd like this, no?"

I smile. "He would. Anything with building or tools, he loves."

Cole's face is unreadable. "You like kids."

"I do. Pass me that book? No, the red one."

He hands it to me in silence, and I study him again. He's being polite, civil. Cordial. So am I. It's... odd. And nice. And that's when my suspicion hits with full force.

"You want a repeat of the night at the hotel," I say.

Cole's eyes snap to mine, and I can tell by the sudden fire in them that I'm right. "So what if I do?"

"Were the plants a part of the seduction scheme? The glue gun?"

"Would you take the plants down if I said yes?"

"No."

"Then yes, sure, they were."

I cross my arms over my chest. This doesn't make sense. That night had been beyond my wildest dreams… exciting, daring, dangerous. Sexy. He'd been fantastic in bed.

"You'd be risking so much."

Judging from the faint amusement in his eyes, he's finding my whole act amusing. "I would?"

"Yes. Sleeping with someone you've made a business deal with. Not very professional."

He hands me another book and nods at the top of the heart. "You're nearly done, Skye. Don't stop now."

I take it from him in an angry movement. This whole conversation, him here… it's beyond frustrating. I could have a repeat of that night—the night I'd been dreaming about for so long—but only if I was willing to sleep with the enemy. With him.

Because despite his cut-glass jawline and his casual laughter, he will tear down this business if he doesn't deem it worthy. I'd read enough online about his ruthless business decisions to know that's true.

"You're the last person on earth I would sleep with," I say. "You're the reason I might be unemployed in a month and a half."

Cole supports the bookheart with strong, capable hands. His handsome face is set in clearly composed lines. He doesn't look remotely flustered by this conversation. "Everyone in the business will be compensated. You won't be empty-handed."

"*If* I sleep with you."

His eyes flash to mine, and for the first time since I've known him, there's actual anger in them. "No. Absolutely not."

"That's not what you're suggesting here?"

"No. Fucking hell, no. You'd think that of me?"

I look over at him. His jaw is working, a faint flush spreading up his neck. There was one headline that had stood out in particular when I'd searched his name. *Cole Porter sued by former business partner, alleging malpractice over his departure.*

"I don't know what to think," I say honestly. This man is effectively a stranger, and I need to remember that. "We don't know each other very well. And you *are* trying to tear down the place I love, Cole."

"A very unlucky coincidence," he says darkly. "Tell me. The night we spent together at the hotel. Why did you leave me that note? Truthfully?"

Now my cheeks flame with the memory. *Thanks for the night, stud.* "I didn't want to push it," I say.

"Push what?"

"I don't know. Myself? My luck?" I throw up my hands. "I don't sleep with random men at bars. This is me," I say, sweeping a hand over my casual clothes. "I spend my days here. I'm currently glue-gunning. And you're... well, *you*. I knew that even before I found out you *owned* the whole damn hotel."

His wolfish grin is back. "I'm thinking of turning *Legacy* into a chain of bars. All because of you."

"Oh, God help us."

"But you enjoyed the night."

I look up at the ceiling. "Yes."

"I wasn't planning on propositioning you like this. You beat me to it. But of course I want a repeat of that night. Don't you?"

I look at the shelves around us, and force myself to picture Cole in a hard hat, tearing them down one by one. "No."

"If things were different—if I wasn't me, and you weren't you—you wouldn't want to sleep with me again?"

He's asking the impossible. I push away from the finished bookheart and stand. Waves of power and raw eroticism are wafting off him, and I don't know if I want to punch him or pull him close.

"That's a hypothetical," I say.

"Yes. It is."

"So it doesn't matter what the answer is."

He smiles, like I've just confirmed something, and I shake my head at him. "Look, it doesn't matter. It's impossible. We're enemies. Rivals. You're my nemesis, my least favorite person on earth."

Cole runs a hand along his jaw, the playful look in his eyes back. "Huh. I can see how that might be a problem, yes."

"A small one. It's not personal."

"Right, of course not." He looks like a million bucks, even in the dim lighting of our bookstore reading room. In a different universe he would be the commander of armies, or crowned an Olympic athlete. His smile turns crooked. "Well," he says. "Have I made you speechless? That must be a first, for you."

"I'm not." I unplug the glue gun and roll up the cord with brisk movements. "I was just thinking of how to proceed. I think I might install the heart tomorrow. I'll need some nails, and a hammer."

Cole opens his mouth to speak, but I hold up a finger and cut him off. "And I don't need any help. No deliveries. Thanks."

"So independent." He runs a hand along his jaw, looking so arrogant that I can't help pushing the boundaries.

"This must be a new experience for you, huh?"

"Glue-gunning? Yes."

"Women saying no to you," I clarify, sitting on the table next to him. Playing with fire again.

"Hmm. You mean that as an insult, but I hear it for the compliment it is."

Infuriating man. "Tell me, in the spirit of getting to know one another better, is destroying innocent businesses a hobby for you or more of a regular pastime?"

Cole pushes back his chair and stands, forcing me to tilt my head back to see him. "It's usually just business," he says. "But in this case, it's definitely more of a hobby. I made an exception for you."

I grit my teeth. "Destruction is such a cliché, though, for men. You don't have some weird Napoleon complex, do you?"

"Hmm. If I remember correctly, that would only work if I was either short, or more crudely, below averagely sized." He leans in, the scent of linen and man washing over me. "You know that's false on both accounts."

"Why are you *really* here?"

His eyes narrow. "You've already figured that out, Skye."

"So it was that good for you too, huh," I conclude softly. "You could have any woman you want, and you're trying to get another night with a lowly bookstore clerk."

His eyes flit down to my lips. "It was average."

I scoot closer and watch in triumph as his eyes drift lower, to my body, to where my legs are splayed for him to fit between them. "Average, Porter? You wouldn't be here if you thought it was anything less than fantastic."

His hand races up my arm, along my jaw, strong fingers tipping my head back. His eyes look nearly black. "I'll admit it if you do," he says.

My knees lock on either side of his waist. "Never."

He bends to kiss me, but I race to kiss him first, and we collide with a fury. It's lips and mouths and then, as he slides his tongue against mine, all heat.

My hands on his neck. His around my waist, pulling me closer.

I melt against the hard lengths of his body. Images of him in bed rise up, unbidden, behind my eyelids. How his mouth feels on my skin. How his body moves above mine.

I shiver as he traces his lips down my jaw. A strong hand grips my hair and tilts my head back to give him better access. My neck is my weak spot. Always has been, and Cole seems to remember.

I wrap my legs around his waist and hold on as his lips are followed by the soft scratch of his five-o'clock shadow.

"Damn it," I growl and pull him back up to my lips. He groans into my mouth, his hands dropping to grip my hips.

I want to get his suit off him. I want to hit him. I want to tear him limb from limb. I want to cry and ask *why did it have to be you?*

My hands hover above the buttons on his shirt, undecided. He breaks apart long enough to growl a rough taunt against my lips. "Coward."

I tug at his hair. "Asshole."

"Since before I met you."

His hands grip my thighs and I'm pulled closer, until I feel the hardness of him against me.

"Fuck." His bruising kiss takes my breath away. It's not like it was the night we slept together at his hotel. That had been a game, step by step, both of us learning and indulging in our shared passion.

This is a wildfire. There's no finesse to my hands on his neck, or his lips on mine. It's a fight and we're both aiming for victory.

I scoot back and flinch as I knock over a pile of books. Cole ignores it, switching his attention to my collarbone.

Books.

Bookstore.

Between the Pages.

I push at his shoulders. "We can't."

"Why not?" He doesn't stop kissing my neck, and my eyes drift half-closed in response. "We've done it before."

"Not when I knew who you were."

He pulls back, eyes dark and voice darker still. "You wound me."

"Hah." I slide off the table, taking a few unstable steps away from him. Fire is still racing in my veins.

He narrows his eyes, and then casually, like nothing has happened, he reaches up to fix the collar of his shirt. "Always a pleasure, Skye."

"This changes absolutely nothing."

"I'd be surprised if it did." He stops next to me, and his hot breath against my ear makes me shiver. "Thanks for clarifying a few things."

I sweep my hair back and try to get my breathing under control. "I *detest* you."

"Sure you do." He stops by the door to the bookshop and gives me his trademark smirk, the one I'd found darkly charming that night at his hotel bar. "Just think how good hate sex we'd have." And then he's gone, and I'm left alone again, heart beating a fiery rhythm in my chest.

8

COLE

I ignore the burning in my muscles as I finish another lap in the pool. My shoulders, my arms, my back are all on fire. I'll have to stretch out the muscles later, but for now, the ache is pleasant.

I'd once read that Olympic swimmers will swim ten to twenty miles a day, just to train. It's a number I've never been able to reach, though most days I tell myself it's because of a lack of time and not ability.

Swimming gives me time to think. It always has, even when my life runs at a million miles per minute, and all I have is this hour for myself in the water.

My thoughts today have drifted from the new investment my firm is considering to my little sister and back around again to Between the Pages.

Because inevitably these days, all my thoughts seem to lead back there, and especially to the bookstore clerk with fire in her veins.

I should get her out of my mind. She'd realized what I wanted and said no. She'd even outlined why it would be a bad idea. She'd been right, too. It would be unprofessional. Complicated. Messy.

And yet, the time I spent with her was some of the most fun I'd had in months. Not once had she tried to suck up to me; to drop hints about monetary needs or expensive restaurants she wanted to try. The women I'd tried to date in the last few years invariably did, as if I'd become terrible at choosing or if the choices available to me had narrowed with success.

Skye held my success against me. It's hard not to smile at the memory of her anger. She's entitled to it, but the way she argues and fights is... well, it's admirable. She's refusing to go down without a fight, and damn it if that doesn't make me want her more.

I finally pull myself out of the pool when the giant clock on the wall reads 7:30 a.m. I've already overstayed my usual hour in the water.

Bryan and Tyra are waiting for me when I arrive at the office thirty minutes later. They're the picture of competence; Bryan has his laptop under his arm and Tyra a smartphone in each hand. The key to good business strategy, which I've been asked a thousand times, is always this; hiring the best of the best. Your business will go absolutely nowhere if you can't delegate.

But that's never the answer business panels and newspapers want to hear. They want me to say things like *inner drive* and *ambition. Either you have it or you don't.* It's all bullshit.

"Good morning," Tyra says. She hands me a coffee and I take it in stride, sinking into one of the chairs in my office. "The Cowell project is on schedule. They just phoned in their latest numbers."

"Good."

"Your interview with *The Inside Tribune* is out today," Bryan says. "Should be circulating already. I'll have a copy of the interview on your desk in an hour."

"Perfect." I don't know if I want to read it. Melissa Edwards had asked leading questions, and the story will inevitably be spun in a way I'll barely recognize.

Bryan sees my frown. "It's great for publicity. And what's great for publicity—"

"Is great for business," I say. "I got it. What else?"

Tyra hands me a thick binder. "The finalized hotel development plans. And, per your instructions, there are two options for the lobby. One that includes Between the Pages, and one that excludes it."

I thumb through the glossy papers. It's a document made for investors, not developers, so the graphics look stellar. I have to give props to the graphic artist, too, for managing to make the inclusion of the small bookstore work with the ultramodern look of the hotel.

It doesn't look bad, but it doesn't exactly look right, either. I'll have to schedule a meeting with the head architect for the project.

"There's this, too." Bryan hands me a printed invitation to a book reading. It's well-designed, with the logo of Between the Pages at the top. "It's tonight. Mrs. Stiller from the bookstore emailed it over to our office." He clears his throat. "I think it's meant as a joke, or a taunt."

"They're not going down without a fight," Tyra notes. "I doubt it'll be enough, though."

My eyes scan through the invite. Seven p.m. All welcome. *Marks the beginning of our mid-season sale.*

"It was sent to our office email?"

"Yes," Bryan replies. "I was CC:ed."

In the bottom right corner there's a small symbol, like a stamp. I have to lean in close to read what it says. *Buy local, support your community, say no to big business.*

I want to laugh.

Instead, I put the invite on my desk and lean back. "Anything else?"

Bryan and Tyra run through the morning report. I'm listening, but mentally I'm already changing my plans for the evening. There's a dinner I can easily cancel; I wasn't the main guest anyway.

It's been over a week since I last spoke to Skye in the bookstore and she called me out on my proposal, *and* said no. But she'd sent this invite to our office. Karli might have been the sender, but Skye was the instigator—no doubt in my mind.

Charles drops me off outside Between the Pages a quarter past seven. It's lit up from the outside; fairy lighting hangs in the window display.

I open the door to a crowd. It's packed in a way I've never seen it before, the large reading room table moved to make room for chairs. People are gathered around it in a semicircle, people in all shapes and sizes.

Karli is sitting in one of the main chairs next to an older woman reading from a red book. I retreat to one of the corners, melting into the background, and scan the crowd. The author is reciting a passage about spring, something about seasons and buds and flowers, but I'm looking for a certain bookstore employee.

I find her in the opposite corner.

Skye is in a bookstore T-shirt and a pair of tight jeans, her long hair loose. It falls in waves down her back and frames her face, currently frowning as she fiddles with a microphone system. There's a healthy flush to her skin.

I want to smile. She's the architect of this whole thing, but of course she's not on the makeshift stage to take credit next to Karli, but working away behind the scenes.

Judging from the crowd, it's a popular event, too. People are listening in rapt silence. All around us, handwritten *sale* signs hang over dark-wooden bookshelves. The place looks spectacular.

The author finishes her passage with a dramatic pause and the audience erupts into applause. Karli accepts a microphone from Skye, her frown turned into a wide smile now. It makes me want to smile too.

"Testing, testing," she says, to a few laughs. "All right, we're back up and running. Many thanks to Nigella for coming out and sharing her book, *The Seasons*, with us here today. We'll be back shortly with a Q&A session—prepare your questions!

Please feel free to mingle, look at our sale section, and grab a bite to eat in the meanwhile. Your support means the world to us. Thank you."

More applause. I watch as Skye takes the microphone and darts around the shop to the back, returning with a tray overflowing with aperitifs. They've really gone all in with this thing.

I lean against one of the built-in bookshelves and wait for her to notice me. It takes a while, giving me ample opportunity to see the softness in her features as she talks to one customer after another. Her serviceable smile, her pealing laughter. I know that'll be gone the second she sees me.

And then she finally does, her gaze sweeping across the bookstore but stopping dead when it lands on me.

I wink at her.

Her eyebrows rise, and then she's advancing, hands on her hips. "You came to our book reading?"

"My office received an invitation. It would've been rude to decline."

To my surprise, she gives me a beaming smile. She's always been beautiful, but with that joy on her face, she's breathtaking. "Well, I'm glad you're here. Look around—see all these people? Watch it and weep, Porter. Our sales are already up compared to last quarter."

"Oh, I can imagine." I nod at one of the sale signs. "You took my advice, too. Again, I might add."

The smile on her face disappears, replaced by the challenging expression I'm used to. "I'd be insane not to accept advice from the most eligible billionaire bachelor in Seattle."

I groan. "Don't tell me you read today's article too."

"Oh, yes. How could I not? You were on the front page."

I silently curse Melissa Edwards and my PR team for thinking the interview was a good idea. She'd taken my words and run with them, and I'd barely recognized the man I read about in the article.

"I was talked into it," I say. "And in my defense, journalists always exaggerate."

"So you're saying you're *not* the most eligible bachelor in Seattle? Why, Cole, if you're not careful you'll come across humble."

I give her my trademark smirk. "The title was accurate. It was the content that skewed on the ridiculous."

"Well, I thought it was very informative," Skye says, leaning closer. "I hadn't realized just how ruthless you can be in business."

The smile on my face freezes as I realize what she's referring to. The exact passage I'd wanted omitted, about my former business partner and his now-wife. It had ended up in the article anyway, as it always did, because it made for a good story. Cole Porter, asshole extraordinaire.

Seems it had reached Skye too, not that she needed another reason to dislike me. "Ruthless, efficient," I say. "It's all just semantics."

"It was motivational," she says. "I'll have to out-ruthless you on this project."

"Well," I say, looking around the packed store, "it looks like it's working. You're a worthy opponent, I'll give you that."

Skye purses her lips. There's a feverish look in her eyes, and up close, her flushed skin is pronounced. "Is that why you're here tonight? Corporate espionage? We still have five weeks left to turn this around."

"Am I that obvious?"

"Yes," she says. "You should have worn a trench coat and a newspaper with holes in it."

I nod, playing along, but I'm really just looking at her. There are circles under her eyes.

"I'll think about that for next time. Have you been organizing this on your own?"

She looks across the room again—at the milling guests, Karli entertaining the author, the plate of sandwiches quickly emptying. "No, Karli and I did it together."

"Hmm. But you made the invitations and flyers, I'm guessing? I appreciated the little addition in the bottom right corner."

She smiles. "I only added that to your invitation. Not very subtle, I know."

"Well-played. Have you had anything to drink?"

"No." She frowns. "We're not serving alcohol."

"I mean water. You look a bit... are you okay?"

She pushes her hair back behind her ear. "Yes, I'm great." A voice across the room calls her name—"Skye!"—and she turns from me. Karli is holding the mic up high. "It's time!"

I watch as Skye sets up the mic system again and hands Karli a set of questions. As the question and answer sessions starts, she's off again, clearing off the tray of food and talking quietly to customers throughout the store.

I stay in my corner, out of sight and out of mind, occasionally answering emails on my phone. Skye is in the opposite corner, across the crowd, the both of us boxers preparing to square off. She sways slightly on her feet, and as I watch she reaches up to furtively wipe her forehead. She's clearly not doing very well.

After the author's Q&A session is done, Skye heads to the register. The line is long—it curves through nearly the entire store, obviously not equipped for this many people.

"Excuse me," I say, pushing my way through throngs of people to reach her. She looks like she's ready to collapse. "Pardon me."

"Hey!" someone calls. "No cutting in line!"

I raise a hand. "I work here!"

The look Skye sends me is furious. "What are you *doing*?"

"Let me help." I nod toward the waiting masses, moving to her left side. "You handle the payment, I'll pack."

There's a pause, infinitesimal, where Skye has to decide between her pride and her need. The latter wins. "Fine," she murmurs, turning to the next customer with a beaming smile.

"Thanks for coming tonight," she says.

The man gives her an uncertain smile back. "My pleasure. I've walked by this shop a thousand times and never gone in. Can't imagine why."

"It's easy enough to do."

"Well, that's changing now."

I hand him the bag of books. Judging from the weight, he really enjoyed Between the Pages' new sale. "You're welcome back any time. Thanks for your support."

Skye and I work in tandem, her with payment, me packing. Money is flowing into the register—a much-needed boost to the business. And as the line empties out, so does Skye's small talk. I glance over only to see her hands shake.

"Let me," I murmur, but she shakes me off. This close it's clear she has a fever. Stubborn woman.

As the door shuts behind the final customer, Skye slumps against the register. "Wow," she breathes. "We've never had a line before!"

"Having a sale worked."

She rolls her eyes at me. "Yeah, yeah, I know it was technically your idea."

"That's not—"

"Skye!" Karli calls, still in the adjoining room together with the author. She hasn't noticed that I'm here, but she will soon, with the store emptying out. Skye shoots me a conflicted look. Her skin, which had been flushed just an hour ago, is now pallid. "Thanks for helping."

It's a clear dismissal, and I know I should leave, but… "You look awful."

She frowns. "Well, thanks for that too, I suppose."

"No, you look sick."

"I might have a cold. I'll be fine."

In the other room, Karli offers the author a ride home, her voice carrying across to us. Skye sighs, looking like she's about to keel over.

"She's leaving?" I murmur. "You're to clean up and close shop alone?"

"She has an early parent-teacher conference tomorrow. I offered to handle the late night."

"Does she know you're sick?"

"I have the *sniffles,* and no."

I cross my arms across my chest. "You can't do everything alone, Skye."

"Watch me."

"If you're pulling these numbers, you two should hire—"

"Stop arguing," she says, and with more force than I thought she could muster, she pushes me into the adjacent storage room. "And be quiet."

In the darkness, I'm standing next to boxes and boxes of books. How much inventory do they have? I lean against a few of the boxes and openly eavesdrop on the conversation on the other side of the curtain.

"Oh, there you are, Skye! We're heading out. Thanks for tonight," Karli says. They exchange pleasantries and goodbyes, a door finally closing. The bookstore is quiet once again.

"I'm coming out now," I declare loudly.

There's no response. When I emerge, Skye is holding on to the counter with both hands, taking a few deep breaths.

I'm at her side in seconds. "Skye?"

"I'm fine. I'll be fine."

"Come on. Have a seat." I wrap an arm around her waist and help her over to a chair in the reading room. The fact that she doesn't protest tells me everything I need to know about just *how* sick she is.

"Let me take you to a doctor."

"No, no. I just need to finish here and then lie down for a bit."

"You're burning up."

She sinks into the chair, boneless. "Mmm. Maybe."

"How could you not tell Karli this?"

"I needed the event to go well. It *had* to be a success," she murmurs, looking around the room with glazed eyes. "There's so much to clear out."

"Tell me what to do."

She gives a weak laugh. "You'll help?"

"Yes."

"All right. Well, we need to stack the fold-up chairs. The

plates need to be cleared away. I can... I should close the register. I can do that."

We work in silence. It doesn't take me long to clear away the chairs and the trash—the bookstore isn't that big. From the corner, Skye works with painfully slow movements at the register.

And she'd said that she had a cold. The woman has no instinct for self-preservation. "All right," I say finally, "the place looks *immaculate*. Can we go now? You need to rest."

She sways at my side, but doesn't respond.

"Skye?"

"Yes," she mumbles. "That's me."

I touch her forehead again and her eyes drift closed in response. "You're cool. Your hand is, I mean. It feels good."

"Okay, we're getting you home right away." I help her to the front door. "Do you have your purse?"

She nods, pointing to the bag tucked under her arm. "All set." She's a warm weight against me, not protesting my supporting arm.

"Where's your car?"

She shakes her head but stops abruptly, frowning in pain. "Ow. My head."

"Do you often get this sick?"

"No. The flu. My nephew had it last week. Must have caught it."

"Your car?"

"I walked to work today," she says, and I want to curse. Of course she did, and had planned to walk home after she closed up shop, late and in the dark. It's almost ten.

She takes a step away from me and sways, but stays on her feet, fumbling with the clasp of her bag. "I'll call a taxi," she mumbles. "I can get home. Thanks."

"No way am I putting you in a taxi right now. Tell me your address, and we'll get you home, and tomorrow you're going to a hospital." I wrap my left arm around her and use my right to dial Charles.

"We're ready."

"I'll be there in five," he says, hanging up.

Skye shivers beside me, despite the late summer warmth and her high temperature. "Who did you call?"

"My driver. Will you tell me your address?"

Skye looks up at me, but her eyes aren't narrowed in suspicion or her usual challenge. There's gratefulness there instead and something else, a bone-deep tiredness. "14 Fairfield Point. It's close."

By the time we get into the backseat of my car, Skye has her eyes closed and her head back against the seat.

Charles shoots me a look in the mirror. "Everything OK, sir?"

"She's sick. I'll give Dr. Johnson a call. Hopefully you can pick him up after you drop us off."

Skye doesn't protest—she's no longer listening to our conversation. It's not a good sign for someone who always wants to have the last word.

I call Dr. Johnson and keep an eye on her the entire car ride. It's late, but he says yes. He always does for me or my family.

"Come on," I tell Skye as we slide to a stop. "Time to get out."

She makes a valiant effort at opening the door but it barely budges, her arms weak with fever. Charles is there an instant later and she shoots him a delirious smile. "Thanks, Cole," she mumbles.

Charles gives me a look that is more concerned than amused. With his graying hair and mustache, we look nothing alike. "I'll head to Dr. Johnson's right away."

"Excellent."

I wrap my arm around Skye and take her purse from her dangerously lax grip. She doesn't protest as I help her unlock her front door, or as we walk the flight of stairs up to her apartment.

I push her door open as soon as she unlocks it. "God," she breathes. "Finally home."

And then she does something I don't expect.

She faints.

I catch her before she sails to the floor, my arms under her in a heartbeat. Her body is limp and far too hot as I carry her into the small apartment and kick the door closed behind me.

"Damn it," I tell her, not that she's listening anymore. "And you didn't want a doctor?"

I find her bedroom, laying her down gently on the queen-sized bed. Taking a seat next to her, I touch both her forehead and her wrist. Fainting is one thing, but being unconscious is quite another.

"Skye?" I ask. "Can you hear me?"

Her eyes blink open. They struggle to focus, finally landing on my face. "Hey," she says weakly. "What are *you* doing here?"

I want to laugh in relief. Instead, I pull my hand from hers and start untying the laces of her shoes.

"You're sick."

She covers her face. "So that's why I feel awful."

"Yes." I get both of her shoes off and she immediately turns over, snuggling deeper into bed. With one hand she searches for the comforter and I help pull it up and over her. Her eyes drift closed.

As she rests, I explore the rest of her apartment. It's not hard to find a tall glass of water or a small towel from her bathroom, which I run under the faucet. I gently put it on her too-hot forehead.

She sighs a breath of relief. "That's good. Very good."

"I'm glad."

"I'm sorry," she murmurs.

"For what?"

"This."

"Don't be," I say. "We all get sick. No fault of yours."

Her hand flits over my arm, down to my sleeve, her fingers gripping the fabric. "Will you stay? Just for a little bit?"

I take her hand in mine. "Of course I will," I say, finding that I don't mind the prospect. Not at all.

9

SKYE

I dream the most absurd things.

Vivid colors and swirling images of faces. I see Karli and Timmy and my sister Isla. I see my mom. I see Cole, and whenever his face drifts into view, he's wearing a concerned frown. He's usually smirking, so I know it's a dream.

I dream that there's a strange man in my apartment, too. Cole lets him in, even when I beg him not to.

"It's the doctor," he tells me in a voice that brooks no arguments. Even convinced he's a dream, I don't argue.

The face of an older man with a kind smile swims in front of me. "Hello," he says. "I'm Dr. Johnson. I've been told you think you have the flu."

"Mhm."

"How are you feeling?"

"Hot."

He opens his bag and then I'm poked and prodded, my temperature taken and heartbeat listened to. I close my eyes gratefully when he's done, seeking the blissful half-dream again.

"She's running on one hundred and four. No wonder she fainted."

"She's been pushing herself very hard with work," Cole

adds, but he doesn't add that he's the reason I have to. I consider pointing it out, but my tongue feels heavy.

The doctor puts a hand on my forehead. "How's your head doing?"

"It hurts like hell," I mumble. "Except there's no Virgil to show me around. It's not nearly as nice as Dante's."

Cole's voice is exasperated. "She's an English Literature graduate."

They head into my living room to talk, their voices hushed. It's draining to try to listen. It's not long until I'm fighting a losing battle with my eyelids.

"She needs rest and a lot of fluids."

"I shouldn't take her to the hospital?"

"Not for a flu. If it gets worse, call me. And I want her to take these. Two pills every four hours."

"All right."

"Does she have someone you can call? Can you stay here overnight? She shouldn't be alone."

"I'll stay," Cole says.

"If her throat starts feeling sore, make her some tea. Keep the cold towel on her forehead. I'll leave this thermometer with you—call me if she's running one hundred and four for more than a couple of hours."

"I will."

There's more talk that I don't catch, and a door closes. I snuggle deeper into my bed and lose the fight with my eyelids. Every piece of my body is exhausted.

Cold hands put the wet towel on my forehead back into place. It feels divine. "Thanks," I murmur.

"Anytime, Holland."

It's the last thing I hear for quite some time.

I wake up to a strong hand on my shoulder and something cold pressed to my lips. "Skye, I need you to swallow. Two pills, that's all."

The room is dark and I have to blink a few times for things to come into view. Cole is sitting beside me.

"Come on."

I open my mouth like a toddler and he pops two pills in my mouth. I reach for the glass of water he hands me, and he helps support me as I drink. I'm breathless by the time I finish and collapse against the pillows again.

"Jesus Christ," I say.

"Still Cole, last time I checked."

I want to laugh, but all that comes out is a low wheeze. My throat hurts.

I try to roll over, but my jeans snag uncomfortably. I'm still in my work clothes. High-waisted pants.

"Ugh. Off, off, *off.*" I toss back the covers and try to get the button undone. My fingers tremble with the effort.

"I'll help you." Cole's hands are cool and strong around mine. He finds the button and zipper in seconds and helps pull the skintight jeans down my legs.

His hands stop at my ankles. "Socks on or off?"

"*Off,*" I groan. "I'm so warm."

He tugs it all off and I feel about a thousand times better once they're off my skin. I feel like laughing, seeing this large, well-dressed man at the edge of my messy bed, in my small bedroom, taking off clothes. It's ridiculous. It must be another one of my fever-induced dreams.

A while later, I blink my eyes awake to another cold compress against my forehead. "Skye, is there someone you want me to call?"

I smile at the male voice. It really is a lovely voice, all deep and powerful. "Nope," I say. "No one at all."

"Your sister?"

Another wheezy laugh. "Noooo. She wouldn't care."

The beautiful voice is silent, and I snuggle into my pillow

again. It's fluffy like a cloud. My entire bed is. It's the best bed in the world.

"I find that hard to believe," the voice says, and I don't know why or what it's referring to.

"Your voice is lovely," I mumble. "Great voice. Excellent."

The next time I hear it, it sounds amused. I should know the person it belongs to, but I can't for the life of me remember who it is.

"You're delirious with fever."

"And you don't know how to take a compliment, Mr. Voice."

"Maybe I'm just not very used to them from you."

I open my eyes and peer to the other side of the bed, but I can't make anything out in the darkness. "That's stupid. I love to give compliments. I give them to my friends all the time."

The bed dips, and then a large, cool hand curves around my forehead. I lean into it. "You have great hands, too."

A masculine snort. "Yes, you definitely still have a fever. It should break soon."

I don't want to talk about fevers or sickness. I fumble blindly for his wrist and keep his hand glued to my forehead, to where his skin is cool and just a little rough. It feels like heaven.

"This is nice," I breathe.

He snorts again. "Glad you're enjoying yourself."

"*We're* friends, aren't we?"

The voice is quiet again, and for much longer this time. Figuring he won't answer, I content myself in stroking the skin of his wrist and relishing in the feel of his hand on my forehead.

"Well," he says finally, "I'd like to be."

"Me too," I breathe. Having this voice in my life forever seems like a first-place prize.

He laughs, the voice washing over my feverish senses like a cool wave. "I wish you'd remember that when you're no longer feverish."

"Of course I will." My hands claw up his arm, up his sleeve, until I find the very solid chest of the man the voice belongs to. It's like steel beneath my hands. I feel too weak to explore it, which must be one of life's cruel jokes. Deliver me a delicious man in bed and render me too weak to take advantage of him.

He lets me examine in silence, until finally, his hands capture mine. "Sleep, Skye."

"Mhm. Okay." It does feel good to relax against the pillows again, and darkness beckons. But there's something I need to know first. A memory that flashed through my pounding head, clues that my tired brain puzzled together with the voice and the hard chest. "Hey. We've slept together, right?"

He gives a low, dark laugh, and I want to bottle it so I can have it on demand. "Yes, we have. Weeks ago."

"Mhm. I remember." I turn over so I'm closer to the voice. "I think about it *aaaall* the time."

Brief silence. "You do?"

I don't see why he seems surprised. Even in my fever-addled brain, I know the memory is one of my favorites to revisit.

"Best sex of my life," I mumble.

A hand flits across my hair, smoothing. "You'll really hate yourself for saying that later. And me, for being here to listen."

I try to laugh and break into a cough instead. He's there, pushing me up to sitting and handing me a glass of water. When I can breathe again, I collapse against the pillows in a worthless, energy-less heap.

His voice is the last thing I hear. "I think about it too," he says quietly. "All the time."

I blink my eyes open to faint sunlight streaming in through my curtains. My head feels like it's made of lead bricks, my mouth cloudy. Ugh.

A cold compress slips from my head to the bed beside me. Something large moves and I startle in response.

"Hey, it's just me." Cole is sitting up against my headboard, a book in his hand. There are circles under his eyes.

"Hey," I whisper.

He reaches over and puts a hand on my forehead without hesitation, like he touches me all the time. He must have, during the night. I remember fever and sweat and whispered conversations in the dark.

I close my eyes at the feeling of his skin against mine. "Much better," he declares. "I think your fever broke a couple of hours ago."

I glance over at the clock on my nightstand. 6:50 a.m.

I sit up with a jolt and immediately groan. Everything hurts. Pain shoots up my neck and my head, and there are sharp pains in my joints. If this is the flu, it's the worst bout I've ever had.

"Woah." Cole's arms cradle me as I sink back into the pillows. He fluffs one of them for me. "Steady there, tiger."

"I have to get to work."

"Absolutely not, you don't."

"Between the Pages…"

"I've texted Karli from your phone and let her know that you're taking a sick day." His voice is firm and I reluctantly relax back into the pillows.

There's so much to be done, and there's no one to cover for me, but even I have to admit that I'm not up for it. My head is still pounding from my feeble attempt at sitting up.

Cole's hands push my hair back and out of my face. "I thought I'd be assaulted for making that decision for you."

"I'm taking a day off fighting."

He puts the book down. "Finally."

I take a few deep, steadying breaths, and gradually the pain in my head abates. I turn on my side and look at him.

He's still in his slacks and sweater, but he's taken off his shoes, his sock-clad feet looking big and vulnerable at the end of my bed. Rumpled hair. Tired eyes.

"What are you reading?"

He shows me the cover. "Agatha Christie. I realized I've never actually read anything by her."

"She's a classic."

"So I've been told." He sweeps a hand out toward the other

side of my bedroom, where books are stacked high. "You really are a bookstore clerk, aren't you?"

"Mhm. And a failed writer."

His eyebrows rise, and I know I shouldn't have said that, but there's no energy in me to fight right now. All I want is to lie in this bed forever, my eyes closed, making lazy conversation until this flu passes.

He scoots down until his head is on one of the pillows. "You said you were a writer when we met."

"I haven't published a book, though."

Cole looks thoughtful. "Isn't it quite rare to have published a book by your age?" He nods at the stacks of books that line my wall. I don't even have a shelf. "Name any one of those writers who were published by twenty-six."

"Dostoevsky," I say. "Bram Stoker. And... mhm, David Foster Wallace."

He smiles wryly. "You have to outsmart me at every turn, don't you?"

"It's kind of my thing."

"All right, but can you at least admit that they're outliers?"

I sigh. The last thing I want to talk about is my own inadequacies. "Yes. Like a thirty-four-year-old billionaire developer."

Cole grimaces. "People like to remind me of that."

I curl up on my side and ignore the protest of my sore throat, annoyed that I'm talking. "Tell me about it."

"About what?" He looks the least composed I've ever seen him, and I decide that this is the Cole Porter I would be able to like, *if* we weren't enemies.

"About people reminding you about your success all the time. It must be exhausting."

Cole gives me a crooked smile. "I can't tell if this is a trick or not. I'll complain, and then you'll tell me I'm not part of the oppressed class."

I blink at him. "No. No, I won't. I'm genuinely curious."

He lies down on his side, so we're facing each other in the dim morning light of my bedroom.

It feels surreal, having him here. "You must be invited everywhere," I say. "To everything. Even events you have no interest in attending."

His smile is self-mocking. "All the time."

"By people you don't know as well, right?"

"Oh, yes," he says. "I showed up to a few things in the beginning before I realized I'm just invited like a trophy."

That strikes me as profoundly sad, and I tell him that, but he just laughs. "Not really. It's a nice problem to have."

"I suppose. I'm not invited to a lot of things. But when I am, I always go."

"I'm sure you do."

"The newspaper spread about you that I read yesterday. No, don't groan! I have a very serious question about it."

His smile is gone, a sudden seriousness there instead. "You do?"

"Yes. Do you save all articles published about yourself? Do you keep a binder? I would, if it was me."

His lips twitch. "You're cute when you're feverish."

"Ugh."

"You don't like being called cute?"

"Not by you. Not at the moment, at least." If anything, I want him to think of me as *sexy* or *sensual*. Irresistible. The things he'd said to me that first night in the hotel. At the moment, I feel about as cute as a potato, unwashed and sweaty.

"Noted." Cole turns over on his back and stares up at the ceiling. "My mother saved all the newspaper articles in the beginning. I don't know if she still does."

"I guarantee you she does."

He smiles, and it's a soft, private one. "Probably. I should ask her."

I rise up on an elbow, suddenly distraught by this new version of Cole Porter, the one taking care of me when I'm sick and who answers my questions in a deep, soft voice.

Somehow, we're in an alternate universe.

"You stayed. All night. Why?"

He glances over at me with narrowed eyes. "You were seconds from collapsing last night. You *fainted.*"

"Oh."

"Do you remember a doctor being here?"

"Mmm. Faintly. You called someone?"

He nods. "And I've already checked in with him this morning. You're prescribed bed rest, lots and lots of fluids, and more of the pills on your bedside table."

I'm speechless for a bit. My head is still spinning, and I close my eyes against the light of day. "Wow."

"How do you feel now?"

"Better. Compared to last night, I mean. Whoa."

He reaches over and fluffs my pillow. "I'm surprised," he says.

"About what?"

"I thought I'd be chased out the second you woke up without a fever. You know, being your number-one enemy and all."

I want to laugh, but all I can manage is a smile. "No energy," I say. "It's a strategic retreat."

"A truce," he corrects.

"Yes. It's nice," I murmur, turning over again. Sleep is already trying to reclaim me and there is no point in fighting it. I don't have the power to.

The last thing I hear is a cell phone ringing and Cole's faint curse before he answers it. His footsteps retreat in the apartment, but one sentence reaches me. *Cancel my meetings.*

And then I'm lost again.

I'm disgusting.

It's the first thing I feel when I wake up again. The clock on my night table reads eleven a.m. My eyes feel like they've been glued together, my hair a mess, and my mouth tastes like copper.

The bedsheets, my own T-shirt… I've sweated all night long.

I need a shower.

I swing my legs over the edge of the bed and sit for a while, catching my breath. I'm in panties and a T-shirt, and that's all.

Cole.

He must have helped me off with my pants, and my shoes, and... he'd stayed. Called a doctor. Cancelled his meetings. The ground shifts beneath my feet. *No, Skye,* I tell myself, and compartmentalize that somewhere far away. I can't process that right now. One thing at a time. Shower first. Contemplate enemy's kindness second.

My bedroom door is open and there's a voice from the living room. Cole's talking to someone on the phone.

"No," I hear him say. "Absolutely not. I know it's your life—don't go there, Blair—but if you're asking for my permission, it's no."

I'm too intrigued to stop listening, so I inch closer to the open door. Whoever is on the line talks for a very long time.

Cole sighs. "Of course I want you to be happy. What kind of question is that?"

I'm eavesdropping. Snooping, really. And yet I can't find it in myself to move away.

"Yes," he says finally. "I'll see you on Sunday. We can talk more then."

His voice drifts closer and I scoot back in bed just in time. Cole's eyebrows rise when he sees I'm awake. He leans against the door post, still in the same clothes as last night.

"You're up."

"Yes."

He flashes his phone. "Did I wake you?"

"No, no. Not at all."

"Good."

I nod as well, but I have no idea what to say. He stayed. It's nearly midday, and he's still here, postponing world domination.

"How are you feeling?"

"Better. Thirsty. In desperate need of a shower."

He gives me a crooked smile. "Hungry?"

"A bit, yeah."

"Go have a shower. I'll fix you something to eat."

I'm too stunned to protest. "All right." I head to the bathroom and hear him grab my keys from my hall side table, my front door clicking closed behind him.

Wow.

I feel weak as a lamb as I strip off my soaked T-shirt and slide my underwear off. The shower is marvelously uncomplicated. I shower with cold water, enough to cool my hot skin, before turning it back to hot and soothing my aching muscles.

I stare at my nice, expensive shampoo and conditioner, and they stare back at me. Do I have the energy?

It feels like it takes all the willpower I possess, but I squeeze out a dollop of shampoo and start to massage my painful scalp. Everything hurts, but the smell of my products helps. Caramel and florals.

I emerge from the shower five years younger and about a hundred times fresher. Looking into the mirror, my cheeks are flushed and my eyes are shiny.

"Damn." I look as sick as I feel. I think of all the things I probably said to Cole last night. Of the fact that he showed up to the book reading, answering the invitation we'd sent to his office in person. It was meant to be a victory statement. *Look at us doing well!* And instead, he'd gotten another night in bed with me, but without any of the benefits. Had he stayed out of kindness? Out of pity? *Out of interest?* I don't know which option scares me the most.

I wrap myself in the largest towel I own and crack open the bathroom door. The coast seems clear, and I hurry across the living room.

My couch looks slept on. There's a coffee cup on the table. Guilt and embarrassment knot together in my stomach. "Save Between the Pages," I murmur to myself. "That's all that matters."

I'm half-dressed when I hear the front door opening. Hurriedly, I pull on an oversized T-shirt and grab a sweater from a drawer. There's nothing sexy about me right now. The woman he met at the hotel bar—the woman who knew what she wanted and didn't hesitate in going after it—feels a million miles away.

"I'm back!" he calls.

I push the bedroom door open. He's unpacking a massive bag of groceries on my kitchen table. A carton of orange juice. A loaf of bread. Peanut butter. Jam. Apples.

"Woah."

"Your fridge is practically empty. I got you a bit of everything from the convenience store next door." He runs a hand through his thick hair, now a mess. "It's been a while since I went food shopping."

He means it, too.

I step closer. He got a packet of cookies and a chocolate bar. A large bottle of lemonade. A box of Advil. It's the ultimate stay-at-home-sick day package.

"Thank you."

He takes a step back and nods at me. "Sure, sure."

I pick up the packet of cookies, mostly to have something to do. "White chocolate chip?"

"Ate them a lot growing up."

"Ah."

"Yeah."

I clear my throat. "I'm sorry you had to miss work for this. I didn't mean... you didn't have to, you know."

His lip curls into a half-smile. "I know. But then, you told me you didn't have anyone to call."

I turn away from him to hide the embarrassment on my face. Awesome, Skye. What other painful things did I tell him?

He glances down at his watch. He must be itching to get away, and here I am, pitiable and keeping him from his work. "Well," I say. "Thanks for making sure your opponent remained in good shape."

"My pleasure," he murmurs. "Does this mean the truce is over?"

"I'm considering it. I have a meeting scheduled with my advisors later today."

He smiles at my lame joke, but I think it's more out of pity than humor. "You have the day off," he says. "We spoke about that this morning. Do you remember?"

"Yeah, I do."

He takes a step toward the front door, like he's already itching to get away. "Good."

Courage, Skye.

"Look," I start. "I'm really sorry about last night. About… this. Thanks for staying. I didn't mean to put that on you."

He cocks his head to the side, and despite the lack of sleep, the lack of a shower, he still looks like something out of a catalogue. It's not fair. "I didn't mind," he says.

"I know your time is valuable. Anyway, I just wanted to say that. And that I'd appreciate it if this didn't affect our professional relationship."

"Our *professional* relationship," he repeats, all trace of humor gone from his face.

"Yeah. Between the Pages. The two-month deal." I swallow down the lump that seems to form when I think about the bookstore closing.

"It won't."

"Good." I'm nodding like a deranged person, wrapping my arms tighter around my chest.

"Like you said, I had to ensure my opponent was in good shape."

I nod again. He's said several times that he enjoys winning against someone who puts up a fight. I can oblige with putting up a fight, that's for sure, but not with letting him win. "And you did. You could become a nurse. If your empire fails, I mean. Something to fall back on."

He grabs his phone from the hallway table and slips it roughly into one of his pockets. That's all he had with him, I realize. "Excellent advice."

I rub my neck. "Yeah. Well…"

"See you around, Skye."

"Bye," I whisper, but he's already out the door.

I sink onto the couch and cover my face. *Damn.* I got what I wanted, and still, I feel like we've just had an argument. And we hardly even know each other.

Through my splayed fingers, I peek out at my apartment. He was here. He saw the mobile of crystals that my eccentric mother made me a few years ago and insists I keep hung for good vibes. He saw my overflowing laundry hamper. The bodice ripper I'm currently reading, very incriminatingly lying on my bedside table.

It was nice of him to stay. At the same time, he's trying to destroy the store. So why do I feel like I was rude in sending him away?

I bury myself under blankets, munching on a white chocolate chip cookie that I fear will now always remind me of Cole Porter, when my phone vibrates.

It's him.

Cole Porter: *These are Dr. Johnson's contact details. He's been informed that you're better, but if you take a turn for the worse, contact him immediately.*

The doctor, whom Cole arranged to make a late home visit. Something twists inside me, and this time it's not pain or sore muscles or even embarrassment. It's guilt at my rudeness.

And beneath it, something far more dangerous.

Feelings.

10

SKYE

It takes me two days to rest and get better. Two whole days of being weak, of climbing on the walls, of sleeping fourteen hours a night. It's a pause in work that neither Karli nor I can afford, not when we're working against the clock.

She only laughs on the phone when I point this out, on my second day of sick leave. "Skye, you're *sick*. Take the time for yourself."

"But—"

"No buts!" Her voice softens. "Look, I know what this place means to you. It's the same for me. But we're not going to run ourselves so ragged that we get sick in trying to keep it afloat. Eleanor wouldn't have wanted that."

I slump on the couch at her admonition. Eleanor, who had been Karli's grandmother, but had never wanted to be called anything but her name. *It'll age me, honey,* I'd heard her say more than once.

Eleanor, who had always cheered on my dream of being a writer, even when my own family didn't understand it. I missed her so much it ached, sometimes.

"You're right."

"Besides, we're still on a high from the book reading. *Thirty-four* individual purchases in one evening. Can you believe it?"

"Hardly." I stretch my legs out on the couch. "Did you get a call back from Chloe?"

"Yes, she agreed to be our new accountant! I've sent her all the reports on our finances today. So far it's looking fairly good, I think. We're not profitable yet, not... not in the way Porter Development wants. But we're getting there."

Something in me squeezes painfully tight at the words *Porter Development*. It's confusion, and anger, and something else I can't quite name. "Awesome," I say. "I'll be back tomorrow."

"You sure?"

"Yes. I already feel a lot better. I'm creating an Instagram profile now, for Between the Pages."

"Skye! You should be resting!"

I smile at her concern. "I will be. Soon. I promise."

Karli is a good friend. I lie back on the couch, my head spinning faintly, and stare at the cracked plaster that runs through my ceiling. She's been with me through thick and thin. A sister, even if she isn't one by blood.

The contrast with my sister Isla is too clear. When she'd called yesterday and asked me to babysit Timmy, and I told her I was sick, she harrumphed and told me to get better soon. *We all need you,* she had told me sweetly, the subtext all too clear.

Karli isn't like that. Nor, it seems, is Cole.

The CEO and owner of Porter Development had been here, earlier this week, putting cold compresses on my feverish forehead all night. *Cancel my meetings,* he'd said on the phone. He'd seen me at my weakest. And, my vain heart is quick to point out, at my decidedly most unattractive. I'm not sure what to make of that.

One thing is clear, at least. He might be trying to tear down the bookstore, but I can no longer conveniently pretend that he's a bad person to boot. I stare up at the ceiling and let the realization flood through me.

It doesn't change much, in the end. We're still at odds, firmly in opposite camps on an issue, and we haven't spoken since he left my apartment a few days ago. *Don't overthink it,* I tell myself, and open our text conversation. The last thing I sent was a plain thank-you after he gave me the doctor's details.

Skye Holland: *Here's Between the Pages' new Instagram page, in case you want to follow our rise to the top more closely.*

Silly.

I regret it almost immediately after I send it, despite the rush of adrenaline pulsing through my veins. I want him, and I want him to not be who he is—the developer trying to destroy my job and my friend's store—and I can't reconcile those two things.

An hour passes without a response. I take a shower. Open the manuscript I'm trying, and failing, to write.

When I get a text, it's from Mom, who wonders if I'll come by for dinner on Saturday and to please bring Isla and Timmy along. I want to sigh. Rare are the times she wants to have dinner just to hang out, but I type an obliging *of course* and forward the details to Isla.

My phone finally buzzes with the response I want.

Cole Porter: *Glad to see you've finally hired a PR consultant. Those twenty-seven followers will really help you.*

I roll my eyes at the response.

Skye Holland: *You forgot your thermometer at mine. I was going to return it, but now I think I'll keep it.*

Cole Porter: *Oh no. That was my favorite one.*

Skye Holland: *Really? It's not even gold-plated.*

Cole Porter: *The horror. Do you feel better?*

I blink at my screen for a few seconds. Before I can type a response, another message from him pops up.

Cole Porter: *I'd hate for my main opponent to be benched. Makes winning less special.*

Skye Holland: *Restored to perfect health, thank you. Maybe I was just allergic to you?*

Cole Porter: *We both know that's not true.*

Yes, I think. We both do.

Something uneasy rolls through me. It's not guilt, exactly, but it's close. He'd gone out of his way at the book reading, showing up initially to check on our progress, but staying and helping.

Three things I remember clearly.

1) The way his body felt against mine.

2) The reason I went to the hotel bar in the first place, all those weeks ago. It had been to live. To push boundaries. To be reckless.

3) The kiss we shared in the bookstore a week ago.

He'd admitted that he wanted to sleep with me again. That he wanted a repeat of the night at the hotel, when we'd spent the entire night doing... well. My cheeks flush at the memory. It had been more animalistic and honest and open than any sex I'd had with previous boyfriends. No limits, full communication, and Cole's sly smile put to good use.

Maybe it's time to be reckless again. I glance over at where my laptop sits, innocent-looking, on my coffee table. When I'd told my sister I'd started writing a novel, months ago, she'd chuckled. *What do you have to write about, Skye?* she'd asked, before seeing the look on my face. *Oh, I'm sorry! I didn't mean it like that.*

But she had.

And the worst part is, she was right. I'm twenty-six. I've lived my whole life—including my college years—in the same city. My group of friends are scattered, my job limited to stacking books. A major in English Literature and a minor in Creative Writing isn't necessary for that.

It's not a comfortable thought. I turn over on the couch, seeking another of the blissful naps I've been taking all day, but this time it takes a long time for sleep to claim me.

I feel a lot better the next day. So much better, in fact, that I'm back at the bookstore fifteen minutes before my shift starts. Karli laughs at me.

"So eager, huh?"

I shoot her a blinding smile and get right to work. Customers filter in and out, and I give them all my new, invigorated smile. Four weeks are gone, and we have four weeks left before the deadline is up.

A quick glance around the bookstore reveals all the changes that have happened. The plants, the bookheart window embedded in the wall. The sale signs. It's true that we're going through parts of our inventory quicker than before.

Karli leaves two hours before closing, and I'm left with my thoughts, the radio, and the book I'm currently stacking.

It's a classic. We sell a ton of these every start of the new school year. The author is male, famous for his cross attitude and sparse writing. He smoked cigars and whiskey. He fought in several wars and travelled across Europe, from city to city, for years. He made mistakes and friends and foes and lived to tell the tale.

It's an author who *lived*.

I look down at the picture of him on the jacket of the book, the thick mustache and beard. Maybe it's time to be reckless, too. After all, the authors I admire don't live tame lives.

Maybe it's time to stop making excuses for not writing that book. To give in to the bad ideas and the good ones alike. To give in to *someone* who might be a bad choice, but who will inevitably make for a memorable experience. *Live a little, Skye. Don't be so scared.*

My bravery trip lasts all through the end of my shift, even as I close up the bookstore with more hope than I've had in weeks. It sends my fingers flying across the screen to send Cole a text.

Skye Holland: *Let me drop off the thermometer before you file a police report against me.*

Not brave enough to wait for a response, I drive home and jump into the shower. Forty minutes later my hair is clean and dry, and I'm putting on mascara in the mirror. He might have seen me feverish and sweaty, but I want to remind him of what I can look like when I make an effort.

Slipping into the same tight-fitting dress I'd worn to the hotel and some matching lingerie—the only matching pair of bra and panties I own—I grab my phone. He's responded.

Cole Porter: *I'm in the Amena Building. Top floor.*

That's the only thing he writes, no instructions, no proper address. It's so like him that I smile down at the phone. Perhaps I should tell him I'm coming over right away, but he might object. I might lose my nerve. Riding my new bravery high, I decide not to.

Thirty minutes later I'm parked outside of the Amena. It's a giant high-rise in central Seattle, a beautifully sleek building. It's the kind of modern look-but-don't-touch architecture that I've always wondered who would choose to live in. Cole Porter, apparently.

My mother would call it *soulless,* and not figuratively, either.

I smooth a hand over my dress. *Reckless, Skye.* The great writers of old travelled the world on pennies for experiences. In comparison, I'm trying to seduce a man who's already shown his willingness. It's not remotely comparable.

I walk into the lobby of the Amena like I belong there. My kitten heels echo painfully loud across the stone floor.

A doorman stops me. "Can I help you, miss?"

"I'm here to see a friend," I reply. "Cole Porter. He's expecting me."

I hope.

The man looks me over once before directing me to a receptionist, seated behind a copper-plated desk.

"For the top floor," he tells her.

She gives me a professional, practiced smile. "Good evening, miss. What's your name?"

"Skye Holland," I say, feeling lesser by the minute.

"Thank you."

As I watch, she makes a call, and then I'm forced to stand there while she informs the person on the other line—Cole, perhaps?—that he has a visitor.

My attempt at recklessness is now a four-person show. I should have figured that rich people come with a retinue. Tugging on the already modest hem of my dress, I give her a smile as my fate is decided.

She finally hangs up. "Welcome to the Amena. Gordon will escort you upstairs."

"Thank you."

He leads me to an elevator at the back of the lobby, only accessible by keycard. Inside, there's only one button, and it's for the top floor.

Wow.

Cole has his own private elevator.

And he willingly spent the night next to me in my little apartment to make sure I was okay.

The ride feels eternity-long, ascending toward the heavens, my heart beating frantically in my chest.

It finally slides to a stop and the doors open to reveal Cole, pacing in a hallway like a caged animal.

He stops when he sees me. "Skye."

"Hey." I step out of the elevator and give him a half-smile. "Your own elevator? Very impressive, Porter."

He ignores me. "Are you okay?"

"Yes, I'm perfectly fine. The pills you gave me did the trick. So this is your place, huh?"

I step past him and around the corner. Gray walls, floor-to-ceiling windows. The sparse furniture is severe and beautiful in a way that's clearly meant to be admired, not used.

"Yes." A strong hand wraps around my wrist and I'm stopped from going further. "You came awfully fast."

"I realized something." My breath catches as his gaze travels down to my lips, my neck, down my body. The tight black dress and the kitten heels. My hair, blow-dried and long down my back.

His eyes blaze when they return to mine. "Ah, Skye, you kill me."

I inch closer and put my hand on his shoulder, slowly running it down the hard planes of his chest. "Don't you want to know what it is I've realized?"

He closes his eyes. "I think I can guess."

"Let me give you a clue. The thermometer was a pretext."

"I'm gathering that, yes." His hands reach out and grip my hips, fingers digging deliciously into my skin. "Have I finally convinced you to be reckless?"

"Yes." I rise on my tiptoes and press a kiss to the sharp edge of his jaw. "But this is a separate thing. It can't interfere with the business deal."

"Entirely separate," he agrees.

Boom. Something sounds eerily like pots slamming together. Cole takes a step back, his hands releasing me. "Fuck. Give me one minute. Let me handle something."

"You have a guest?"

"One minute. Don't leave, Skye." He disappears down the hallway with brisk strides, and I'm left in the larger-than-life corridor.

I inch further down and peek into his place. That's when I see the two glasses of wine on the coffee table. One has a faint, but distinct, lipstick mark.

Voices reach me. One is dark and deep and delicious, even at this distance. The other is unmistakably feminine.

Shit.

Shit, shit, shit.

I tiptoe back into the elevator to avoid the sound of my heels against the stone floor. Everything inside me feels hot with embarrassment.

The elevator requires no keycard to reach the bottom floor. It barrels down, and my self-esteem with it, even though I know I have no reason to feel upset. Did I think he'd been celibate the entire time since he'd met me? No, because I hadn't thought about it at all. Hadn't even crossed my mind.

I give the doorman and receptionist a little wave on the way out and ignore the surprise in their eyes.

"Good evening, miss," Gordon says, his voice growing in strength as I hurry past. "Would you like us to call you a cab?"

"No thank you!" I half run out of the stupidly fancy building.

My smile falters the second I'm back out in the warm evening air. Once I reach my car, I take a few deep breaths in the driver's seat. *It's okay*, I tell myself. I was reckless. I learned a lesson. And I'm never going down that particular path again.

I drive home on autopilot, my mind running over the interaction over and over again. The idea that he would get rid of one female guest to make room for me… would we pass one another in the hallway?

Hi, and bye?

Unease rolls around in my stomach. There's a reason I haven't had a proper boyfriend since college. I don't do this. I'm not good at it.

Especially not when the dating game involves casual sex and hook-ups.

My phone rings, vibrating inside my bag, but I ignore it and focus on the road.

"You tried, Skye," I tell myself out loud. "Maybe being reckless just isn't for you."

My phone rings again.

I ignore it again.

When I've parked and closed my apartment door behind me—back to my familiar, homely chaos, away from brutalist glass and severe furniture—my phone rings a third time. This time I look at the screen.

Cole Porter.

I press decline.

A message appears nearly immediately after.

Cole Porter: *Answer your damn phone, Skye.*

I don't. Another text appears.

Cole Porter: *Didn't think you'd chicken out like that.*

Oh, hell no.

With my hands nearly shaking from anger, I find his contact information and press dial. He answers on the first ring.

"Chicken out?"

He scoffs. "Knew that would get to you."

"Glad I'm so predictable," I say, "but I didn't chicken out. You were clearly busy, and I didn't want to be rude and force your guest to leave."

"You're right," he says. "I did have a guest."

It's something I knew already, but it still hurts, irrational as it is. "See?"

"My sister."

"Oh."

"And while I very much appreciated you showing up unannounced, it did present somewhat of a dilemma."

"Of course." My heart sinks, both with embarrassment and relief. Way to be reckless, Skye. "I'm so sorry."

"An apology? From Skye Holland?"

"I'm capable of it. God, Cole..."

He continues as if I didn't speak. "Now, you never gave me back the thermometer. I thought that was why you showed up."

I sink down onto my couch. "It was just a pretext."

"Yeah, well, I'm here on the same one." There's a knock on my front door. "Let me in, Holland. I want my thermometer back."

11

SKYE

I open the door and there he is, face set in determined lines.

"You followed me home?"

"Yes."

"What about your sister?"

"She understood." Cole steps past me into the apartment, closing the door behind me. There's a fierce purpose to his movements. "I told you to *wait*, Skye."

"I thought you had a woman over!" My voice mirrors his, and I throw my hands up in frustration. "One you're not related to, I mean."

"And that would have bothered you?"

"Yes!" The question sinks in and I shake my head. "No. I mean, of course you're allowed to see women. However many you want. It's not like you need my permission or anything."

"Good to know." He takes a step closer and I react in kind, taking a step back. "But you were still bothered by the idea?"

He's goading me to admit it, and damn him, but the words flow out of me of their own accord. "Yes. I didn't want to meet her. Or take her place. "

"Take her place, huh? Tell me again why you came over."

"Thermometer," I say, putting as much haughtiness as I can in the word. Wanting him wouldn't be so damn hard to admit if he didn't draw it out like this—if he didn't make me spell it out.

His mouth twitches. "Dressed like this? Not likely."

My eyes drift to his lips, to the stubble along his jaw. "I didn't think you were this slow. You must have figured it out by now."

"Oh, I have," he says, eyes burning. "I just want to hear you say it."

"You want me to admit defeat? Never."

"Not defeat. A truce." His smile curves, crooked and sly. "You want me as much as I want you."

Every part of my body wants to admit it, would say anything to have his lips on me again. For a few perilous seconds, I fight the impulse, but it's a losing battle. I reach up to twine my arms around his neck and surrender. "Fine," I say. "I want you. *Stud.*"

Dark humor glitters in his eyes. "Finally," he murmurs, bending to press his lips against mine. It's just like the kiss in the bookstore, powerful and deep and insistent. His mouth is demanding and I give in to its power. Strong hands run down my arms and raise goose bumps in their wake.

Despite everything—the fact that we don't know each other very well, the competition over the bookstore, the vast class difference between us—it's the same as it was in the hotel room. It's uncomplicated, our bodies knowing one another intimately.

I press myself against him and he growls low in his throat. The sound reverberates into me, a moan of my own taking shape. He kisses down my neck and I swear my eyes roll into my head a little bit. "Bedroom," I tell him.

The shake of his head is faint. "Right here."

I crawl back on the couch and he follows, covering me with his body, the weight of him bearing me down.

Cole returns to my lips. I run my hands up his back as he kisses me senseless, a tongue seeking entry. Strong hands reach down and push my dress up so I can wrap my legs around him.

"This feels familiar," I murmur.

His dark laugh washes over me. "Painfully so," he says, pushing against me until I feel his hardness.

It undoes something in me. I pull his face down to my neck and bite his ear, my heels digging into his thighs. "Fast," I say. "Slow *later*."

He sits back, pulling off his sweater and T-shirt in one smooth motion. Tan, taut skin is revealed in all its glory. Hair on his abdomen, disappearing down into the black slacks.

I arch up to pull down my zipper, and he helps, peeling the tight dress off my skin and revealing it to his gaze.

His hands roam. My hips. My arms. My stomach. His gaze soaks up my body, my lacy lingerie, and I burn everywhere it touches.

"Sure you want it fast?" he asks, voice dark and coarse.

I undo his belt buckle and turn his former words on him. "Chickening out, Porter?"

He laughs, but it's a short, heated sound. "Fuck no."

I pull down his zipper at the same time as he reaches around and undoes the clasp of my bra. The lace falls down my arms and he tosses it aside.

"I'm pulling rank," he says, standing up and kicking off his slacks. "Come here."

Strong hands grip my thighs and I'm lifted up, held against his body. He knocks something over on his way to the bedroom.

"Leave it," I say, though with his lips against my throat, it doesn't seem like he's even noticed.

He tosses me on the bed and climbs over me. My legs around his waist. His hardness against my heat, even through our underwear. His silky hair under my fingers. I'm overcome with sensations.

Cole breaks away with his trademark smile. "No hesitation tonight. You were more unsure that night at the hotel."

"Only at first." I pull him down again and rake my nails lightly over his back.

"Only at first," he agrees, flipping us over so I'm on top. His hands grip my hips and his eyes are on my breasts, my body, unmistakably hungry.

I grab his wrist and pull it to my chest. He cups obligingly, strong fingers pinching my nipples. "This, I remember," he says, and sits up to put his mouth on them. He bites. I gasp.

This is what the hotel night had been like. No awkwardness. Full communication. The combination had made for multiple orgasms and more playful sex than I'd ever had before.

Heady waves of need pulse through me with each pull of his lips. I run my hands over his wide shoulders, the deep grooves of his back. I've missed this body.

Cole leans back and inspects my breasts—both of them full and heavy, the nipples now taut and red. "Perfect."

I push him back and he falls onto the bed, laughing. "So impatient, Holland."

"Very." I reach down and stroke him through his boxers, and his laughter dies immediately.

"This is separate," I remind him.

"Entirely," he agrees.

I pull the waistband down and grip him hard. He hisses in painful pleasure.

"We'll have sex."

"Yes," he growls. *"Please."*

I stroke, once, twice. He's throbbing in my hand, steel and velvet combined. "And afterwards, we go back to hating each other."

The black of his eyes flashes. "Yes."

He reaches out and tugs my panties roughly to the side. And then he does the same to me, the same power play, letting his fingers tease and circle until it's difficult to focus on stroking him.

"Fair is fair," he says, voice breathless.

I feel the same way. Every touch of his fingers increases the ache inside me. There's not much more of this I can take.

Cole flips me in one strong move, and then he's moving down my body, hands on either side of my panties. I raise my hips off the bed and he pulls them down my legs. "What did you think of the lace?"

"Very nice." He puts his hand on me, fingers spreading me,

before one of them sinks deliciously deep inside. "But I like this better."

Something inside me warms at the praise at the same time as need claws through me. Judging from the dark of his eyes, he feels the same.

"And so wet already," he says. "Fuck."

"Already warmed up."

Cole draws his finger out slowly. "Clearly."

He sits up between my legs and spreads them wide, eyes not leaving mine. He grips himself and slowly runs the throbbing head along my center. Every time it touches the top of my slit, I mewl. He's giving me just enough to keep me on the edge.

"Quit teasing."

"No," he says. "This is payback."

"For what?"

"For leaving me that note instead of your number."

I rise up on my elbows and slide my hands up my sides, cupping my breasts. His gaze shifts to my nipples as I roll them between my fingertips. "Two can play that game," I say. It's the kind of exhibitionist sex I've never had before—lights on, no shyness. There's no space for awkwardness with him around.

Still watching me, he reaches down and circles my clit with sure, practiced fingers. Fire races through me like an ember to a flame and I collapse against the bed with a moan. It's more than I can bear, and it seems like it's more than he can, too. We lose the game at the same time.

Strong hands grip my hips and pull me tighter. The pressure at my entrance increases, delicious, not enough, I want—

"Condom," I breathe. "We need one."

His exhale is shaky. "Right. In your bedside drawer?"

"I don't have any."

"For fuck's sake, Holland. Who wouldn't—"

I push against him. "Stop wasting time. Do you have one?"

"I might. Let me check." He disappears and I'm left on the bed, physically aching from the lack of him. When he returns, it's with determined strides.

I lay back and watch him, his v-shaped physique, the wide shoulders and trim waist. He's cut like a swimmer. It's unthinkable that I'm not nervous or self-conscious around him, but here I am, comfortable and so turned on it's painful.

He tears off the foil and rolls the condom on with one practiced move. "Had one in my wallet," he growls. "Thank God." He kisses me so hard I think I might bruise, both of us gripping each other eagerly. He grabs my thighs and pulls me close. I reach down and guide him.

And then he's inside me.

"Shit," he growls. "You feel so good."

I want to echo the compliment—he's stretching me out in the most delicious way—but then he starts to move and speech eludes me completely.

Cole grasps my ankles and puts them on his shoulders. His fingers dig into my thighs, using me as leverage to push himself deeper.

"Touch yourself," he orders. "I want to feel you come around me."

And that's why I haven't been able to forget the night at the hotel room. He'd demanded that I show him where I wanted to be touched, and he'd wanted to see it, to learn. To touch me that way himself.

I reach down and circle my clit in the way that always brings me to the edge. It's easy—I'm already close—and Cole looks down, eyes transfixed.

It empowers me. I circle again, and again, and he's groaning now. "Fuck. I'm close."

He bends me over until I'm nearly double, and I'm gasping, I can't breathe, he's so deep. My hand is still working. I'm teetering on the edge, dangerously close to losing control. The abyss is beckoning.

And then he rolls his hips while inside me and I'm lost, to pleasure, to him. To us.

Somewhere through the climatic fog I hear Cole groan loudly. He jerks into me, hands gripping my thighs.

Seconds pass. Minutes.

My legs are lowered gently to the bed as he stands, tying off the condom. I admire his backside as he heads to the bathroom. It's all I have the energy for. My limbs feel loose and heavy. Moving is beyond me at the moment, possibly for all future.

He laughs at me when he returns. "Are you all right?"

"Much better than all right."

"Glad to hear it." He sits down on the bed, propping up a few pillows. Making himself comfortable. It reminds me of when I was sick and woke up to him reading on the other side of my bed.

A bit flustered, I turn over on my stomach. His gaze dips down to caress my body, and I revel in it, feeling powerfully feminine. He might only have seven percent body fat, but he certainly doesn't mind mine.

"So," I say.

"So," he echoes. "Let me guess. You're going to say that this was a one-time thing?"

I try a smug smile of my own. "No. I was going to discuss ground rules."

"Rules? You really know how to talk dirty, Holland."

"Hah." But... interesting. "Would you want me to?"

One of his eyebrows rises. Naked, with his just-fucked hair, he looks too good to be true. Which he kind of is.

"Absolutely." He glances over at my stack of books. "I've never slept with a writer before. Will you use similes? Metaphors?"

"Tons," I tell him. "A lot of alliteration."

"You're turning me on already."

I reach for my pillow and slide my arms underneath it. "Ground rules. No one knows we're sleeping together."

"Who would I tell?"

"*Especially* not Karli, or anyone in your business."

He looks at me like that's obvious. "I don't gossip."

"Didn't imagine you did, but it needed to be said. Too much is at stake," I say. Like my business. My reputation. *My heart*, my head warns, but I wave it away. Just because I've never had a friends-with-benefits situation before doesn't mean I can't.

Cole leans over, running a hand along my back. I close my eyes at the pleasure of the simple touch. "What we do in bed won't interfere with anything outside of it. I can keep the two separate if you can."

"Good," I murmur. "Because outside of bed, I still hate you."

His laugh is rough. "I wouldn't have it any other way."

"So we're agreed. This is just sex."

"Just sex," he agrees. "Uncomplicated, no-strings-attached sex."

I glance at his chest, his shoulders, the sharp cut of his jaw. The man is sex on a stick, and I'm sure he's used to this kind of situation. Not to mention the glittering amusement in his eyes when we spar. The curve of his smile, sly and teasing. Enemy or not, I'd have to be a fool to throw that away.

"Hot-as-hell sex," I correct softly.

His answering grin is all masculine pride. "You're coming over to mine on Saturday."

"Oh?" I say, reaching out to run a hand over his chest. "I am?"

"Definitely." He reaches out to flip me over, his body moving over mine. "We've only just begun."

12

COLE

Nick slaps me on the shoulder. It's his normal greeting, has been since we were in our early twenties. I slap him back. "Man, it's been weeks since I've seen you around."

"Sorry about that. Work has been… well, *a lot.*"

"Is your new development set to start?"

"Yeah, within a few weeks," I say, taking a sip of my whiskey. Skye would have my head for phrasing it that way, but I know better than explaining the business deal I made with Between the Pages to Nick. He'd tell me all the ways it was a terrible decision.

He nods, leaning back in the booth. "Ready to lose on Saturday?"

"Hah, you don't stand a chance. I'm not losing three sets in a row." I lean back, draping my arm over the back of the empty chair next to me. "Blair might swing by toward the end. Promised her a game too. That okay?"

Nick nods, even though his face tightens. For some reason, he's never gotten along with my little sister. "Sure."

The circles under his eyes look deeper than usual, even if he's otherwise the picture of health. "Business booming?"

He snorts. "You could say that, yes."

I recognize the wolfish glint in his eyes. "What failing company are you taking over now?"

"NDA," he says. "I'll tell you in a week."

I grin. Seattle society has never known what to make of Nicholas Park. Brilliantly wealthy, but very obviously new money. Talented and efficient, but with a penchant for ruthlessness.

We'd been classmates in college and had stuck together ever since, both of us drawn to winning and accomplishment like moths to a flame.

"The number of enemies you make in a month must be hard to keep track of," I say. "Do you keep a list? A little black book?"

He smirks. "Of course. I'll make a copy for you in the event of my death."

"So I can track down your murderer?"

"Yes. I have complete faith in you."

I snort. "I don't. But I'll hire the best private detective that money can buy."

Nick tips his glass to me. "I'd expect nothing less."

In my pocket, my phone vibrates. It's usually something I ignore when I'm with family or friends, considering how many hours of the day I work.

"Give me a moment."

He nods and looks out over the hotel bar. Another one of mine, but not Legacy, thank God. I haven't been back there since that first night.

It's Skye. She's sent me a photo, no text, of the crowded storage room at Between the Pages. On the wall is a small dartboard with the nearly unintelligible logo of Porter Development taped over it.

Arrows pepper it.

I grin at my phone.

Cole Porter: *Not a single arrow is in the bull's-eye. There's room for improvement here.*

Her answer is immediate—like she was waiting by the phone.

Skye Holland: *It's hard to aim when I'm overcome with anger.*

Cole Porter: *If I'm to be vandalized, at least try to do it properly.*

It's easy to picture her face, amused and annoyed in equal measure. *Asshole,* she's saying to herself right now.

Nick is shaking his head at me. "You're smiling at your phone? Don't tell me it's Blair."

"No." I lean back in the booth, looking at him. Nick has always given it to me straight. Sometimes brutally so. "Remember the girl I told you about?"

"The one who worked in the building you're demolishing?"

"That's the one."

"What about her? No, don't tell me. You've started sleeping together."

I shrug. "Yeah. It's casual, though."

"To you, maybe," he warns. "It always *starts* casual."

"Mutually agreed casual, actually. She still can't stand me on a personal level."

Nick chuckles darkly. "I like her already. So what? The two of you are having hate sex?"

"Yeah." From my side there isn't much hate at all. She regularly likes to remind me of hers, though. Nick isn't the only one talented at making enemies at work.

"Perfect setup, man. It'll blow up in your face, but enjoy it while it lasts."

"There's a risk, but it's minimal," I say.

Nick grins. "When was the last time you did casual?"

"It's been a while," I admit. "But once upon a time it was the only thing I did."

He raises a finger, warning in his eyes. Whatever he's about to say, I don't want to hear it. I don't want my ex dragged into whatever psychoanalyst babble he's going to attempt.

To my surprise, he doesn't. "Enjoy," Nick says, "but you guys are heading toward a deadline. Don't forget she's eventually going to cut contact with you completely."

My whiskey tastes sour. "Oh, I won't."

Our evening doesn't run long. There was a time when Nick and I would've been out till late, both of us chasing shots and skirts, but that's over a decade gone.

He puts a hand on my shoulder. "I won't dry your tears on Saturday when you lose," he says.

I repeat the gesture. "Tennis is a gentleman's sport, but I'll make an exception for you."

Nick's answering smile tells me that I'm going to have to fight for victory—just the way I like it. Nothing feels good when it's unearned.

Maybe it's the whiskey, or the text she sent me, but I dial Skye's number as soon as I'm alone.

"Cole?"

"Hey," I say. "I have a dartboard at home."

Her voice is half-amused, half-annoyed. "Why am I not surprised?"

"You need to practice aim."

"Rude," she says. "You're right, but still."

"Are you busy? If not, come over and practice."

A pause. "Is this a booty call, Porter?"

I can't help it. I laugh. "Casual sex usually involves some form of planning, yeah. It doesn't just happen spontaneously."

There's silence on the other line. It's the first time we've spoken since the evening at hers, two days ago. We'd agreed to it then—she was the one who set the strict guidelines—but perhaps she's changed her mind. Backed out of the whole thing. For all of her refreshing feistiness and attitude, she's surprisingly innocent at heart.

"Skye?"

"I'll come over," she says. "Give me half an hour."

"I'll send a car."

She snorts. "Under no circumstances will you do that. I'll drive myself."

I find myself smiling a long time after I've hung up, thinking about her soft voice laced with steel as she refused my offer. Independent Skye Holland in action, indeed.

Forty-five minutes later the bell of the elevator rings out in my hallway, and there she is in all her glory.

"You're late," I call.

"Only by fifteen minutes." The sound of boots being unzipped, a jacket tossed to the ground. "It's a school night. I can't stay late."

"Are you telling me to hurry?"

"Yes."

"A master never hurries." I grab a bottle out of the wine cooler and open it with an easy move. Skye walks into my kitchen on bare feet, wearing a short-sleeved sundress. Her brown hair is loose over her shoulders and gleaming. I've always thought she's pretty, but under the dimmed lights, her face is arresting. Dainty nose. Sparkling eyes. Temptingly curved mouth.

I clear my throat. "Wine?"

"Yes, please." She takes a sip, looking up at me through dark lashes. It's a brazen look—confident in its ability to seduce.

"I'm glad you came over."

"I told you I would."

I lean back against the counter, sweeping my eyes over her form, stopping at her neck, her cleavage, her hips. It's completely inappropriate, which is the point. She shifts her feet from under my scrutiny. "Well," I say finally. "I had my doubts."

"Oh?"

"Yeah. Is this the first casual relationship you've had?"

She ignores me pointedly, walking around the concrete kitchen island. "Do you ever cook here?"

"Sometimes. You're evading the question."

Skye sits down on one of the high chairs and looks around. I wonder what she thinks of my place—of the stark, minimalist design. It's a world away from her apartment, with its knick-knacks and lack of bookcases and complete hominess.

"You must hate my place," she says, as if she's realizing the same difference.

"Not at all." If anything, it reminds me of my old apartment. Of the house I grew up in. Of family and warmth.

"What instructions did you give your interior designer? Luxury Buddhism?"

I chuckle. "I didn't give any. The place was furnished when I bought it." Not to mention I'd been in a rush, not wanting to stay one more night in the place I'd lived with my ex.

I put my glass down and walk around the counter to where she's sitting. Her dress has ridden up and I put a hand on her thigh, smoothing over soft skin. "Is this the first time you've had an arrangement like ours? Explicitly casual?"

Her lips open, invitingly full, even as her brown eyes shutter. "Perhaps," she says. "I don't usually sleep with men I'm also trying to win a business deal against."

"Oh, you don't?"

"No. You're kind of my first in that regard."

I put a hand over my heart. "Honored."

"You should be." She pulls away from me, sliding off the chair and continuing her perusal of my kitchen. I sit back, watching as she stops at my stove, my microwave. At the fridge.

"You don't have any fridge magnets," she says. "I don't think I've ever been to a home without any."

I put a hand over my mouth to hide my smile. "Well-spotted."

"How come?"

"Well, how does anyone get theirs?"

"Hmm." She runs a hand over the handle and opens the fridge. It winks emptily back at her. A few bottles of juice, some fruit. There's rarely food in it. I'm just not home enough.

"This is sad, Porter." She holds up a half-opened jar of pickles, sitting alone on a shelf. "This is what you live off? I doubt it."

There's no way to hide my smile now. She's stalling, and it's adorable. "A pickle a day, you know."

"This is all wrong." She closes my fridge and moves on to the dining-room table. There's a bowl of something on a side table—are those decorative lemons?—and she grabs one. "Fake fruit. This is how the rich live?"

"Tell you what, I've never noticed those before."

Her mouth turns into a frown. "No wonder you don't have any food in your fridge. You don't know how to spot it."

I'm grinning wide now, reaching her in a few quick strides. "If you want a tour of this place, all you have to do is ask."

"Will you provide commentary?"

"Not sure I know enough about this place to do that, as you've so brilliantly illustrated."

She slips her hand in mine. The movement is effortless, like we've done it before, her skin warm against mine. "Lead the way."

I pull her through the dining room, heading to the living room and the large central fireplace. "Keep all hands and feet inside the ride at all times," I say. "And no distracting the driver."

She tugs at my hand, pulling me to a stop in front of a framed picture on the wall. It's my mom, sister and me at Blair's graduation. I'm wearing a pair of dark sunglasses and a suit, looking, as Blair so lovingly put it, "Like a complete jackass."

"This is your family?"

I rub my neck. "Yeah."

"Your sister is gorgeous."

What's the appropriate response to that? *Thanks?* "Uh-huh," I say, wondering if she'll comment on anything else. This is… well, it's the kind of conversation that's decidedly *not* part of a casual sexual relationship.

But she just gives me a wide smile. "Come on, tour operator. I want to see the bedroom."

"Wow. All right, but that's kind of forward, Holland."

Her eyes widen. "But—"

"No, no, what the lady wants, the lady gets. Even if you're making me feel cheap." I pull her forward, her laughter trailing behind us.

"Not my intention!"

"Deny it all you want."

She steps past me to the bedroom, laughter dying on her lips when she spots the giant bed. Another feature that was already here when I bought it, but not one I've complained about.

Her hand slips out of mine as she walks around to the nightstand, finding the book on top of the small pile of reading material. Her hair falls forward, obscuring her face from view. My hand aches to feel it through my fingers.

"Of course you want to see what I'm reading."

She smiles absentmindedly, turning it over to read the back. *"The History of Aviation?"*

"Yes." I reach up to undo my tie, tossing it aside. "You're stalling again."

"Maybe I'm just evaluating you. Just because I'm a booty call doesn't mean I'm a done deal, you know."

"Evaluating me based on my reading habits?"

She nods, looking through the rest of the pile. I run a hand through my hair and watch in agonized silence as she bites her lip. "Oh," she says, the sound a soft exhale. "This book is excellent."

I tug at the collar of my shirt. "This is excruciating."

"You're not used to being judged." Her voice is silky, the same tone she used at the hotel all those weeks ago. Confident and seductive. And seeing her stand so close to my bed…

"Not in the bedroom, no."

Her lips quirk into a smile. "Poor little developer."

"You got one word right, there. The last one."

She puts the books down and turns to me fully. Eyes blazing, she reaches up to the top button in her summer dress. Her quick fingers undo the first one.

"So?" I say, mouth dry. "Did I pass?"

Two more buttons come undone. The white lace of her bra

peeks through, the smooth curve of her breasts visible. And her fingers don't stop, either—soon her flat stomach is revealed. I stay rooted, afraid a sudden movement will make her stop.

"You did," Skye says, shrugging the dress off. It pools at her feet. "I love it when you look at me like that."

I drag my gaze up to hers, a Herculean effort. "Oh?"

"Yes," she breathes, her voice containing bravery and shyness and want in a heady mixture.

"Then take off that bra, too."

She bites her lip but obliges, her eyes still on mine. It slides off her arms and then she's standing in front of me clad in only her panties and her long hair. Delicately curved collarbones. Flared hips. Soft thighs. Freckled breasts with nipples that are already hard.

"Fucking hell."

Her smile is warm. "Yeah, that's the look."

"You know what I like so well already, do you?"

"You're easy to read." Skye slides up the bed, her eyes locked on mine—yes, don't look away—as I reach to unbuckle my belt. Her breath makes a hissing sound as I push my pants and boxers down. It's difficult, being so painfully hard.

"See?" I say, stroking myself. "All because of you."

Her beautiful skin flushes, and it races up her cheeks, her neck, down across her chest. It's one of the first things I'd noticed at the hotel bar. She'd mouthed off to me, but she'd blushed while doing it.

"Come here." I grip her ankles and pull her roughly to the edge of the bed. She gasps when I grab a hold of her panties and tug them off, down long legs and off one ankle.

Beautiful.

I settle between her legs, my hands on her hipbones. "*Just* a booty call," I mutter against her skin.

"What?"

But I don't answer with words. I make sure she shatters instead—enjoying every minute of it. Skye's back arches when she comes, in a way that is as natural as it's arousing. Her gasps are real, and every last one of her hissing breaths makes me throb.

She collapses against the bed and finds my head, her fingers threading through my hair. I rest my forehead against her inner thigh and breathe through my arousal.

This, I could do forever. Making her come that first night together had felt like success, and after the third time, like victory. Especially when she told me she rarely came with men.

"I want you to fuck me," she breathes.

I groan. "Fuck. So do I."

"Hard, Cole. Really, really hard."

Hate sex, I think, Nick's words finding me again.

I flip her over, my hands on her hips, pulling her ass back to me. I want her too much to think clearly, to think of anything beyond her body bent before me.

"Yes," she breathes, arching.

I've never put on a condom faster than I do right then, with Skye's demanding eyes on me. "Hard," she growls.

She doesn't have to say it twice.

Pushing inside her feels like heaven and both of us moan at the sensation. She's beyond wet, and so tight, and fucking hell I could do this forever. Fuck her forever.

Except I can't. Each deep stroke increases the sensation, the need inside me, and I won't last for shit this time around. It's too good. I grip her hips—they're the perfect handhold—only to abandon them for her round ass. Watching myself slide in and out of her. Hearing her gasp when I go deep.

"Cole," she mewls, hands fisting in my covers. She falls forward onto her elbows, her legs moving closer together, making her feel even tighter around me. It obliviates all thought.

"Good girl," I growl, fucking her harder and faster, giving her everything, my hands in her hair, and then she's moaning and I've lost control and her body is so beautiful underneath me and I can still taste her on my tongue and it's all over. I erupt with my hands gripping her hips, pinning her in place, buried deep.

She whimpers against the coverlet. "Oh my God."

I brace my hands against the bed, covering her completely, and try to focus on breathing. How is every time I fuck her better than the last?

"You OK?"

I huff a laugh and pull out of her, tossing the condom aside. "I was going to ask you that." I collapse onto the bed, my breath furious. She turns over onto her back beside me.

"Yes." Skye is in no better shape—her arms and legs spread out like a starfish, staring up at the ceiling. "Wow. That was…"

"Fucking unreal," I mutter.

"Yeah, that's about right."

I look over at her. Flushed skin, glazed eyes. Beautiful hair that spreads across my bed like brown silk. "Not too hard?"

She shakes her head, vigorously enough to make me smile. "No. Perfect amount."

"You feel unbelievably good against me, not to mention around me. I'm always surprised I manage to last at all."

Skye turns to look at me, amusement and embarrassment evident in her eyes. Is she not used to compliments during sex, either? If so, it makes me seriously question the men she's been with before.

"Is this the part where I compliment your dick?"

I laugh, reaching over to flick her pert nose. "Only if you want to."

"In that case, I'd say—" The shrill sound of a phone ringing cuts through the air. It's a tune… it's familiar. Skye scrambles into sitting.

"*This?*" I ask. "You have the theme song to *The Office* as your ringtone?"

"Yes." She rummages through the pockets of her dress, fishing out a battered old iPhone. "Hi, Isla."

I put my hands behind my head and eavesdrop openly, listening to her talk. "Yes, dinner is tomorrow at seven. I can—"

Her face shutters at whatever Isla says. Her cheeks, already flushed from sex, turn dark red. "You're *impossible*."

Whoever is on the phone didn't like hearing that, that's clear. Skye turns away from me, still nude, her hair long down her back. My gorgeous bookstore clerk, smart and strong and brave. "Okay. Yes, of course I will. Do you want him to stay over at mine too?"

A pause.

"Yes. Fine. I'll pick him up at six. And Isla... Don't go too crazy this weekend, all right?"

Skye hangs up, a frown on her beautiful lips. It doesn't belong there. "Whoever that was," I declare, "was an idiot."

She breaks into a surprised laugh. "Where did that come from?"

"Call it a hunch."

"Well, I can't outright agree to that."

"Your sister?"

She nods. "I'm babysitting Timmy tomorrow. I don't mind that part at all, but her bailing on a dinner with Mom isn't cool. Especially not..." She trails off with a shake of her head. "I don't want to bore you. It's silly."

It doesn't sound silly, but I don't push. I watch instead as she clips on her bra. *Bye, breasts,* I think. *Until next time.* I pull on my own pants and watch in amusement as she searches for her underwear.

"Where did you toss them?"

"No clue. I was more interested in what they covered."

Skye blushes again. "Well, I do need them back."

I help her look, finally finding her panties atop my dresser. I hand them to her with a flourish. "For you, miss."

"Thanks."

We head into the living room, Skye quietly doing up her buttons. "It's a school night," I say, "but I'll never kick you out after sex. Stay as long as you'd like."

Her smile is crooked. "So we can braid each other's hair?"

"Hmm. Perhaps a pillow fight?"

"I have an advantage in the first game, you in the second. Sounds fair."

"The fairest." I slip my hands in my pockets, still without a shirt. "I'm going away for a few days, by the way."

"You are?" She sways closer and I reach out, running a strand of her hair between my fingers.

"Yes, for business. I'll be back by Tuesday."

"Going to conquer more of the world?" Her eyes, flecked with hazel, look just like they had in the hotel bar that first night. Teasing and confident, with no trace of dislike. The way I prefer.

"What do you think I do for a living?" I slide my hands around her waist. "I don't think I want to correct you on it; I sound much more powerful in your imagination."

She chuckles, hands wrapping around my neck. "And egomaniacal."

"That's another very good word."

"My vocabulary turns you on, huh?"

I tip her head back and press a series of slow, shivery kisses to her lips. "Most definitely."

She kisses me back—soft, warm, inviting. "Then take a thesaurus with you."

I fill my hands with her ass. "Not nearly as appealing as you. All hard angles, no curves."

"Thanks for comparing me favorably to a book." She slides her arms down my chest, my arms, ending the kiss with a smile.

"I know it's the highest compliment in your book."

"More true than you know."

I lean against the wall and watch as she presses the button for the elevator. She looks respectable again—cute, in her boots and dress—but nothing can hide the just-fuckedness of her long hair, gorgeous and wild.

"Don't miss me too much while I'm gone," I say.

She steps into the elevator and gives me a crooked smile, the one I like the most. "Don't worry, Porter. I still hate you."

The elevator doors close and shutter, sending her barreling down from me one floor at a time. "I know," I say out loud, "but we'll work on that."

13

SKYE

Monday morning starts with a bang.

Chloe accidentally slams the front door to the bookshop on her way in, an expensive handbag dangling on her arm. She pushes auburn hair back and gives Karli and me a winning smile.

"Hey! So sorry I'm late!"

"Oh, don't worry about it. We've had a fair bit of traffic coming through, so there's no rush." Karli grabs the financial ledgers from behind the counter. "We'll have to go through the books in the storage room. I hope you don't mind?"

"Not at all." Chloe's smile goes from professional to warm when she sees me. "Skye! You're finally here when I'm here!"

I hug her. "It's good to see you again."

"Oh, likewise. It's been far too long." She leans back, running eyes over me assessingly in a way that reminds me why we're friendly, but not friends. She's always been a tad too critical. "You look good."

"Thanks. So do you."

"We'll have to catch up after Karli and I have spoken. I want to know everything that's new with you."

She follows Karli into the storage room, chatting about numbers. We'd been lucky to get an accountant on such short notice, and I'd never heard a bad word about Chloe's professional qualifications.

All the same, we'd need someone brilliant to sort through our expenses and newfound income to find a way to win the bet. I'd understood enough about bookkeeping to realize that looking profitable and being profitable weren't necessarily the same thing. If we could reschedule some payments, cut down on expenses... well.

I sit by the register while Karli is gone, using the time between customers to work on our Instagram profile.

It's really grown since Cole mocked it for only having twenty-seven followers. We're up to nearly four hundred and counting, and we had the hundreds of articles I'd read on how-to-grow-your-Instagram to thank for that. Organic engagement. Outreach. Consistent posting. Hashtags.

Oh well. If Between the Pages fails, perhaps I have a future as the world's least experienced social media consultant?

Two teenage girls come in around noon, giggling to one another. They straighten when they see me. "Hi there! Can I help you with anything?"

One of them steps forward. "Hi. Yes, please. We're looking for, like, a book made out of hearts? As a window in a shelf?"

"No," the other one says, "a *heart* made out of *books.*"

Excitement rushes through me. "Yes, we have that! It's right down here..." I lead the way to the wall in between the reading room and contemporary fiction.

The first girl clears her throat. "Is it okay if we take pictures of it?"

"Of course! And," I add, because I've learned *something* from all those articles, "don't forget to tag us if you post it online."

Both girls give me a smile. "We will."

It's a small thing—maybe a silly thing—but it makes me stupidly happy to see the bookheart working as I'd hoped. It's part of the mystical charm of this place. What booklover could resist?

I return to the register and smile at the excited shrieks from the back, one of the girls instructing the other how to pose. Why hadn't I made it earlier? It makes me want to text Cole. *Take that, Porter. Profitability, here we come.*

Or, perhaps more accurately, *Thanks for helping me make it. It's working.*

I don't send him either of them. He's been gone for two days, which is no time at all, but it feels like an eternity. I'd gone twenty-six years without really good sex, and now that I've had it, I'm determined to *keep* having it.

I look over at the bookshelf of political classics. Machiavelli. Sun Tzu. Clausewitz. All of them dealt with power and enemies, with manipulation and subterfuge. I doubt they'd approve of sleeping with your enemy.

My eyes drift lower, to literary classics that are more daring. Protagonists who did crazy things—lived on the road, fought Greek gods, braved insurmountable odds.

I chose messy, I think. *I wanted life experience. This is it.* It's exhilarating and difficult in equal measure.

And dangerous, especially as I sometimes have to remind myself of why we can't last, of who he is—the person trying to turn Eleanor's legacy into a shiny new hotel with plush carpeting and chandeliers. This is a mess entirely of my own making.

After work I treat myself to a bit of self-care. I close the fourteen internet tabs on my computer titled everything from *How to save a small business* to *Create tote bags for your company!* I pour myself a bath. I light candles. I turn on gravelly jazz, the old-school kind that makes me feel like I'm in a speakeasy wearing a bedazzled dress without a care in the world. For tonight, it's exactly what I need.

No worrying about the future allowed.

The water is heavenly against my skin, dissolving both my worries and my sense. Cole is my release. My escape. My chance to do something I absolutely shouldn't. He makes me feel wanted and alive, accepted on my own terms.

My phone is lying next to the bathtub, and before I lose my nerve, I dial his number.

"Skye?" His voice on the other line is surprised, but undeniably pleased, too. It gives me strength.

"Hey."

"Is anything wrong?"

"No, not at all," I say, bending a knee in the tub. Some water splashes out. "Does something need to be wrong for me to call you?"

"Of course not. Are you *swimming*?"

"I'm taking a bath."

There's a pause, and then his voice is back, dark and hoarse. "You're calling me while you're in the bathtub?"

"Yes. I was feeling a little out of sorts, but then I realized why. I haven't told you that I hate you yet today."

"Ah," he murmurs. "You haven't had your daily dose."

"Exactly."

I hear a door close, and then footsteps quickening. "Where are you?"

"Hotel," he says. "I was in the lobby, but I'm heading to my room now."

"Oh."

There's a faint electric beep, and then another door closing. "Tell me more about what you're doing."

"In the bath?"

"Yes."

I slide deeper into the hot water, until only my shoulders and head are above the surface. "I'm almost entirely submerged."

"Submerged, huh. That's a good word."

"It is. I'm your thesaurus with curves, remember?"

"Oh yes," he says. "I remember."

"Plus I've taken creative writing classes."

"Mhm." His voice sounds faintly strained. "Put them to good use for me and paint me a picture. Make me wish you were in my hotel bathtub."

My cheeks are burning, and not just from the heat of the

bathwater. Are we doing this? "All right," I say. "My bathtub isn't big, but it's enough for me. My hair is up in a bun, but it's slowly coming undone. I have a few candles lit."

"Oh?"

"Yeah. The water smells like lavender. I added some oil. But no... well, there are no bubbles. None at all."

Fabric rustles on the other end. I imagine him undoing a tie, lying back on the bed, his phone to his ear as he listens to me.

"Damn it, Skye. All I can think about is you naked in the bath right now."

"Well, that would be a pretty accurate picture."

"I want you to pinch your nipple."

My breath catches in my throat, but I obey, sliding my hand down to do as he says. It rises between my fingers. "I wish it was your hand."

His voice is heated. "It would be my teeth."

"You know, nobody has played with my breasts as much as you do."

"A crime," he says, "that I very much enjoy correcting."

My hand drifts lower, empowered by his words. "Are you in your room now?"

"Yes. I'm on my bed."

I find the spot between my legs and circle. The water is oily and the motion practiced, need already pulsing. A soft moan slips out.

"Fuck. Put the phone on speaker, Skye. Touch yourself for me."

And his voice... I circle faster, my breath quickening. "If you do the same?"

"It's always a negotiation with you, isn't it?"

"Always."

Through the phone, I hear the distinct sound of a zipper being undone. My hand moves faster, circling, the pressure building. His breathing is heavy on the other end, the phone on speaker next to the tub.

"Talk to me," I say. "I like your voice."

It sounds like he's smiling when he replies. "So you keep saying. All right. Are you touching your clit for me?"

"Yes."

"Good girl. Slide your fingers further down, slip one inside for me."

Dear God. I do what he says, a moan escaping me at the sensation. "I wish it was you."

"My hand?" he asks. "Or my cock?" I sink deeper into the bathwater without responding, and a throaty laugh comes through the phone. "You're blushing now. I can tell."

"Maybe."

"I'm so hard for you here, Skye. I want to fuck you so bad."

My fingers are circling faster now, my breath coming in gasps and moans. It's his voice. His words. The picture of him on his hotel bed, stroking himself, hard because of me.

"You are," I say.

He growls. "Damn it. Tell me you're close, don't hold back, I can't—"

"I'm close. I wish my fingers were your tongue. I wish you were inside me."

"Oh baby, me too."

I close my eyes at the endearment and flick my fingers back and forth. Pleasure starts deep inside, spreading to my stomach, my legs, my entire body. It's too much. I moan, my body arching, my orgasm exploding through my senses like a tidal wave.

Through the phone, Cole groans loudly, cursing.

And then both of us are just breathing.

"Wow," I murmur. "Are you still there?"

"Barely. Fuck. I should've taken off my shirt."

My laughter is breathless. "That was so hot."

"Beyond. I wish I was there, though. Fucking you in a bathtub is now high on my list of priorities."

I glance down at my narrow little tub. Unlikely, although I'm sure he'd find a way to sex me senseless anyway. "So do I. My fingers are good, but they're not you."

He groans. "Don't. If you keep talking, I'll get hard again, and my dick is already sore from how hard I was stroking."

"Famine. Disease. Thirty-seven times eight."

Cole laughs, the sound rich and full in my small bathroom. "Thank you. Crisis averted."

"Have you conquered the world yet?"

"Only half," he says. "Some people resist my rule. Curious, that."

I snort. "Put me in touch with their leader?"

"Rude."

I sink deeper into the warm water, my body feeling languid and loose. "Two girls came into the bookstore today. They wanted to take a picture of the bookheart."

There's a pause, long enough that I wonder if I've ruined everything by mentioning the store. It's the reason we'll only ever be casual, after all.

But then he laughs. "You're feeling pretty good about that, I'm sure."

"Yes. I think the word is 'vindicated.'"

"That's a good one," he says. "You have an eye for that sort of thing, Skye."

I have no idea what to say to that. "Is the weather nice in LA?"

"It's always nice. But I've been in back-to-back meetings, so no chance of enjoying it, I'm afraid."

"Poor little developer."

"The poorest," he agrees, a smile in his voice. "So tonight I was your booty call, as you so flatteringly put it?"

I want to protest, but when I open my mouth to, they all fall flat. He's right. "Yes," I admit. "I'm happy you picked up."

"I'm happy I was the one you called."

There is no one else, I want to say. But that would reveal more than I'd want to. "Honored is the right word," I say.

"All right." His voice is teasing. *"Honored."*

There's a knock on his end, audible even on the phone. "Damn it, I need to go."

"Take care," I say, and regret it immediately. What was I doing? Signing off an email?

"Later, Skye."

The phone call ends and I sink further into the bath, and then further still, until my head is under the water. It seems like an accurate description of how I'm feeling—in way over my head.

The next morning, there's a delivery to the bookstore. *Skye Holland*, the packet says. *Fragile*.

Karli is on the phone when it arrives, and I quickly carry it out to my car and away from her eyes. My suspicion is confirmed when I tear up the cardboard, too eager to wait.

It's a box filled to the brim with bath salts, bath bombs, bubbling bath oil. It smells like Bath & Body Works on steroids. And below it, a small bullet vibrator. *Water-friendly*, it says on the box in pink letters.

I want to sink through the ground. I want to open the box and test it.

And attached, a small handwritten note.

Booty call me all you like.

14

SKYE

A low whistling in the bookstore makes me smile. Timmy is bent over his oceanography book, intent on finishing his homework, whistling on and off. When it comes to anything animal-related, he's more than motivated.

I hardly have to help, either—and as much as I like doing so, that's getting tougher and tougher. Parts of his math homework have already begun to look alien to me. At least I can be helpful in his English class.

"Are whales and dolphins friends?" he asks, not bothering to look up.

I smile down at the cash I'm counting at the register. "I don't know. They don't live together, and I don't think they spend a lot of time together, but they don't *dislike* each other. Does that make sense?"

"Yeah," he says, scribbling something in his notebook. "Kind of like you and Mom."

I lose track of my counting completely. It's an offhand comment, like he's stating something obvious. "What do you mean?"

He looks up, pushing his glasses back. "You don't spend a lot of time together."

"We do," I say. "Some."

"Not much." His voice is cheery with a child's triumph. "Either I'm with her, or I'm with you, but I'm not with *both* of you at the same time."

"Hmm. That's true, buddy. But we're definitely better friends than dolphins and whales."

He nods, returning to his homework, like my answer explains everything.

Maybe it does, and maybe it's not particularly complicated. But at the same time, Isla's been getting on my nerves in a way she never used to. Just tonight, she'd ignored me when I'd said *I'm busy tonight*, guilt-tripping me into changing plans to look after Timmy. It hadn't been big plans—yoga, dinner, calling Cole again—but I'd looked forward to it.

Just thinking it feels traitorous. I love having Timmy around. His shoulders bent over his homework, the vulnerable nape of his neck, the cheerful whistling... he's the best nephew I could ask for.

But would it hurt Isla to plan ahead for *once* in her life? Sometimes, I'd appreciate more than a few hours' warning. And Timmy deserves far better.

Not that she gets that. Where reason is concerned, my sister has always had a mind like a colander. She hears what she wants to hear and siphons off the rest.

Timmy leans back, ink on his fingers. "Did you know that sea turtles can live to be a *hundred?*"

"They can? That's impressive!"

"And so old!" He flips a page in his book, and even from this distance I can see the outsized drawings of orcas on the page. "Have you ever been to the aquarium?"

"Yeah, but it was a long time ago. Do you want to go?"

"Can we?"

"Of course. I'll talk to your mom and figure out a good time. Maybe this weekend?"

His smile is massive. "You're the best."

"No, you are." I walk around to the reading room table and ruffle his unruly hair. Freckles dance across the bridge of his nose. "I'm almost done with closing up, and then we'll head home. Do you want to make homemade pizza for dinner? I have dough in the fridge."

"Yes, let me just finish my homework first." His voice is so serious that I have to bite my lip to stop a smile.

"Of course, sweetheart. Take as long as you need." He turns back to the page, and I smile all the way to the cash register. Isla's son, the picture of studious. I might not see eye to eye with my sister, but we both think Timmy's the best kid around—and we're both right about that.

I wipe down the counter with a wet rag. There's not a customer in the store, but that's not unusual for a Tuesday evening. Besides, customers have been filtering in and out all day—and our sales are definitely on the rise. The thought makes me whistle, too.

But then the door opens, the bell sounding, and there he is. Without warning or prior notice—a day before his trip was supposed to end.

Cole's eyes find mine right away. They're blazing with purpose, his suit jacket stretched taut over wide shoulders. No tie. Undone top button. The determined lines on his face hit me with force and all I can do is stare.

He crosses the distance between us in long strides. "Did you get my delivery?"

"Yes. But—"

He bends me back with the force of his kiss. It's demanding, lips moving across mine with a clear message. *We're finishing what we started when you called me in the tub.* And then, when his tongue slips inside, something far filthier. *We're using that vibrator.*

Or maybe that's just my mind.

I push him back, breathless. "Cole—"

"I came back early."

"Welcome back." My eyes flit to the reading room. "We're not *alone.*"

He leans back, his arm dropping from my shoulders to my waist. "Karli?"

"No."

Timmy peers at us through the cased opening, a smile on his face. He ducks his head as soon as he sees us looking.

"Hi again, kid!" Cole calls loudly. "Sorry to interrupt your time alone with your aunt."

"That's okay!" Timmy calls back. I extricate myself from Cole's arm. How will I explain this? Not to mention to my sister, when he inevitably tells her about it?

Cole must have read this and more on my face, because he shoots me a smile. "Don't worry," he says under his breath. "We'll handle it."

"Okay. Yeah."

"You need to close up the store?"

"Yes."

Timmy has closed his book—homework forgotten, apparently—and is leaning against one of the fantasy bookshelves. "You know a lot about baseball," he tells Cole, without a shred of the shyness he usually shows around strangers.

Right. They've met before. I release the breath I've been holding and force my shoulders to relax. Beside me, Cole is the picture of ease.

"A fair bit, yeah."

"There are tryouts at my school," Timmy volunteers. "Later this year, I mean."

I blink at him. "You're going to join the team? That's awesome!"

He shoots me an exasperated you-wouldn't-get-it look, coupled with an eye-roll that says I'm being embarrassing. All of a sudden he's ten going on fifteen, teenager savvy and all.

Cole nods knowingly. "Tryouts are scary," he says. "I get it."

"Yeah."

"I've had to do a bunch of them."

"You have?" Timmy takes a step forward, his hand itching at

his side. He's started writing up anything he considers important lately.

"Yes, for the swim team. It's not the same sport, but I can give you some pointers."

Timmy nods enthusiastically, pointing to the reading room table. "Let's sit," he says, like they're about to have a meeting.

Cole shoots me a crooked what-can-I-do kind of smile. "Is that okay?"

"Yes. Yes, absolutely," I say. His charm is irresistible, it seems, both to ten-year-old boys and their old-enough-to-know-better aunts.

I close and lock the register. I turn off the lights upstairs, and double-check the back entrance through the storage room. And all the while I listen to snippets of their conversation, Cole asking Timmy if he's played before, if he has a good baseball racket to practice with.

Something about it strikes me as a distinctly masculine conversation. Peering around the corner at them, Timmy is wide-eyed and enthusiastic, watching Cole as he explains something that is beyond me. *Coach. Pitch. Angle.* Bracing a strong hand on his thigh, he's the picture of male vitality. It's something neither Isla nor I can provide.

By the time I'm finished, they're still deep in conversation. Timmy has half a page filled with notes. I lean against the cased opening. "Hey, guys. Ready to head out, Timmy?"

The grin he aims my way is blinding. "Cole said he'd take us to a baseball game! To see the Mariners!"

Oh no he didn't. I give Cole a withering look, but he just gazes levelly back at me. "I have VIP season tickets. Might as well use them. The kid needs to see proper games if he wants to start playing one day."

"Please say yes, Auntie," Timmy says, almost bouncing with barely concealed excitement. "You don't even have to watch. You can bring a book!"

That makes me smile. "We'll go, if our schedule matches Cole's. He's very busy."

"There's a home game tomorrow night," Cole supplies helpfully. "And I'm not too busy."

What he's offering... well, it goes well beyond the casual status we'd decided on. Warmth spreads through my chest and brings a smile to my lips. Regardless of Cole's motivations, this will make Timmy's week.

And judging from his puppy-dog eyes, I will quickly lose my best-auntie-in-the-world status if I say no to this. It's a long way to fall.

"Let me call your mom," I tell Timmy. "If she says yes, we're going tomorrow."

"Yes! Yes, thank you so much. Thank you, Cole."

"My pleasure. I don't go often anymore. It'll be fun, kid."

Cole walks us to my car, parked just across the street. Timmy doesn't protest when I say that Cole and I need to talk on our own for a minute or two. Instead, he gives Cole a thumbs-up and a cheerful *see you tomorrow!*

When the door closes, I turn to Cole, rubbing my neck. "This is really nice of you."

His lips twitch with a smile. "Are you about to say thank you?"

"Yes, I might be. I... Cole, it's too much. If it was for me I wouldn't be able to accept it."

His hand lands on the curve of my waist, comfortable, like it belongs there. "Nonsense."

"Thank you," I say, my voice sincere. "Truly."

"But...?"

I lower my voice. "What part of this is casual, though? It'll complicate things."

He tips my head back and presses a kiss to my lips. It's soft and warm, the kind of kiss you give someone when you know there'll be lots more opportunities. "We won't let it. And your nephew will love you for eternity."

I smile, a bit crookedly. "Buying a kid's love, huh?"

"It's the way I was raised." He kisses me again, deeper this time, running his hands down my arms. "Tell him I'm just a guy you're dating. Your sister won't know the difference."

"You're right."

"Wear a baseball hat and sunglasses to the game, and no one will recognize you." He flicks my nose again—it's quickly becoming a habit of his—and grins. "This is still casual."

"Good," I say happily. "We'll go, but we're still enemies."

He laughs, releasing me. "I'm counting on that, Holland. And don't forget to bring a book."

———

Normal game day experiences for me have included waiting in line. Lines to get in, lines for the security check, lines to get a hot dog or a pretzel. Apparently the one percent doesn't live like that.

With Cole's VIP tickets—and VIP status—Timmy and I are ushered along through a separate entrance. We ride in an elevator instead of taking the stairs. It's almost ludicrous, and when Cole sees my expression, he gives me a not-so-subtle elbowing. "I don't make the rules."

I elbow him back, his chest a solid brick wall. "Do you have different snacks too?" I ask. "Gold-infused soda? Truffle-flavored popcorn?"

"No. That would be ridiculous." A pause. "But the caviar-flavored pretzel is to die for."

I laugh, keeping a hand on Timmy's shoulder. "Sounds delicious."

Timmy's wearing his favorite baseball shirt, complete with the team's logo and winning colors. I'd pulled out one of my own—about two sizes too big and twenty years too old, one of the few pieces of clothing I have from my dad. I've tucked it into a pair of jeans, a baseball cap low on my head.

Cole isn't in a suit. It was so jarring at first that I had to needle him. "Not used to seeing you without a tie," I'd said, which was a mistake. In his eyes, the rebuttal was clear as day.

You're used to seeing me without anything at all. Check mate—there was nothing I could say to that in public.

We're escorted to a terrace-like seat. The pitch unfurls before us, green and endless. Four padded chairs and a table with a monitor embedded, and on it, stats about the players are already circling.

"*Wow,*" Timmy exclaims, climbing into one of the chairs. "Look!"

Batting practice is done, it seems, and both teams are milling on the pitch, preparing for the national anthem.

Cole hands me a menu with the entire snack selection. "What do you want?"

I scan the lists, a smile on my lips. "No caviar pretzels. Damn."

"They must be out."

"Then what will you have?"

He snorts, pulling out one of the chairs for me. "The normal ones are nice, too. A bit of sea salt. Melted butter."

I pretend to shiver in pleasure. "Perfect. Timmy, do you want a pretzel?"

His eyes are glued to the pitch with an almost feverish intensity. "Yeah," he says, but in a way that confirms he hasn't been listening for a second.

I smile at the back of his head, noting the spot where his hair curls. It's always curled right there, from the time he was a toddler. "Two pretzels, then, one for us each. And some soda?"

Cole uses the screen to order. All around us, people are taking their seats, clad in Seattle green, white and blue. Seated in our own little terrace, we're attracting a fair amount of curious looks.

"Good thing I remembered to wear glasses and a cap," I stage-whisper to Cole. He smiles, throwing an arm around the back of my chair.

"Anonymous brunette number one," he says, letting his fingers trail lightly over my shoulder.

"Glad I got the number-one spot," I tease.

"Of course. I'm a gentleman."

An attendant delivers our food and a chilled bucket of beer, shooting Cole a practiced smile.

Timmy pays the food no mind. He's standing up, arms around the railing. On the table is his notebook and pen, brought along for research purposes. Cole asks him questions about the opposing team, in from out of state, and to my surprise Timmy knows nearly all the answers.

"When did you learn all this? Both of you?"

Timmy's voice is proud. "I keep up with the Major League."

"Of course you do," Cole says, arm still around my chair. "You love the game."

I laugh, propping my legs up. "Okay, okay, I get it. I know nothing."

"We'll teach you," Timmy offers generously. "It's starting!"

And so it is. We stand for the national anthem, and then I watch, nearly as entranced as the two boys, as the batter hits with the sound of a whip. It's been a long time since I've seen a baseball game, even longer in such an enthusiastic crowd. It's exhilarating.

Timmy cheers and high-fives with Cole, occasionally giving me one, too. Next to me, Cole is outwardly relaxed with a beer in hand, but his eyes don't leave the pitch. He wasn't joking when he said he was a fan. He hasn't shaved today, either, and his five-o'clock shadow is pronounced. It looks good on him.

He looks at me, quirking an eyebrow. "You're here to watch the game, not me."

"But you're so much more interesting than a ball."

He chuckles. "Is that a compliment, Holland?"

"Yes. Don't get used to it."

"No risk." He tightens his arm around me and looks back at the game. On impulse, I lean forward to press a kiss to his cheek. He doesn't turn his head, but his lips curve into a smile.

Timmy is ecstatic at the first break between innings, so excited that he hasn't taken a bite out of his pretzel. He discusses moves with Cole, who indulges my nephew in every part of the game he wants to dissect. And to my delight, *both* of them seem to be enjoying themselves.

Someone clears their throat next to us. "Didn't know you'd be here today, Cole."

A tall man leans against the entrance to our terrace, a rogue grin on his face. His hair is dark ink and cropped short, eyes taking in Cole, Timmy and me with dark amusement.

"Nick." Cole nods, a look in his eye that's impossible to interpret. "You didn't tell me you'd be here today, either."

The man snorts. "Glad we've established that. Hello," he says to me, extending a hand.

"I'm Skye," I say, as we shake.

"Nicholas Park."

The name rings a faint bell. He sees it in my eyes, because his smile widens. "Yeah, that one."

Wow. Arrogant, much?

Cole clears his throat, as if he was thinking the same thing. "Nick runs a venture capital firm."

Timmy takes a step closer to me, watching this display of masculinity with bright eyes. I put a hand on his shoulder.

"Just came by to say hi. I won't bother you guys, out on a family outing." Nick's eyes are shining with sly amusement.

"Thanks," Cole says. "I'd invite you to stay, but then again, I don't really want you to."

My exhale is audible—Timmy is staring at Cole with an open mouth—but Nick just throws his head back and laughs. "Of course you don't. And you know what, I was considering going easy on you next time we play. But now I won't."

Cole snorts. "As if. Well, good luck trying."

Nick's gaze shifts to me and Timmy. "Pleasure meeting the two of you," he says, and then he's off, striding down the steps to his own VIP seating.

That's when the name registers. Nicholas Park, Seattle's most hated billionaire. Destroyer of companies. Hedge fund manager extraordinaire. Not a builder, like Cole. No, Nick deals with destruction.

"Wow."

Cole reaches for another beer. "Sorry about that."

"*That,*" Timmy declares, "was awesome. You just said…"

"I only said that because we're friends," Cole says. "And because Nick isn't offended by anything."

"Still, though. *Awesome.*" The hero worship is clear in Timmy's eyes.

Cole reaches out to punch him lightly on the shoulder. "Game's starting."

It is, but I only spend one-third of my time watching it. One-third I'm looking at Timmy, happy at his happiness, and the other third is to sneak glances at Cole beside me.

Here, at the baseball game, he seems so ordinary. *We* seem ordinary, like this is something we do all the time. He's relaxed and smiling. Still too attractive by far—there is nothing ordinary about his broad shoulders or square jaw—and yet it's dangerously easy to pretend that we're more than we are. Dangerously easy to forget the bookstore, the demolition plans, the expiration date on our casual relationship. I push the thoughts away, like I have so many times before with him. *Live in the present.*

By the seventh-inning break our team is in the lead, and you can tell. All around us, people are cheering and laughing, toasting with beer bottles, waving foam hands around.

The between-inning entertainment begins and up on the Jumbotron excited fans cheer, captured by the panning camera.

"You really go here all the time?" Timmy asks, finally reaching for his pretzel.

"Fairly often, yeah," Cole says. "More often in the past, though. When I didn't work so much."

"What do you work with?"

"I'm in construction. Buildings, you know," he says, as if his job was that simple. His gaze flickers to me—challenging me to add what we're both thinking. *And occasionally tearing them down.*

"Coooool," Timmy says, and then shoots me a look, like I might be offended. "Skye is really cool, too."

Cole's smile is crooked. "I think so, yeah."

"She always lets me eat candy when I've finished my homework."

I hold up a finger. "One piece, after math homework."

"Whenever I stay at her place, I get to watch TV late, too. We watch a lot of nature shows."

Cole chuckles at that. All my bad habits are being exposed here, apparently. "Anyway, are you Skye's boyfriend?"

I open my mouth, but no response comes to mind. I'd told him before that we were friends. Apparently, I hadn't been convincing enough.

Cole shakes his head. "No, but we're very good friends."

Timmy cocks his head. "Most friends don't kiss, though. At least not any of mine."

"You're right," Cole says, lips twitching again. "It's not usual. We're more like boyfriend and girlfriend in that way."

"So…" Timmy breaks off, glancing at me furtively, perhaps wondering if he's going too far. "You're friends who *might* become boyfriend and girlfriend? But you don't know yet?"

Oh, dear God.

Cole gives a decisive nod. "That's exactly right."

Is it? I sink back into my chair, a jumble of conflicting emotions racing inside me. And that's when I notice people around us are cheering far louder than usual. It's still a between-innings break, isn't it?

It is.

And Cole and I are on the Jumbotron. Surrounded by a heart.

I watch the screen in a dazed sort of horror, seeing Timmy's massive grin when he realizes we're on TV. My own face is half-hidden, the baseball hat pulled low. Cole's is set in determined lines.

"Damn it." His voice is nearly lost in cheering around us. *Kiss. Kiss. Kiss.*

I pull my hat down lower. "This is on camera!"

"They won't see you." And then he's kissing me, pushing me back into the chair with force, an arm around me. His lips are warm, his back broad.

Covering me from view.

He pulls back an inch. "Duck your head."

Obediently, I duck my head as he sits back, pulling me against his chest. Applause and whistles sound all around us. And then it's over. The camera moves on, the cheers die down, and breath returns to my lungs.

"*Wow,*" Timmy is saying. "We were on TV!"

My voice is faint. "Imagine that."

"Damn Nick," Cole says, his hand fisted on the edge of his chair.

"This was his doing?"

"Undoubtedly."

I shake my head, trying to clear it. The game is shown on TV. The odds that any of my friends are watching, not to mention my family, are low. Nearly infinitesimal. But they're not zero—and that's enough to make my stomach turn.

I put my hand on Timmy's shoulder to distract myself. "What player is your favorite? Do you want to show me, on the touch screen?"

He launches into a discussion about pitcher strength and technique and I listen intently. Ignoring my emotions yet again where Cole is concerned.

The game begins again and Timmy's attention is glued, although he occasionally turns to us to point out something extraordinary. I lean into Cole, and his arm tightens around me. "Stop worrying about the kiss cam," he murmurs. "No one will be able to recognize you."

I play with the hem of my baseball shirt. "But people will recognize you, right?"

His voice is reluctant. "Yes."

"And wonder who you're with."

"Probably," he says. "But you're Anonymous Brunette Number One."

I put my feet up on the little table. "Sometimes it's good to be plain."

"There's not a plain thing about you," he says, pressing a kiss to my temple. And despite it all, the words make me blush.

After the game, Timmy has two full notebook pages of notes. He's talking excitedly about the tryouts with Cole, who as it turns out, is an expert at amping up Timmy's confidence.

"It's not going to be easy, but that's okay. If it's easy, what would be the point? And if you don't get into the team on the first tryout, you try again. And again. And you practice."

Timmy is nodding, brown locks flying. I smile at the two of them. Whatever comes out of this night, it has been worth it for the giant grin on my nephew's face.

The attendant allotted to us shows up again, a box under his arm. "Before we go, there's something here for the youngster amongst you. The team heard that you're a big fan."

Timmy's eyes are the size of saucers. He looks at me once, and I nod encouragingly. "Thank you."

"You're welcome. Now come on, let's get ahead of the crowd."

Timmy holds the package like it's the Holy Grail. Once in Cole's car, he opens it with reverent hands. There's a baseball shirt signed by the players and a set of three baseballs.

"This," he declares, "has been the best night of my whole life!"

Cole grins at me. "I can't complain either, kid."

I smile back at them both, my heart full, even if the happiness feels as fragile as a soap bubble. One thought of the bookstore and it might pop.

15

COLE

Blair has her hands on her hips. "You were on kiss cam for the whole arena to see, but you won't tell your own sister who it was?"

I groan, leaning against the wall in my hallway. "How did you even find out about this?"

"It was shared on Facebook."

"You're joking."

"Nope." She shakes her head, golden locks flying. "The caption nearly made me gag, though. *Who is eligible bachelor Cole Porter smooching?* Ew."

"You're friends with people who'd share something like that?"

"We're *not* turning this around on me." My sister peers around the corner, clearly itching to be invited in. "Is this the same girl you had to rush off to see two weeks ago?"

"Yes. And—how many times do I have to say this—it's not something I want to talk about."

"Come on, Cole. I had to see this on the news!"

"Facebook isn't news. Not yet, anyway."

"Not to mention I haven't seen you around in ages." She drops her purse on the hallway table, already reaching for the clasp of her jacket.

Damn it. Any other day she'd be welcome, but on this beautiful Sunday morning, I happen to have a guest.

The kiss cam participant, as it turns out.

"That's not true," I protest. "We played tennis last weekend, and had brunch."

"Nick was there."

"So?"

She wrinkles her nose, and I sigh, knowing the dislike between Nick and Blair runs both ways. Why they don't get along is beyond me.

"Fine, don't answer that. But Blair, I can't hang out right now. This afternoon? Let's call Mom and take her out to dinner."

"Don't deflect. I know your ways, Cole. Let's talk about this." She tugs off her jacket and hangs it on a peg, her blonde hair newly cut to shoulder-length. Blair changes like the wind. "Since you're being so cagey about it, is it serious? That would be a first after Elena."

I scowl at the mention of my ex's name, especially with Skye right around the corner. "Blair, please leave."

"Okay, okay," she says, starting down the hallway to the kitchen. "Let me just get a glass of water first and I'll be— Oh. Hello there!"

Skye is sitting by the kitchen island with a bowl of cereal. She gives a small wave, glancing down at herself. "Hi there! Sorry for…" She sweeps a hand over herself, my button-down nearly drowning her. A beautiful flush is climbing up her neck.

"No, no, I'm the intruder," my sister chirps. "Now I understand why Cole wanted me out of here as soon as possible."

Skye's eyes flick to me with curiosity. "Blair, this is Skye. Skye, meet Blair. My sister," I sigh. "My very *nosy* sister."

Blair laughs, unfazed by the critique. "That's me, always with my nose in his life. It's really nice to meet you, Skye."

Skye stands to extend a hand to my sister. My shirt reaches her mid-thigh, but she still tugs it down. "It's a pleasure to meet you, too. Oh, the questions I have for you!"

Blair grins with delight. "You do?"

"Definitely. Like, does your brother have an aversion to fridge magnets?"

I groan again. "This is not happening right now. Blair, I'll call you later."

"But I just arrived!"

"Nope. Elevator is that way." She gives me a pout, but I'm relentless, and eventually she shakes her head at Skye.

"He's always been this bossy. I'm sure that was another of your questions."

Skye nods, her smile echoing Blair's. "My very next one."

"It was really nice to meet you. Until next time!" Her voice trails off as we walk down the hallway. Stepping into the elevator, she gives me two thumbs-up and a mouthed *she seems nice!*

I shake my head at her as the doors close. The last thing I need is the cheerleader-like support from my little sister, especially when Skye and I are... well. *Casual.*

She's still eating cereal when I return, a smile playing on her lips.

"Really sorry about that," I say.

"Don't be. She was amazing."

The surprise on my face must be evident, because Skye laughs. "As long as you don't tell her that I work in the bookstore, then no harm's done, right?"

"Right."

Skye slides off the chair and pads to the sink on bare feet, putting her empty bowl down. "Besides, I kind of feel like we're even now."

"Even?"

"You've met a member of my family. I've met a member of yours."

I rub my neck. "I suppose that's true, yeah."

She leans against the kitchen counter, her hands braced behind her. "Thanks for the game last night," she says. With her hair still mussed from bed, my shirt folded up to her elbows, she looks gorgeous. "Whatever else is going on, whatever happens

155

with Between the Pages, thanks for that. You made Timmy incredibly happy."

I lean against the kitchen island. "He's a good kid."

"He really is, and he has a serious case of hero worship going on right now."

I grin. "And I'm the chosen object?"

"Oh, yes. My sister has already texted me twice to ask about my 'boyfriend,'" she says, adding air quotes.

"I told him I wasn't."

"Yes, well, then we kissed in front of him. I think he's drawn his own conclusions."

I snort. "Smart kid. Sorry about your sister, though. I know all about nosy siblings."

She turns around, turning the faucet on to wash the dishes. "Yeah."

"Are you two close?"

A long pause, the only sound that of running water. "Yes and no," she says finally. "She's a difficult one, to be honest."

"Older?"

"Yeah, by five years, but she's always acted as the youngest. A bit wild. Timmy's father isn't in the picture, and never was. I think that's why he took to you so quickly." She holds up a sudsy finger my way. "You're like the epitome of masculinity, something he's in short supply of, being raised by a single mother, his aunt, and his grandmother."

My eyebrows shoot up. "Did you just call me the epitome of masculinity?"

"Yeah." Her cheeks color beautifully. "Don't get used to it."

"Oh, I'll be dead of shock before that happens." I reach for the towel, drying off her clean bowl. "Tell me more about your sister."

"She often has new boyfriends. They're all nice, but they filter in and out, you know. And she's just like our mother—every new hobby has to be pursued. Her current boyfriend likes cars, so she's suddenly become a car maniac. Goes to shows out of town all the time."

"And you babysit Timmy."

She nods. "My mom and I split it."

Her nephew. Her family. The bookstore. Everything she does, it seems to be for other people, or for a purpose. For Karli and Timmy.

I press a kiss to her neck and her eyes flutter closed. "How's your writing going?"

"Mmm. Good." Her hand grips mine, guiding it to her waist. "Much better than it has in a long while, actually."

"Inspired by me?"

Her laughter is soft. "Maybe."

"I'm flattered." I kiss my way up to her ear. "Look at us being civil. Isn't it nice when we have a truce?"

She wiggles against me, her butt round and soft and enticing. "Yes," she says. "But don't worry. I'm being nice to you because I know we'll win."

"Oh, you will?"

"Yes. We have more customers daily. Sales are increasing. Our accountant basically confirmed it, you know."

I tip her head back, her neck soft and fragile under my hand. She sighs as my lips trail up and down. "Good," I say, my hand running down to the hem of her shirt. Her thigh is silky-smooth.

"Good? I thought you wanted to win."

"Mmm, I do. But the next best thing is you winning."

Her smile is massive as she turns in my arms, backing me against the kitchen counter. Beneath my button-up, I know for a fact she's only wearing panties.

"Charmer."

"Another compliment?"

"Don't get spoiled."

I lift her up onto the kitchen island, her surprised laughter raining down on me. "Spoiled, me? Never."

She opens her legs so I can fit between them, my hands resting on her hips. "Was that the first time you've dried a dish in your own kitchen?"

"Maybe," I say. "Is that another strike against me?"

"Maybe," she echoes, running a hand up my arms. "The swim team, huh?"

"You remembered."

"Of course. Do you still swim? You look like you do."

"Every morning," I say.

She wraps her hands around my neck. "Except today."

"Except today," I agree. "I had better things to do."

I lean in and kiss her, and she kisses me back, warm and sweet. Her hands find their way into my hair, tugging in that way that sends shivers racing down my back. Before long my hands move of their own accord and pull at the buttons of her shirt.

She laughs against my lips. "So eager," she murmurs, her laughter turning into a gasp when I pinch one of her nipples. After she'd told me none of her previous lovers had given them enough attention, I'd made sure to redouble mine.

Her hands tug off my T-shirt. My tongue finds hers. It's a dance we've done nearly a dozen times now, and still, every time leaves me hard and aching. She's irresistible.

"Sorry for staying the night," she murmurs. "I fell asleep last night after we... well." She breaks off, biting her lip, and I grin at her. We'd tried her bathtub fantasy in my master bath, the tub large enough for me to fuck her underwater. She'd been slick like oil after the first two orgasms. The memory, combined with her naked and ready before me, makes it hard to think.

"Do I look like I'm complaining?"

She grins, shrugging off her shirt. "No."

I slide her panties to the side and find her warm and wet. "*Yes*," I murmur. "You're always ready for me."

She presses eager lips against mine, scooting to the edge of the kitchen island. "Like this?"

"Fuck yes." I tug off her underwear. In broad daylight she's gorgeous, pink and sweet and slick. She pulls at the tie of my slacks, pushing them, her movements jerky.

"This casual thing is getting complicated, huh?"

I can only agree. When this began, I had no plans to send her gifts, not to mention hang out with her nephew. Maybe we should talk about that. Set new ground rules.

But then again, she's beautiful and naked in front of me and her hands are stroking and then I'm spreading her legs wide. "That's fine," I say, my hands running up her inner thighs. "Completely fine. Still casual."

Skye nods, a breathy moan escaping her when I run the head of my hardness along her. "It's casual because we say it's casual," she says.

"Exactly. You're not falling in love with me, are you?"

Her chest is heaving. "No, don't worry. I still hate you."

"Good," I say, pushing forward. "We're good."

That's a lie, because she's fucking *fantastic*. I bury myself inside, and she grips me back, hot and slick and tight. I should tell her that but words refuse to form. My body is moving on instinct, fucking her on the kitchen island, both of us watching where we join.

It's over almost as soon as it began. My hand is circling, moving over her clit the way I know she likes, both of us exploding. It's her moans that bring me over the edge, soft and breathless and entirely real.

"Fucking hell."

Skye lies back on the kitchen island, her body limp. Her breasts rise and fall with her heavy breathing. "You could be the worst person in the world," she says faintly, "and I'd still come back for more of that."

My hands tighten on her hips. "So I'm *not* the worst person in the world. It's a small upgrade, but I'll take it."

She smiles up at the ceiling. "So many compliments today. You really are fucking the good sense right out of me."

"I aim to please." Wincing slightly, I pull out of her heat. "Damn. We didn't use a condom."

She rises on her elbows. "I'm on the pill."

"I have regular health checkups," I say. "I'd be happy to give you a copy of my latest clean bill."

She blinks at me. "Wow."

"What?"

"That just sounds very experienced. I got checked last September," she says, that beautiful blush spreading over her cheeks again. "Haven't had sex without a condom since."

Her blush makes me think she hasn't had sex *with* one since then either. Something in my chest constricts, and I pull her up into sitting, kissing her again. "Then we're good."

She kisses me back. "I'm glad I spent the night when this is what I wake up to."

"Me too."

Her hand slips into mine, and then she's pulling me toward my master bathroom again, a glint in her eyes. "Come on. We need to shower."

"Do we?"

"Yes," she says, and then I'm lifting her up, her naked body warm against mine. It's one of the longest showers I've ever taken.

Skye leaves early afternoon. Her hair is half-dried and braided down her back, her cheeks flushed with exertion. She kisses me in the hallway.

It's a sweet kiss, her arms twined around my neck. "Bye," she murmurs.

"Bye," I murmur back, watching her as she retreats into the elevator, a smile on her lips as the doors shut.

When she's gone from view, I lean against the wall and close my eyes.

This is getting out of control, slipping out of my grasp, a lot faster than I had anticipated. A dangerous suggestion had hovered on my tongue and I'd had to force it down. *Stay for lunch. Spend the day with me.*

What would we do? Read books? Watch TV? Go for a walk?

Casual, Porter. She wanted casual, and so did you. She still hates me—she says so regularly. The feeling isn't exactly mutual, but I know we have a deadline. The only hope I have of continuing to see her, and having the best sex of my life, is for the bookstore to succeed.

Which means I have incentive to work against my own best business interests.

"Fucking hell," I say, leaning my head against the wall. I'm thirty-four. I've had my share of relationships, both longer and shorter. Yet somehow, Skye Holland has gotten me to consider betraying my own ambition, the one thing that had always served as a guiding star in my life.

And damn it if that doesn't scare me.

16

SKYE

"Here you go," I say. "And thank you. Your support means the world to us, truly."

The teenager smiles at me, slipping one of our newly minted loyalty cards into his bag. "No, thank you. I've been looking for this series everywhere!"

"It's a great one," I say. "I read all of them when I was your age."

He nods, tugging at his cap. With his dark hair and glasses, it's easy to imagine Timmy like that a few years in the future. "I'm sure I'll be back to get the rest," he says. "Thanks!"

The bell attached to the front door jingles as he leaves and I'm left grinning like a fool. That was our millionth customer of the day.

A slight exaggeration, perhaps, but not by much. There's definitely more traffic today than a normal day just a few weeks ago.

Whatever we're doing is working.

I look around Between the Pages, at the familiar nooks and crannies. At Eleanor's old armchair in the corner. I breathe in the scent of new books. "We're doing it," I tell the store, the armchair, myself. "We're actually pulling it off!"

With less than two weeks until the deadline, Karli and I've

had to make a pact to stop obsessing over the numbers or we'd be calling Chloe thrice daily for her latest calculations. Profitable means we have to be in the green. We can't count on future sales; we can't break even. We have to make *more* than we need to be allowed to stay.

As if my thoughts have conjured him, my number-one enemy calls. I glance around the bookstore to make sure it's empty before I answer. "Hello," I say, a stupid smile in my voice. "Are you taking a break from world domination to call me?"

Cole's voice is dark and velvety. "Yes. Feel honored."

"Oh, I do. Just to be in your presence is a blessing."

He snorts. "If I thought you were being serious, I'd ask if you'd fallen and hit your head. Are you alone in the store today?"

"Yes, Karli has the day off today."

"Perfect. Closing soon?"

"Yes, at six." I'm curious now, craning my neck to look out at the curb. "Why? Are you coming by?"

"I could tell you, or I could show you."

"Mhm," I say. "Show don't tell is one of the pillars of good storytelling, you know."

"You're the weirdest."

"Well, at least I excel at something."

His voice warms. "At many things. See you soon, Holland."

He walks through the front door not ten minutes later. In a suit and tie, his standard look. It hasn't stopped being impressive—nor has the way his thick hair falls over his forehead, or his smile, crooked and ironic.

"See?" he says. "I've learned my lesson. Call first to avoid run-ins with wayward family members and friends."

I step around the counter. "Never too late for an old dog to learn new tricks, huh?"

He bends down to kiss me, his stubble chafing pleasantly against my chin. "I'm only seven years older than you, you know."

"You had that information very handy."

"Of course. I always need ammunition with you." His hand skims my waist, long fingers trailing. "Lest I be accused of cradle-robbing, on top of my elitist and exploitative ways."

His words are spoken lightly, but it brings a faint flush of embarrassment to my cheeks. He sees it—interest immediately flaring in his eyes. "What's this? You only blush in the bedroom."

That intensifies the blush, of course, and I turn away from him. "I'm just so harsh on you sometimes. I was wondering if I should apologize for that."

Cole's eyebrows shoot high. Then he laughs, the sound filling the bookstore completely. "Of course you are, and rightly so."

I rub my neck. "I suppose. Just goes against my nature, you know?"

"Oh, I know." He presses a kiss to the top of my head. "You're a good girl. I figured that out early."

I frown at the lapels of his jacket. "What does that mean?"

"Nothing." He steps away from me, walking down the aisles. His voice reaches me easily. "Things have changed since I was here last. The sale is nearly half the store!"

"We took your advice."

"Are you flying through your inventory?"

I follow him. "Maybe not *flying*. Hurrying?"

"Good enough," he says with a smile, stopping dead in front of the bookheart, positioned in the shelf. "I haven't seen it in real life yet."

I walk around to the other side, and we look at each other through the opening. Framed by a heart, he looks like he did on the kiss cam at the baseball game. My smile is soft. "It's good, right?"

"Yes." He rubs his jaw, leaning in to inspect it. "I was skeptical at first, but I can see how this is a draw. Especially for online marketing."

"Our Instagram profile is growing."

"So I've seen, yes." He glances toward the front door and then back to me. Something in his smile deepens, stretches wide, humor and challenge both hidden within. "Before you close, I want a shot at the dartboard."

"You want to shoot arrows at your own logo?"

"*Yes*," he says. "There are days when I'm more tired of it than you can possibly know."

I'm chuckling as I lead him into the storage room, leaving the curtain open to the main bookstore. "You're very welcome to try."

Cole steps into the small space, looking far too *much* for the cramped storage room by the staircase, ducking his head to avoid hitting the ceiling. I have to bite my lip to keep from laughing out loud at the image.

He pulls out the darts stuck to the board. "Oh, look at this poor logo. It's skewered."

"Kind of the point."

He steps back, rolling the darts around in his open palm. "Ah. The angle isn't very good."

"You're making excuses?"

He holds up his hands, lips curling. "I take it back."

I grin, glancing back toward the front door. No customers. "Come on, then."

He throws the first dart and it reverberates as it hits the board, just half an inch from the logo's center. The next two are thrown in quick succession, hitting dead center both times.

"There," he says, satisfaction in his voice. "That fucking thing cost me 50k to commission."

What? "You're *joking*."

"I wish I was. Ready for some more great business advice? Find a cheaper graphic artist and ignore your business partner's protests."

I shove him lightly, like I'm twelve and don't know how to flirt. My smile feels etched on my lips. "I'll remember that for when I start a multi-million-dollar firm."

He wraps an arm around my shoulders. "Look, just make sure you get as much of your inventory out as possible on sale, all right? All you need to show is that you're profitable. Your profit margin can be razor-thin—it just needs to be there."

"What's this? You're helping your competitor?"

He shrugs, the movement pulling me closer against his body. "I'm feeling generous."

"Do you want us to succeed?" My words are a bit breathless, even to my own ears.

"Maybe," he says. "Maybe not. Maybe I just don't want you to hate me indefinitely."

I have no idea what to say to that.

Cole sees it on my face, because he snorts and steers me back to the counter. "You, speechless. Now I've really seen it all. Come on, close up shop. I'll throw some more arrows while I wait."

"All right." I clear my throat. "Would you like to come to mine afterwards?"

His eyes glitter in response. "I very much appreciate the offer, but no. I have a surprise planned."

"You do?"

"Yeah. But I'm going to follow your instructions to show and not tell."

"What? You can't hint at a surprise and then say nothing more! We're going somewhere?"

His smile is wide now, the picture of a man in complete control and loving it. "I like you frazzled."

"You know my mind is going a mile a minute right now."

He kisses my temple. "I know. You're just going to have to try to keep up."

"Cole!"

He doesn't answer, laughing as he ducks back into the storage room. I grumble to myself as I close up the register, but it's with a smile. The man is impossible. Larger than life. Absurd. The whole thing between us is absurd. A casual relationship that is feeling less and less casual by the day.

Cole helps me to turn off the lights and lock up. His hand is on the low of my back when we finally leave, Between the Pages dark and safe behind us.

"I still don't like the fact that you work alone in the evenings."

I roll my eyes. "We close at six, some days seven at the latest. It's not exactly midnight. Besides, we have cameras installed."

"They only help *after* an incident, not before."

"There's no money to hire anyone else. Besides, there are only two weeks left until we know if we'll even stay open." My words hang in the air between us, a truth we've both been avoiding. I force some cheerfulness into my voice. "We're not discussing that. Tell me what we're doing instead."

He opens the car door for me, the crooked smile on his lips. He knows I chose to sidestep the landmine of a subject. "You might say no. It'd be completely fine if you did. I'd understand. It's a bit… adventurous."

Is he suggesting what I think he's suggesting?

I narrow my eyes at him, and he gazes serenely back at me. "I'm open to trying most… *things*, you know. But now you're making me imagine the worst." I glance toward Charles in the driver's seat before lowering my voice. "Can we discuss this later?"

Cole leans his head back against the headrest. "Your mind went straight there, didn't it?"

"You're not talking about…?"

His smile is massive. "No. But now you're making me wish I was. No, I was going to ask you to be my date to an event tonight."

"Your date?"

"Yes."

"Like, out in public?"

"That's usually the way it works, yes." His eyes glittering, he leans in closer, setting a large hand on my thigh. "Brooks & King are having a social tonight."

"*No way.*"

"Yes. I'd said no months ago, but when I received yet another email about it today… well. It might be fun."

Fun. That's a mild way to put it. Brooks & King is one of the biggest publishing houses on this side of the country. When I'd been a student, I'd followed their vacancies religiously, looking for updates on traineeships and junior positions.

He'll be recognized. If we go together, I might be, too. "We can't take any pictures together," I say.

"Agreed."

"Maybe I need a code name. Do you think Skye is too uncommon?"

Cole's lips quirk, and leaning back against the headrest, he's watching me through hooded eyes. "That's where your mind went first?"

"It's a legitimate concern," I say, but there's no seriousness in my voice. "Oh, Cole. Are you really sure? Can we go?"

His thumb smooths over my thigh. "Absolutely."

"Thank you. Oh! We'll need to stop at my place. I can't go dressed like this!"

"We're already on our way."

I lean back in the seat, closing my eyes at the rush of excitement pulsing through me. *Brooks & King!* And Cole, doing this for me. He said he wouldn't have gone to the event otherwise.

A small portion of my mind is telling me to focus on that. To dissect it. To face the facts—his actions, from giving Timmy the best night of his life to this event, are making it harder and harder for me to stay emotionally uninvolved. *Hush,* I tell it. *A bit more living and a little less thinking.* At least for tonight.

Back in my apartment, Cole has a seat on my bed while I get dressed. "Seen it all already," he says by way of explanation, but judging from the way his eyes rake over my body, he's enjoying the show.

"First row seat, huh?"

He leans back on his hands, eyes darkening. "You're stunning."

Empowered, I change into a matching set of lingerie. While

he watches, I slide the red lace underwear up my thighs, tugging them in place on my hips.

"For later," I say.

Cole's jaw clenches. "You have about two more minutes to get dressed, and if you're not done by then, we're not leaving at all."

"Is this testing your self-control?"

"More than you can imagine."

I laugh, slipping into my silkiest black dress. It hangs off my shoulders on two spaghetti straps and falls nearly to my knees, but hugs my form. It's indecently decent. "I'm done," I say. "I want to sleep with you, but I really want to go to the Brooks & King event, too."

"This is how it starts," he says morosely. "I'm getting replaced."

I grab his hand and pull him out of my bedroom, stopping in the bathroom to put on a dab of perfume. "Not at all. For now, I'm determined to have my cake and eat it too."

Charles drives us to a beautiful villa by Lake Union, a wrap-around porch extending onto the water. Lights illuminate the driveway as he cruises through wrought-iron gates. Cole has fallen silent beside me, but at my quiet intake of breath he smiles.

"It's a nice place they've rented," he remarks.

A valet approaches, intent on opening the car door for us, and nerves reawaken in my stomach. My silk dress feels too cheap; my makeup too simple. I'm here as a plus-one—what do I have to talk to these people about?

Cole steps out beside me and puts a hand on the low of my back. "We'll stay for as long as you want," he whispers in my ear. "Or however short."

My grip on his arm loosens. "Thanks."

We walk up the oak steps together. A small jazz band is playing music in the corner; along the opposite wall is a giant table of books with a small gold-plated sign. *New Releases.* Something in me relaxes immediately. They have books here.

A middle-aged man approaches us, hand outstretched. "Mr. Porter! We're so happy you could make it!"

Cole gives the man's hand a firm shake. "It's a pleasure."

"Did you just arrive?"

"We did, yes." Cole nods to me. "This is Mr. Edwin Taylor, of Brooks & King's executive department."

He extends a hand to me—to me! "Skye Holland," I say, shaking his hand firmly. "I'm Brooks & King's biggest customer."

His eyes light up with delight, darting from me to Cole. "Is that so?"

"An exaggeration perhaps, but a slight one," Cole says dryly. "She's both an avid reader and a writer."

"Excellent," Edwin says, smiling at me. "Well, you should fit right in tonight. The table over there displays all of our upcoming releases. Feel free to look around and talk to our guests. Most of our department heads are here tonight. Ask anything you want, anything at all."

Cole nods, like this is a perfectly normal thing to be offered. "Lovely. We'll talk to you again, I'm sure."

"I hope so." Edwin smiles at me again. "A pleasure to meet you, Miss Holland."

As soon as we're out of earshot from other guests, I turn to Cole, unable to hide my excitement. "The head of their *executive department?*"

His lips quirk. "Figured you'd get a kick out of this event."

"We get to see their releases ahead of time? Before they're announced? That's wild!"

"Yeah."

"And the way he spoke to you... You were invited to this? Why?"

Cole shrugs, ignoring the glances several in the room are aiming his way. I can't tell if it's to admire his looks or his power. "I'm invited to most things. You asked me about it once, actually."

"I did?"

"You were delirious with fever at the time. I'm not surprised you don't remember."

I slip my hand into his. "Probably a good thing I can't remember. It can't have been the only thing I said."

Cole leans forward and presses a kiss to my temple. It's become his thing, and leaning in to his touch, I don't object to it at all. "You were delightful."

"Until I kicked you out afterwards."

"Until then, yes. Come on. Let's get you introduced to all these notorious department heads."

At Cole's side, the world is my oyster, it seems. We're stopped every few feet by well-wishers, investors, publishers, marketeers and authors. I try and fail to remember all the names given to me. Cole nods and listens, but rarely speaks, letting me handle most of the conversations. I do my best, talking about the literary industry, and yet... most of their eyes dart to him regularly. Monitoring his expression, I imagine.

Only a few people are exceptions. Edwin Taylor comes up again to ask my opinion on their new releases, a conversation that Cole politely excuses himself from. The head of modern English poetry wants to talk to me at length after I mention that I work in a bookshop, leading to another fascinating discussion about the future of print media.

I'm on my second glass of champagne when I finally spot Cole again. He's surrounded by men in suits, standing in a semicircle with Cole at its center. With his drink in hand and the smile on his lips, it looks effortless. Like he's enjoying himself. But I've learned when that smile is true and when it's a charming facade.

He excuses himself immediately when he sees me alone.

"Thank God," he murmurs, sliding an arm around my waist. "Never leave me alone again."

"You were the one who left me," I point out.

"Right you are." He takes a sip of his whiskey. "What a mistake."

I peer up at him. "That looked like an ambush."

"Oh, it was."

I glance at the people around us, some already watching us with interest, some looking for an opportunity to approach. "They really wanted you here, huh?"

"They usually do."

I straighten his lapels, a disturbing thought taking place. I pitch my voice low for his ears only. "They want you to invest?"

He nods. "Publishing is a struggling industry. They probably invited every potential investor in the state to this."

"Money opens doors," I murmur.

"Yes," he says dryly, "but they close awfully fast when people realize you have no intention of parting with yours."

I put my hands flat on his chest. "Thank you for this."

He looks down, perhaps surprised at my sincerity. "You're welcome."

"You don't want to be here. I get that, with all these people sucking up to you."

His lips quirk. "Well. I do like *some* people sucking up to me."

"You're impossible."

"Yes," he says, "so you've said before."

Another thought strikes me. "The people that have been nice to me. Do you think they've been genuine? Take Mr. Taylor, for example. Was he nice to me in the hopes that I'd convince you to invest?"

Cole sighs, his eyes draining of amusement. My suspicions aren't completely far-fetched, then. "I couldn't tell you," he says. "And honestly, I've stopped trying to parse it out. You'll drive yourself insane with that kind of thinking."

A realization he's had to come to. Ever since he became someone who's invited to these events, someone to manipulate or coerce. Imagine having to live like that—knowing that the people close to you might be using you. It strikes me as profoundly sad. Maybe that's why he's friends with Nicholas Park. One billionaire doesn't need another, not in any financial sense.

I nod toward the porch, where the light ripples across the

lake. The night is warm and beautiful and the champagne is sweet. "Let's get some air."

"We'll be followed," he warns.

I slip my hand into his and pull him along to the far edge of the porch. It's a secluded corner, with ivy and jasmine growing intertwined up the post. In the dim light, Cole's eyes glitter. "Here? Are you planning on having your way with me?"

"This isn't a spot you go to mingle," I say. "I *dare* them to interrupt us here."

"You have a mean streak."

"You knew that already."

He inclines his head, a smile hovering around his lips. "So I did."

"Do you know what this reminds me of?" I reach over and touch my champagne glass to his whiskey, the amber liquid barely coating the bottom. "The night we met."

"Mmm. The Legacy bar. Best hotel I've ever built."

I lean in closer. "What did you really think that night?"

"That you were gorgeous. I said I was people-watching, if you remember." He swirls his glass around, eyes on me. "But I mostly watched you."

I take a sip of the champagne, cool against my parched throat. "Would you have come up to me? If the creep next to me hadn't tried to hit on me?"

He moves closer, his body shielding me completely from any nosy guests who might follow us out. "Yes," he says. "I don't usually strike up conversations with women in bars. But that night… eventually, I would've had to."

"And later?"

"What did I think later?"

I nod, licking my lips. "When we went to your hotel room."

"*A* hotel room," he corrects softly. "When you went to the restroom, I got management on the phone. They gave me a key card."

My eyes widen. "You did?"

"Yes. And to answer your question... well, when we went to bed, I thought you were cute. Shy, but determined to be brave."

I look down. "I was aiming for gorgeous and seductive."

"Oh, Skye, you were," he says, voice dropping low. "So fucking irresistible, it killed me."

"Shy and seductive don't mix."

His breath is by my ear, his voice a dark caress. "In you they most definitely do. Do you remember when we had sex the first time?"

Oh God. I nod, my nipples tight against the fabric of my dress. "Yes."

"Tell me what I did."

"You made me show you how I touched myself in the mirror." I lean my forehead against his shoulder, closing my eyes at the waves of desire and embarrassment at war inside me. "So you could replicate it."

"That's right." His lips touch the outer rim of my ear. "And then...?"

"Then you did the same thing, but with your tongue." A breath. "I came."

"Yes, you certainly did."

"And then you..." I trail off, swallowing at the memory of him pushing inside me, of his groan at that first sensation. My pulse skitters alarmingly. "Cole, let's get out of here."

His grip on my hand is almost bruising. "Thought you'd never ask." He pulls me back through the throng of people. He takes long strides but I keep up, hurrying along beside him. No one stops us—not until the very last moment. Edwin Taylor smiles at us and offers *both* of us his business card. "If you ever feel like talking new releases," he tells me.

The drive back to my apartment is mostly quiet, but Cole's hand is in mine, his thumb smoothing small circles across the back. Electricity is dancing across my skin from the simple touch. When did we become a hand-holding couple? When did we become a couple at all?

The car slides to a smooth halt outside my building. "Thank you, Charles," Cole says. "Tomorrow morning, please."

"Of course, sir."

His arms are around me the second we hit the sidewalk. I chuckle, pulling him along to my front door. "Tomorrow morning, huh?"

"I'm staying the night." He reaches over my head and pushes the front door open for me with one firm shove. "Hearing you narrate the first time we had sex has me more than a little worked up."

My breath is coming fast when I unlock the door to my apartment. Behind me, Cole locks the door, the sound of a discarded suit jacket hitting the floor a second later.

I slide the zipper down. "Remember the lace lingerie I put on?"

"Fuck yes." His hands are there, pulling, my dress pooling at my feet. "I've thought about it all evening, just like you wanted me to."

His breath is uneven against my cheek as I unbutton his shirt. "Remember when you fucked me against the hotel wall?"

Cole doesn't answer. He lifts me up instead, my legs wrapping around his waist, his voice a growl. "*Yes.*"

I'm airborne and flying and then I'm eased down onto my bed. Cole stands back and tugs off his shirt. I could never get tired of the sight—tan skin, a smattering of hair, the deep V of his stomach. *Never stop swimming,* I think. *Whatever you're doing is working.*

I tug at one of the lacy cups of my bra, teasing my nipple with my fingers. Cole's eyes zero in on my breasts. It's empowering, the effect I have on him. "You're unreal," he murmurs.

I smile at him. "And you're too far away. Come here."

He does, sliding atop of me. I'd expected quick. Hard. Perhaps against a wall, like I'd mentioned. But Cole does the complete opposite.

He kisses me senseless, his body atop mine, tongue moving

slow and deep. A hand skates across my hipbone to my legs, teasing me through the fabric of my panties.

"So wet," he murmurs, lips trailing down to my nipple. "Do you know how good it makes me feel that you're always wet for me?" I want to respond, but then he's biting, and my words turn into gasps. "Like the epitome of masculinity," he continues softly. "You called me that as a joke once. But when you're wet like this for me, fuck if I don't feel like it."

I roll my hips against his hand, reaching down to slide his silken hair through my fingers. "Not a joke," I breathe. "I want you."

"I want you too."

"Inside me."

He rests his head against my hip, his breath a warm gust across my skin. "Fucking hell, Skye. Let me make you come first."

"No. I want us to together." I grab his shoulders and tug him up to me, and Cole lets me, our lips meeting once more. I could lie like this forever—with him bearing me down into the mattress and kissing me. He turns it into an art, something to be appreciated and experienced and savored. But then he throbs against my stomach and desire sweeps my senses away again.

"Skye..." he murmurs against my skin as he strips off my underwear, eyes and hands pausing over every inch of flesh he uncovers. And when he finally settles between my legs and pushes in, both of us groan at the feeling.

I wrap my legs around him. "Yes. Just like this."

Cole comes down on his elbows, covering me completely, thrusting deep and slow. "I'd fuck you forever if I could."

"I'd let you."

His movements are deliberate, hitting spots inside me that make me close my eyes and hold on. Our skin quickly turns slick where it's touching—and we're touching *everywhere*.

"You feel so goddamn good," he groans. I run my hands up his back, lightly using my fingernails, and struggle to form a response. Rational thought is disappearing with every beat of his heart against mine. It's flesh against flesh, man against woman, my breasts against his hair-roughened chest.

He changes his angle, hitting *just* the right spot, and oh! "Yes," I gasp. "Just like that."

Cole's smile isn't ironic or crooked or teasing. It's wide with pleasure. He redoubles his efforts, maintaining the angle and moving strong and sure above me. With every thrust the pressure inside me builds.

It takes me, crests, and I grip him hard. All I can do is hold on.

Cole loses his grip on himself as soon as I do. His thrusts become urgent, shallow, as he buries his head against my neck. His body tightens against me and he groans as he shatters.

The silence that follows is complete. I hold him, thinking that he could fall asleep like this and I would say thank you.

He makes to move and I tighten my legs around him. "No. Not yet."

He laughs warmly against my skin. "So bossy."

"Sometimes," I murmur.

"Never stop." He pushes up on his elbows to kiss me. "God…"

I kiss him back. "It's still just me."

"Funny." He sits up, easily breaking the hold of my legs. "Was I too rough?"

"Not at all."

"Good." A hand moves down to where I'm sensitive, at the clear evidence of his lack of condom. "I prefer this," he says. "Maybe it makes me a caveman."

I chuckle. "Just a man, I think."

He stretches out next to me, his face relaxed, the usual lines of determination or amusement gone. "Well, this man feels ten feet tall." His hand skates across my hip, up to my waist, curving softly over my skin. "You came."

There's no point in denying it, and no chance of hiding it, either. It had been pretty obvious. "Yes. About to gloat?"

Cole's warm laughter washes over my skin. "No. But I do want to hear you talk about it."

"My orgasm?"

"Your story with them. You told me in the hotel room that it was unusual for you to come with a partner."

Oh, God. I want to bury my face in the pillow and hide from the things past me had clearly had no problem spilling. At the time, I'd had no intention of ever seeing him again—and I'd surrendered completely to the skills of his hands and mouth.

Cole laughs again, pulling my body into the hard contours of his. "Don't be shy around me. Not anymore."

"I'm not. And for the record, at the hotel that night, you pretty much fucked all the sense out of me. I can't be held responsible for anything I said."

"Up," he instructs, and I lift my head so he can slide a muscular arm underneath my neck. He's warm, like a space heater. "You thought it was that good?"

"Yes. Why? It wasn't for you?"

He chuckles. "That night was unreal, Skye. But I'm vain enough to enjoy hearing you say it."

"I didn't know that was in question."

"Well, you did leave without saying goodbye." He laughs at my groan, his hand closing warmly around my breast. Absent-mindedly, his thumb toys with my nipple. "I won't start that discussion again. You're deflecting, by the way. It won't stand."

I groan again. "Do you really want to know?"

"Yes."

I release a breath. "Fine. Well, I've had one long-term relationship, in college. Aside from that, my only sexual encounters have been... well, short-term."

"One-night stands," he says.

I purse my lips. "No. Not exactly. I've dated two guys that I've also slept with. Not at the same time, I mean. But things progressed far enough that we slept together, but weren't in a relationship? And then it ended. So three. I've slept with three guys."

Cole's lips are curved in a genuine smile. "You're doing an excellent job at explaining this."

"Yes, well, I wasn't prepared for this grueling pop quiz about my past sex life."

"Only about your orgasms," he says lazily, kissing me. "But I welcome all the information you're sharing."

I shove him lightly and he laughs, arms tightening around me. "How can you blame me? You've already told me I'm the best you've ever had."

"I have *not* said that!"

"Yes you have. Several times." He flips me over, lips trailing down my neck. His shoulders block out the dim lighting from my bedside lamp. "You say a lot of things when you're in the throes of passion. Or feverish."

I groan, but it quickly becomes one of pleasure when his lips close around my nipple. My embarrassment evaporates, fading away in a rush of sensation and dizzying feeling. "None of them made me come," I say softly. "Not regularly. And I wasn't comfortable enough to show them how I wanted to be touched."

He bites my nipple softly before releasing it, looking up at me with eyes that blaze. "What a shame," he says darkly. "And yet... I'm more than happy to pick up their slack."

Cole kisses down my body slowly, like we have all the time in the world, and I lose myself in his touch. When we're like this, it's easy to pretend that we do.

17

SKYE

Karli bursts through the door to the bookstore twenty minutes before her shift starts. "Skye, you won't *believe* this."

I hold up the tote bag I've been admiring for the past half hour. "You won't believe this either. Look. What do you think? I sketched the logo design on it last night."

She pauses in front of the register, a newspaper in hand. "Yeah, that's nice."

"Nice? If—sorry, when—we get the green flag to stay in business, we could produce and sell these. It's cute. It's quirky. It's eco-friendly. It's your neighborhood book bag. This is just a prototype, but—"

Karli slams the newspaper on the register. "*Look.*"

I do.

Cole is on the front page.

They've captured him walking out from a Porter Development building, the skyscraper rising imposing and tall behind him. He's on his phone, and for once, he's not smiling.

The headline screams the accusing words at me. "Billionaire's dirty backstory revealed," I read, murmuring the words.

"You *need* to read this article," Karli says. "Apparently he cut out his old business partner. He was stone cold about the whole thing."

I flip through the newspaper in search for the story. His business partner, his business partner… the one who'd commissioned an expensive logo?

The article is a full spread. Karli is practically seething beside me, pointing out things before I reach them. "He made Ben sign a non-disclosure agreement," she says. "That's why it's his wife who's doing the talking."

"Ben?"

"Ben Simmons. Cole Porter's former business partner." She points to the picture in the spread of Ben and his wife. It's a beautiful image. They're sitting close together on a couch, her hands clasped around his, the picture of support.

I shake my head. "Wait, wait, I have to read." My eyes skim the questions and the answers, each more damning than the last. Elena, Ben's wife, is the one who does most of the talking. *They were school friends,* she answers. *And then to be cut off like that…*

The reporter interjects here—asking about the exact details. Ben's the one who responds to that. *I couldn't tell you. I wish I could, but I was forced to sign an NDA. I would have been left with nothing if I hadn't.*

I scan the rest, every sentence, every question worse than the one before. Something sinks inside me. Could Cole have done this? Cole, who invited my nephew along to a baseball game?

"It's a story. Stories can be twisted," I say faintly.

Karli snorts. "Yeah, but not that much. God, can you imagine that we might have to see him again? He's even more of a snake than we thought."

"Yeah."

"Apparently Ben was the one who actually built the business. He says so, at the end."

I scan the final lines. The reporter asks if it's fair to say that Ben had been the brains behind the operation. *Simmons looks down, a faint smile on his face.* "Cole was my best friend, once," he says. "But no, he was never the smartest of men. He had the trust fund and I had the ideas. It was a good combo until it wasn't."

Anger and fear chase each other inside me, running in aggravated circles. Cole is one of the smartest men I've ever met—so Ben's wrong on that account. But is he wrong regarding the rest? Cole *can* be ruthless. I've witnessed that. He's good friends with Nicholas Park—and that man has quite the reputation for the unsavory.

"He might not honor our agreement," Karli continues. "We have to accept that possibility. What do we do if he doesn't? Would our bargain hold up in court?"

I sink into the chair. "No clue."

"Cutting out his own best friend for profit. *Disgusting.*"

"Seems like it."

Karli's face swims into view, her mouth set in determined lines. "And that was the guy you went toe to toe with, Skye! I'm more proud of you than ever. He might be a sleazeball, but we can hold our heads up high."

Hold our heads up high.

If she only knew, I think. *She'd never look at me the same way again.*

Karli's eyes widen, a sudden realization settling in. "Maybe he'd take it out on you if we win the bargain. Judging by our spike in customers, we might."

"He wouldn't."

"You don't know him. Look at this… he cut off his *best friend!* Made him sign an NDA?" She shakes her head at the article. "And this is the *Seattle Tribune.* They wouldn't publish just anything, either. You can bet this was fact-checked."

Each of her words falls heavier than the next, until I feel bent under the pressure. "Sorry, I have to… Can you watch the register for a minute? I have to use the bathroom."

"Yes, of course. Are you okay?"

"Yeah. One minute."

And in our little three-square-feet bathroom, I break down completely. It's not pretty. It's not even rational. And still, I have to grip the sink to keep my breath from running away from me completely. The article is either a smear piece or a daring exposé.

And I have no idea what to believe.

My first instinct is to call him. To text. To hear him say *It's not true, Skye. Of course it's not. You're a writer. You know how writers write.*

But isn't that exactly what someone who was trying to manipulate me would say? Someone who wants to see this business demolished. Someone who's been damn good at making me think they'd stopped caring about it. He'd hinted that winning wasn't important to him anymore.

That I was important instead.

And I'd believed him.

The baseball game. The publisher event. Was it all a lie?

I shake my head at myself in the mirror. If I was being played for a fool, at least my eyes are open now, thanks to Ben Simmons. That is a good thing.

And if I wasn't... well, I can't let myself consider that, not yet. Not while my chest feels like it's collapsing in on itself. Karli's words come back to me, the ones that carried the most weight. The *Seattle Tribune wouldn't* publish just anything. They would fact check. They had probably reached out to Cole for a comment, even.

The look Karli gives me when I come out of the bathroom is sympathetic. She puts a hand on my shoulder and squeezes. "I'm sorry. Of course this made you think that it's futile, but it's truly not. We might still have a chance to pull this off."

I nod. Inside, I've never felt more like a fraud. I don't deserve her friendship, or her support, not right now. The bookstore is hers, after all. Eleanor was *her* grandmother. Not mine.

"We'll just have to work harder," I say faintly. "We have a week left."

She nods. "That's right. And if push comes to shove, he's not getting us to sign any NDAs!"

I *hmm* in agreement, returning to stacking shelves with my mind whirling. And despite my phone burning a hole in my pocket that day, I don't contact Cole, and he doesn't contact me. He must have his hands full.

He's either devastated by the article or pissed off that his former business partner found a way to circumvent the non-disclosure agreement.

And I'm not sure I want to find out which one it is yet.

The next day marks exactly one week until our two-month agreement with Porter Development comes to an end. Karli has a meeting with Chloe in a few days, and the both of them will pore over the numbers to see if we can present a profitable store.

Karli and I have been ramping each other up constantly. "We can do this," Karli tells me again, as much for herself as for me.

"Oh, absolutely. We've seen more customers these past few weeks than ever before. We're good."

"We're good," she repeats. "We're good."

Her eyes flick to the back wall, and I wonder if she's thinking of the same thing I am. The framed picture of Eleanor in front of Between the Pages from when it opened. It's hung there so long there's a square mark in the wallpaper behind it.

The day is a blur of sales and Instagram updates and hanging sale signs. I hang a huge one in the window display and add a handwritten note that explains our situation. *One week left to make a difference,* I write in the heading. *Do you want our store to remain?*

It's desperate, but these are desperate times.

The doorbell jingles an hour before closing, and not with a customer. Middle-aged. A frown on his features. And wearing a T-shirt with an all-too-familiar logo. This time, it's not peppered with darts.

He walks straight up to the register. "Good afternoon."

I brace my hands against the counter. "Hi. I wasn't aware we had a scheduled appointment with Porter Development today."

He gives me an unpleasant smile and pulls out a construction ruler from his pocket. "I was sent to inspect the property in preparation."

"Inspect?"

"Yes." He taps the ruler against the desk, looking around with appraising eyes. "Take the building's measurements and inspect the construction. After all, we need to know how big of a wrecking ball to bring."

"Nothing has been decided yet," I grind out.

His smile is irreverent. "That's for you to bring up to my boss, or my boss's boss. I'm here on orders, and to the best of my knowledge, we're razing the building within the month."

"Not on my watch."

The man chuckles, like I've made a joke. His voice turns syrupy. "All right, sweetheart."

Sweetheart? The nerve! "What's your name?"

"Max Blakefield."

"Well, you won't be measuring inside this store today, not until you come back here with a scheduled appointment that has gone from your boss or boss's boss to us."

The smile he aims me is patronizing. "I'm to measure the building on the outside, which requires no agreement from you. Free country, after all." He has me beat, and he can see it on my face, because he gives a slick nod. "You have a good day, now."

He strolls out of the bookstore, measurer in hand, like he does this all the time. My fingers ache from clenching so hard around the edge of the counter. If this was a cartoon, smoke would be coming out of my ears, I'm so angry. *A wrecking ball*, he said. *His boss's boss.*

So much for honoring agreements, it seems. Porter Development seems intent on tearing the building down. Are Karli and I going to become the next Ben Simmons?

My hands fly furiously as I write a text to Cole.

Skye Holland: *I close up the store soon. Can I come to yours after?*

His response doesn't take long, and it's thankfully in a text, too. I'm not sure I could've kept my emotions hidden on the phone, and this is a conversation I want to have in person.

185

Cole Porter: *Yes. I'll be home by seven.*

I'm in the lobby of the Amena at six fifty-eight. My fingers twitch at my side, too pumped up on adrenaline and nerves for my own good. Potential scenarios dance in my mind. Him admitting that our casual affair was all just amusement, that he had never planned to honor the agreement. The crooked smile twisted sardonically.

Or, worse, him telling me that the bookstore had never had a shot in the first place, eyes as patronizing as the handyman he'd sent today. My nerves increase with each floor I pass on my way up to his penthouse.

The elevator doors open to an empty hallway. He's not in the kitchen, either. I lean around the corner, peering toward the living room. "Cole?"

"Coming!"

He emerges from his home office, a hand tugging at the tie around his neck. "You came fast."

"I sure did. What happened today?"

"What do you mean?"

"You sent one of your men to the bookstore today."

His face grows still. "I absolutely did not."

"A certain Max Blakefield seemed to think otherwise. He showed up to measure the store for a correctly sized wrecking ball. Said the place would be razed within a month—and that if I believed otherwise, I'd better talk to his boss's boss." I spread my arms wide. "So here I am."

Cole is shaking his head slowly. "I don't know a Max Blakefield. Must be one of our contractors."

"He was wearing a shirt with your logo. Looked like a builder." My eyes snag on his expensive suit, stretching taut across his frame. "A real builder, I mean. He was wearing boots and work pants."

There's a silken thread of warning in his voice. "He was wrong. The company still plans to honor its agreement."

"You mean *you* do."

"Yes," he says, like that's the same thing. But it's not.

"Your employees seem to think otherwise." I swallow hard, lifting my chin, meeting his gaze head-on. "We saw the article yesterday. Karli is doubting that you honor agreements at all."

"Ah." He grinds the word out between his teeth. "So that's what this is really about, huh? And is Karli the only one who is doubting?"

"I have some doubts too," I say honestly. *Doubts about us. What you've been doing. And why you've been doing it.*

"Nine hundred words in a newspaper, and you're rattled. I thought you were a writer yourself, Skye. You know how things are twisted." The words are playful, but his tone is not.

"So it's not true? What he said in the interview?" I ask. Cole just stares at me, and the silence grows heavy between us in a way it never has before. I'm furious about my own vulnerability to him—that I care so much about the answer. That I've given him this power over me.

"Did I make Ben Simmons sign an NDA?" he asks, voice trembling with barely concealed fury. "Yes. Did I cut him off from the business? Yes. And I'd do it again in a heartbeat, Skye."

My chest feels like it's collapsing, constricting, anger and fear choking off a response.

"And now you're wondering about my character," he continues. "What I would do to get what I want."

I give a shallow nod, clenching my fists hard enough that my nails dig into my palm. "They say you're ruthless. That you always win. Maybe you knowingly sent one of your men to the bookstore today to rattle us. Maybe you didn't, but you might as well have, Cole. We made a deal."

"Hold on," he warns.

But my thoughts are leaping from one conclusion to another. "All this time, I thought sleeping with me was fun for you. Good sex. Maybe it was for sport, too. But now… was it to throw me off balance? To gain leverage?"

A swift shadow crosses over his face, jaw hardening. "What?"

"You don't like to lose. Ben Simmons confirmed it. *You* just confirmed it, when you said he'd spoken true."

Cole starts undoing the cuffs of his shirt in harsh, quick movements. "No, I don't like to lose. Neither do you, by the way. We're both competitive."

"So?"

"I can be an asshole sometimes. You've pointed that out yourself. But to the best of my knowledge, I'm not *amoral*."

"I didn't imply that you were."

"You just asked me if I'm fucking you to gain the upper hand in our business deal. Not that I understand how that would help me, exactly. Does your business lose profit, one orgasm at a time?" He shakes his head, an unhappy smile on his face. "I'm not, by the way."

My throat feels like it's closing in on itself. "You admitted to cutting off your best friend. How could I *not* ask?"

Cole braces his hands against the kitchen counter. "You want to know the real truth about Ben and Elena, his loving wife? Ben and I built the business together. I did most of the strategizing and he brought on investors. Always had a good eye for marketing and building a story." He takes a deep breath, shaking his head. "Toward the end, he wasn't pulling his weight. Skipping out on business trips. Making bad decisions without consulting me. But he was my best friend, so I gave him second chances."

"Oh," I breathe.

His voice hardens. "Elena didn't like me working so much. She was *my* fiancée, by the way. They didn't mention that in their little interview." He looks away from me, jaw working. "They'd been sleeping together for nearly two years when I found out."

"Oh, Cole…"

"So yes, I forced him out. It wasn't hard. I had our staff's loyalty, the majority of our shares, our clients' trust. But I left him with more money than anyone should need in a lifetime."

He pushes away from the counter, shrugging off his suit

jacket and dropping it on his couch. "Is that enough humiliation for you? Or do you want to accuse me of something else?"

"Cole..."

"Spare me the pity, please. I've had more than enough of that from my own staff."

I swallow against the dryness in my throat. I feel rooted to the spot, not sure if I should go to him or leave him alone. I'd come here to talk, to get to the bottom of things, to make sense of it all. And I'm left feeling like it all went sideways somehow, without knowing where it went wrong.

"Don't worry," he calls out, not bothering to turn around. "We're just sleeping together. Your business deal still stands."

To my horror, something burns behind my eyes, and I don't know if the tears are from embarrassment, anger, or something far more dangerous. *Hurt.* I hurry to the elevator.

Cole doesn't try to stop me.

18

COLE

The past two days have been an absolute shitshow, from morning to evening. Everyone has read Ben and Elena's article, it seems. Blair calls me to ask if I'm doing okay, as if she's just found out I have a terminal illness. My mom calls, too, and is far less tactful. *Didn't you take care of them?*

Yes, Mom, but I forced them out of my company and my life. I didn't order a hit on them.

From talking to my PR team to my assistant to the board of investors, the entire day had been damage control. "We need to put out a counter-statement," Tyra kept saying to me, one of our company lawyers. "This is terrible for your reputation."

"No."

"Mr. Porter... it's slander."

"It's gossip."

"Gossip that will take root."

I'd squared my shoulders and stood firm. Repudiating the claim would require explaining what really happened, and I'd had quite enough of humiliation to relive it in front of all of Seattle. Coming home from a weeklong business trip early to find Ben and Elena in my master bed had cured me of any masochistic tendencies.

Bryan had agreed on a tactic of silence. "It makes you look

powerful," he'd said to me in an aside. "Not commenting on it makes it seem like you're either above it, or it's true. Both enhance your business reputation." I had nothing to say to that, not out loud, but I made a mental note to give Bryan a raise.

But I didn't expect the biggest fallout to be with Skye.

Shame isn't an emotion I'm used to any more. It had been, when the wound with Elena and Ben had been fresh. But in the years since, it's faded, until the scar barely aches. But after the fight with Skye, it's all I feel.

She came to me with legitimate concerns. The picture didn't look good, and she asked me to fill it in for her. I had—and not in a gentle way. Her feelings had been clear on her face and I'd trampled them with my own hurt and sordid past.

I wince again, remembering the admission to her. Trust Ben and Elena to succeed in screwing me over one last time. Nothing about the situation painted me in a good light to Skye, not to mention the ill-timed visit of one of my underlings to the bookstore.

That's the first thing I get to the bottom of, the day after the fight. Bryan stands straight in my office when I question him. "Did you send someone to Between the Pages yesterday? The bookstore?"

His eyes light up. "Yes, yes I did."

"Why?"

"It was a classic shakedown. They have less than a week left of the deal you agreed to, and we need to remind them of the outcome." He shrugs. "Fairly standard."

My hand grows white-knuckled around the arm of my chair. "You didn't inform me?"

"No. I considered mentioning it, but then we had the article to deal with." Bryan frowns. "Was it the wrong call?"

Yes. A thousand times yes.

But there is no way I can make him understand that without giving away far too much information. "We will honor the deal," I tell him. "If the store is profitable, they stay."

Bryan doesn't comment, but the refusal is clear in his eyes.

None of my team understand why I'd accepted Skye and Karli's challenge in the first place, and I can't blame them for that. It had been nonsensical.

I don't look forward to explaining in front of a board of investors and partners why the next Porter Hotel will have a bookstore incorporated in the ground floor.

The rest of the day is miserable. Skye doesn't text me, and I don't text her. What is there to say?

I snap at my assistant. I have to re-read emails to understand them. My mind seems stuck on her face from the night before… what she'd accused me of, well, it doesn't sit right with me. By the time I make it home in the evening, I'm in such a bad mood that I consider hitting the pool and swimming a few lengths. Having already done my workout that morning, the thought of pushing my muscles further isn't tempting, but I'm far too riled up to remain still for long.

The urge to make things right with Skye grows into an itch that's increasingly hard to ignore. She hadn't handled her questioning well, but then again, I hadn't handled her questions well either.

I'm halfway to the hallway before I've even made the decision. Finding the car keys, pulling on a pair of shoes, tugging on my leather jacket. It's a conversation we should have in person.

But my phone rings as I reach for the elevator button. For a brief moment, indecision is all I feel. It's likely Bryan or Tyra. Some fire to put out or a late-night contract to sign. With a sigh, I pull it out of my pocket, ready to hit decline.

The name on the caller ID stops me. "Skye?"

"Yeah," she says on the other line. "It's me. Hi."

"Hey. How've you been?"

She clears her throat. "Good."

"That's nice."

There's a pause, her breathing soft through the phone. "Actually, no. I haven't been good at all. I... Cole, I'm sorry for jumping to conclusions about the article, and inferring things about our agreement."

"I should have been able to talk about it better," I say quietly. "You were concerned. I get that." I put a hand against the wall to brace myself. "And I promise you, I wasn't aware of the company man who visited your store. Had I been, I would have stopped it. It was unnecessary."

"Yes," she says. "It was."

"Was he rude?"

"Terribly. He called me sweetheart."

"What?"

"Don't worry, though," she says, a tone of both smugness and bashfulness in her voice. "I wasn't very civil back."

Despite myself, I want to laugh. "I'm sure you weren't."

There's silence again, but this time it's warm. Skye is the one who breaks it. "You don't feel like coming over?"

"I don't?"

"You know exactly what I mean, Porter."

I step into the elevator, car keys in hand. "I was already on my way."

"Really?"

"Oh yes."

"Good," she says. "I'll be waiting."

Six days. The number hits me as I drive over. Six days until this ends, until the decision has to be made, until it all comes to a head. It fills me with nothing but dread.

The front door is unlocked when I arrive. "Come in!" she calls out from her perch on the couch. She's in some sort of pajama set—striped shorts and a camisole—looking innocent and domestic. It stirs something in me, seeing her like that, her hair loose down her back. It's a sight I could get used to.

"Do you want some tea?"

"No thanks," I say, hanging up my jacket. "I'm good."

There's a chagrined look on her face as she sets her cup back down on the coffee table. "I'm sorry, again."

"You don't have to apologize."

"No, I do. I... I believed the worst of you."

"I would have too, in your shoes," I say quietly. Most people in the city probably do now.

"Do you want to talk about it?" she asks. "The article?"

"Hell, no. I don't even want to think about it."

"I can imagine you've done quite enough of that," she says with a smile. "Make yourself comfortable."

I do, sinking down into her couch and stretching out my legs. For the first time all day, I feel like I can take a deep breath and have it fill my lungs. It feels good.

Skye gets up and heads to one of the flowerpots in the corner. I watch as she snaps off a browning leaf. "Sorry," she says softly, "but I kill all my plants. I'm determined this one will make it."

"I have faith in you."

She tucks a lock of hair behind her ear and straightens a pile of books on the coffee table. It's such a homely thing to do, and in her pajamas, it's... sweet. This is a proper home. A place to relax and unwind.

I toy with the tassels of a cushion. "That's why my place is like a museum, you know."

"Sorry?"

I clear my throat. "I bought it just a few weeks after I found out about Elena and Ben. I'd been staying in one of my hotels after I found out, having just walked out of our apartment. I never went back there," I say. "Couldn't, actually. Just the idea of it made me sick."

Skye sinks down onto the sectional in front of me, crossing her legs. "It's awful, what they did." Her voice hardens. "And to think she gets to play the supportive wife in that article. Bah!"

The outrage in her voice makes me smile. "I like your anger more than your pity."

"No pity," she agrees. "You did the right thing in cutting them off. But why would they write that article?"

I scoff. "I'm guessing the money ran out. Ben is terrible with finances and Elena has expensive tastes."

"They're the ones in the wrong, and somehow your name is

the one dragged through the mud. Can't you set the record straight somehow?"

I grab one of the books on her coffee table, flicking through it aimlessly. "That would mean admitting to the world what really happened."

"Which wasn't your fault."

"Maybe not," I say, "but I still have my pride."

Skye shakes her head, but there's a fondness in her eyes that I haven't seen before. "Men," she muses.

I snap the book closed. "You love us."

"Much to our own detriment sometimes, yes."

"Why does the bookstore mean so much to you?"

Skye's eyebrows shoot high, but her face remains open, fondness still clear in her eyes. I want to live up to it. "That's a non-sequitur," she says.

"Well, you've asked me personal questions. My turn now."

She tucks her legs up beneath her, her gaze on the bookshelf in the corner. Maybe I've pushed my luck with this one. It's not a topic that the name "Cole Porter" is favorably attached to.

But then she starts to speak.

"I spent a lot of time there growing up. My mom is... well, eccentric."

"You called her bohemian once."

Skye looks over. "You remembered that?"

"Of course."

"Well, she certainly is. A new project every week, a new obsession. She's not a bad mother, but she's an absentminded one. She gets lost in stories and ideas easily. And she's very stubborn about it."

I resist the urge to smile, thinking that Skye shares some of those traits, and admirably so. Stubbornness. Obsession. A love of storytelling.

"So you spent time in the bookstore?"

"Yes. I loved to read and write. And walking home after school, I'd stop at Between the Pages. It felt like the most wonderful place. Eleanor ran it, back then. She started making me tea, even though I didn't like it yet." A smile plays at the corners of her mouth, the look in her eyes a million miles away. "She encouraged me to write. To explore. She put new books in my hands every week and would ask me questions about them. 'And why did Heathcliff act like that?' she'd challenge. 'What are the author's intentions?' When I chose to major in English Literature, my mother and sister didn't understand it. Eleanor did."

"She was Karli's grandmother?"

"Yes. I started working there part-time, when I was old enough. It's more like home to me than my childhood house ever was." She looks down at her palms, as if seeking answers there. "It's the place I love the most in the world."

And I was trying to tear it down.

She doesn't say the words, but the knowledge hangs in the air in between us, tangible and uncomfortable. An unwelcome intruder. For the first time, I want to undo the whole thing. The bargain. The business project. I just want her.

"Skye, I—"

Her phone interrupts me and the cheery theme song fills her apartment. She tracks it down to one of her kitchen counters, the apartment small enough that I can hear the entire conversation.

I settle down on the couch to listen, completely without shame, a hand under my head.

"Hey, Isla," Skye says. It's a name I remember—the older sister, Timmy's mother. This should be interesting.

"No, it's fine." A cleared throat. "No, I'm home alone."

I grin at that.

"Isla, I don't feel like talking about him any more. It's all you ask me about!"

I grin even wider.

"Timmy might have been exaggerating on that point a bit. Anyway, what's up?"

Then she gives a suppressed sigh—I can hear it all the way from here. "Why can't you use your car? Doesn't Jason have one?"

Jason doesn't, apparently, and this is explained vigorously enough that even I hear the mumbled words on the other end of the line.

"Fine, fine. No, okay. I need it this weekend, though." A pause. "Yeah, that's fair." A much longer pause. "All right. Bye."

I'm grinning at Skye when she comes around the corner. She groans, putting a hand to her forehead. "You heard everything, right?"

"Oh yes."

"She's been nagging me about you since the baseball game. Timmy has been laying on the praise thick, let me tell you."

"As well he should have."

She tosses a throw pillow my way and I catch it easily. "It's getting harder to dodge the questions," she says.

"What have you told her?"

"That you're someone I'm seeing casually. She's not buying it."

I reach out and grab Skye around the waist, pulling her down to the couch. She lands on my lap. "Because I'm your first casual hookup."

"*Yes.* How long are you going to lord that over me?"

"Just a few more times." I smooth my hand over her thigh, the skin soft to the touch. "She asked to borrow your car."

"Yes," Skye says irritably. "Last time she had it for almost a week."

I pull her back against me, our bodies flush. She's warm in my arms. "Why don't you stand up to her like you do to me?"

Skye relaxes against me. "Like I do to you?"

"Yes. You have no problem telling me when I'm being an asshole. The first month you told me regularly that you hated me."

"I still hate you," she murmurs, fingers trailing up my arm.

I grin. "See? No problem at all. Stand up for yourself with her, too."

Skye is quiet for a beat, but when she speaks, her words are not about her sister. "I really was awful to you, wasn't I?"

"Well-deservedly so."

She rolls her hips, grinding against me, and my body reacts right on cue. It's impossible to hold her and *not* want her. "But you enjoyed it."

"Very much." I bite her ear, moving down lower, pressing a kiss to the soft skin of her neck. "I don't know what's more fun, arguing with you or sleeping with you."

Skye chuckles and rests her head against my shoulder. She grabs my hand and slides it down her front, right to the waistband of her shorts. It's all the cue I need.

"Sometimes we do both at the same time," she says, her voice breathless.

I slide my hand under the elastic. "Mhm," I say. She's like silky velvet against my fingers, soft and smooth and responsive.

"Remember what we did in your bathtub?"

"Yes." I use an arm around her waist to secure her to me, using my thigh to spread her legs further apart. Skye shudders as I slip a finger inside.

"Do you think we could manage it in a shower?"

I smile at her suggestion, at the way she's spread, at the self-confidence. Standing, I grip her around the waist, hoisting her up against me.

"It'll be a tight fit," I say, "but then again, so are you."

Skye doesn't blush. She kisses me instead, warm and enthusiastic and willing, drowning out the number pounding in the back of my mind. *Six days left.*

What happens then?

19

SKYE

I'm in the storage room when my carefully constructed double-life comes crashing down around me. It's done in a heartbeat. I should have been able to predict it—and the fact that I haven't makes me question not just my morals, but my intellect too.

I overhear the whole thing.

"Want to see something cool?" Timmy asks Karli, having arrived earlier than usual from school.

She indulges him with a smile in her voice. "Absolutely."

"This is one of my signed baseballs. I brought it along to school today to show my friends."

"Wow! Where did you get that?" she asks.

I'm out of the storage room and halfway through the room, but I'm not fast enough. There's no stopping what's said next.

"I went to a baseball game last week." The pride in Timmy's voice kills me. "Skye and Cole took me. We had the *best* seats."

"Cole?"

"Yeah. Skye's boyfriend. He gave me tips for the coming tryouts, too."

Karli turns to me, where I stand breathless and guilty in the doorway. "Skye?"

"Yeah."

"Which Cole is this?"

I can't talk. I can't even breathe, wondering if the guilt is like a shining beacon from my eyes.

It must be, because hers widen with horror. "Skye!"

"I'm sorry. I should have told you."

"*How?*"

Timmy's eyes are moving from one of us to the other, and I shake my head at Karli. She catches on immediately. "Sorry," she tells Timmy. "That's lovely, and I'm glad you got to go to the game. Skye and I just need a moment, okay?"

He nods sulkily and gives me a reproachful look through his glasses. He hates being left out of the conversation, but he dutifully turns back to his homework.

Karli follows me out to the register. "How could you, Skye?" she asks in a low voice. "You hated him more than I did!"

"I know. I still do. I... remember the one-night stand I had?"

"The unreal hotel guy?"

"Yes. It was him. I didn't know it then, of course. And then he walked in here and I was so angry... and then it somehow turned into more." I run a hand through my hair. "I barely understand it myself, Karli."

Her mouth is a tight line. "So that's why he agreed to the two-month deal. I thought he was just a bull and you'd waved a red flag."

"Yes, well, that too. He's competitive."

"How could you not have told me something like this? Our business relationship with Porter Development concerns me too. It's my livelihood, Skye!"

"You're right. I'm sorry. I wanted to, several times, but I was afraid of what you'd say, or worse, what you'd think of me."

Her eyes soften, but it's just a tad. "Relationships are complicated. Emotions are complicated. You should have given me a chance to understand."

"I should've." I lean against the counter, my heart pounding like I've been running sprints. "We've kept it very casual. He doesn't have anything to leverage against us, Karli."

She puts a hand on my shoulder. "Skye, for Christ's sake, of course he doesn't. But what about *you*? What's going to happen when this all ends? I don't want you getting hurt!"

I take a deep breath. "I don't think I will. At least, not if we win."

It's a half-hearted joke, and she smiles, but it's probably for my sake. "I hope so, and I hope he's been treating you right through all this. He was my enemy before, but then it was just business. If he hurts you, Skye... well, then it's personal."

She looks so determined, and so fierce all of a sudden, that I get a lump in my throat. "Thank you, Karli."

She pulls me into a hug, far warmer than I deserve. "I'm still angry at you for not telling me," she says. "But I'm still in your corner, as always. Tomorrow, when Timmy's not here, I want you to tell me *everything*."

"I'll tell you. I promise."

"Good." She holds me at arm's-length distance, a faint smile on her lips. "You're living your own grand story at the moment, it seems."

A surprised laugh escapes me. "Yes. It's awfully exciting. Perhaps too much. I'm barely holding it together."

"Well," she says, "just make sure you write about it when it's all over, okay? Remember what Eleanor used to say. It's your mistakes that give you the best stories."

Despite Karli's calm acceptance, I feel guilty for the rest of the day and unable to fall asleep at night. Seeing Cole and I through someone else's eyes—someone who isn't ten years old and my nephew—made the whole thing feel less somehow. Almost cheap. A daring adventure in the dark can look very different when it's brought out into the harsh light of day.

I shake my head at myself. Focus on Between the Pages. That's the whole point of this thing, anyway. To see this place torn down would tear me apart, and besides, Cole and I have no future. We'd never discussed it, but it was clear in the way both of us spoke. With five days until the deadline for delivering our financial reports to Porter Development, our time's numbered and the clock is ticking.

And our final meeting with Chloe is here. It's the last time we'll be able to go over the financials before the deadline, the last time we'll be able to course-correct.

"She'll be here at five," Karli says for the third time, rearranging the loyalty card display on the register. "She said she'd bring her calculations with her."

"Awesome," I say, sorting through the register.

She taps her fingers against the counter. "How can you be so calm?"

"Because I *know* we've managed to become profitable."

"You *know* it?"

"Yes." I give her my most confident smile. "You and I have both seen the numbers go up. How many more customers have we had in the last week than usual?"

"Well, a lot. Your flyers helped, and the book signing event. And the Instagram page. Oh Skye, we should have started with these changes ages ago!"

The thought had struck me, too. "Yes. But it's never too late to learn," I say. "They'll see that we've turned it around."

Karli's smile is grateful, even if it's tinged with the same fear I'm concealing. "You're right. We just have to breathe in and breathe out," she says. "There's nothing more we can do today."

"Easy as that." I look around the bookstore, at the artful crown molding around the built-in bookcases, at the beautiful wooden beams. Eleanor had added detail after detail over the decades, changing a newer building into something that looked centuries old.

There are markings with my height in the storage room. Eleanor had insisted on it, once I became a regular, when she was the one who helped me with my English homework.

I keep my smile in place for Karli, for the customers, but

inside I'm just as afraid. For two months, this moment has been my guiding star, and the possibility of failure feels like an ice-cold hand around my heart.

When Chloe *finally* sweeps into the bookstore, it's with a professional smile and another expensive bag on her arm. Karli gives me a single nod, and I nod back. *Here we go.*

We take a seat around the table in the reading room. Chloe's manner is measured, professional, as she opens up her laptop. Nothing in her behavior hints at either success or failure. *A good sign,* I tell myself.

"First things first, here is your monthly accounting report." She pushes a sheet with colorful graphics our way. "Your sales are up, which is very impressive, especially in this financial climate."

I nod, looking over the numbers. Nausea sweeps through me at the thought, but I ask it regardless. "So? Has it been enough?"

Chloe sighs in defeat, and somewhere inside of me, something cracks. It might be my heart. "I've tried," she says. "I really have. But no, it hasn't been. It's not enough to push you into the green as a business."

"You've got to be kidding."

Chloe gives me a sad smile. "I'm so sorry, Skye. Truly. I've run the numbers every which way, but there's no way I can spin it so you look profitable."

Karli opens and closes her mouth, no sound emerging.

"But we've had more customers," I say faintly. "We've both seen the large uptick. We've sold for *more* than previous months, you just said so."

"You have, yes. But not enough. I'm sorry, but there's the large inventory and the high fixed costs. You're just barely breaking even. This place hasn't been truly profitable for months, and it's a hard thing to turn around in such a short period of time."

"How? We've done everything!"

Chloe turns her laptop around for us to see. And there, clear as day, are the numbers in accusing red. Two months' worth of combined accounts.

"On a deal like this, they're going to check my bookkeeping, so I can't fudge either."

Karli clears her throat. "We'd never ask you to."

I would. Staring down at the wooden table, my gaze snags on a small act of vandalism. Someone had carved the word *hope* into the old wood. Someone who hadn't yet learned how pointless that emotion was.

"When do we have to send the numbers to Porter?" I ask.

"In four days' time," Karli says. "But surely that's too little time to…?"

"It is. Even if you triple your daily sales, it won't be enough." Chloe pauses, and it's the look on her face that kills me, that tells me this is real. "I'm more sorry than you realize. I know this wasn't what you hoped for, when you hired me."

"It's not your fault," Karli says immediately. "Thank you for doing this for us, and for agreeing to the time pressure and deadline."

She's taking this better than I am. I just stare at Chloe's screen—at the big red deficit—and feel like I'm falling, like this is a nightmare, one I've been dreading, and now that I'm here I can't wake up.

I'm glad Eleanor can't see us now.

Chloe gives me a hug before she leaves. My movements are on autopilot, and maybe she sees that, because she invites me over for dinner.

"For old time's sake," she says kindly. "Whenever you feel up for it, let me know."

It's nice, and I nod, but my insides are tearing themselves apart. How can this be? I watch in a daze as the front door shuts behind Chloe, the jingle of the bell obscene.

Karli turns to me. "I can't—"

"We did *everything*—"

"You did so much!"

"Oh, I'm so sorry!"

She wraps her arms around me, and me around her, and for a long time there are no words.

"We tried *everything*," Karli finally murmurs. "Thank you, Skye. Thank you so much for believing in this. For negotiating those two extra months for us to try."

I shake my head. "For nothing. I got our hopes up—"

"Nonsense. Between the Pages has touched so many lives in the past two months. It's reached more people, and that's because of *you*."

"Us both."

"Yes, well, I can't take credit for half of your inventions." Karli leans back, her eyes glittering. "We knew this day would come. We'd accepted it, months ago. We'll learn to accept it again."

I can't accept it. Not yet, and maybe not ever. "How are you taking this so calmly?"

"Because this place had a five-decade run," she says, her voice turning fierce. "Eleanor's dream lives on in me, and it lives on in you, Skye. *That's* what matters."

Eleanor. We failed her.

When she died, she'd given me a set of leather-bound old editions and a beautiful note. *Follow your dreams, Skye, and never doubt that you're a born writer.*

I still doubted.

I still needed this place.

Pulling out of Karli's embrace, I reach for my phone with a trembling hand. "Maybe I can talk to Cole. Convince them to keep this place anyway. We *have* gained more customers, after all. That's good?"

The smile Karli gives me is kind, but it's not hopeful. "Honey, he's a businessman. I don't like him, even if you've told me the article didn't paint a fair picture, but he's still out to make money. And we're not a good bet."

"Yes we are." I swipe left to open my phone and click open my texts.

Skye Holland: *Can I come over after you're done with work?*

His response is immediate.

Cole Porter: *Yes. I'll finish up early for you.*

"This can't be the end," I tell Karli, my hand a fist at my side. "It just *can't*. I won't let it."

20

SKYE

I knot my hands into fists to keep them from shaking and watch the elevator screen's meticulous count of all the floors we barrel past. Twelve. Fifteen. Eighteen. Twenty. The Amena building is one of the tallest in Seattle. In a different world, I'd make a joke to Cole about it. *You couldn't settle for just a mid-rise, could you?* Maybe I'd quip that he was compensating for something, and he'd make a crude joke back.

Tonight is not that night.

The elevator bell dings as it slides to a smooth stop at the top floor, opening straight into Cole's home, if you could call his modernist fortress that.

I walk down the hallway without stopping to take off my jacket. My mind feels blank and foggy—too much has hit me in too short a time. The bookstore is closing. Cole's tearing it down. Karli and I failed.

"Skye? Thank God you're here." Cole emerges out of his home office, shrugging out of his suit jacket. "I can't wait to bury myself in you."

My handbag slides off my shoulder and lands with the sound of metal on hardwood.

His eyes find mine. "Skye? Are you all right?"

"We met with our accountant today. We're not profitable."

For a moment he's completely still, eyes locked on mine. And then he's crossing the space to me in quick strides. He opens his arms but I can't. Not right now, and not with him.

I take a step back and he stops. "We failed," I repeat.

"Fuck." He slides a hand through his hair. "I'm so sorry, Skye. Truly."

"We turned things around. There were more customers there. You saw it too, didn't you?"

He gives a faint nod. "I did."

"And we followed your advice. Practically *everything* is on sale, Cole. We're flying through the inventory, and our Instagram page is growing, we engaged the entire neighborhood, and we got a new accountant and...and... I can't think of *anything* else we could have done. It's heading in the right direction. We could still become profitable, it just needs more *time*."

"You've worked so hard," he says, and the expression on his face kills any last shred of hope I'd harbored. "I don't know what to tell you. I'm sorry. More sorry than I can tell you."

I swallow hard. He's sorry, because he's going to tear it down anyway. *He's sorry.*

"I know how much this meant to you, to prove yourself."

He says it like he expects me to walk into his arms—to have him console me—before he tears it down in two weeks' time.

Karli and I failed.

Correction: I failed. I was the one who made the crazy bet with him, who pushed through the late nights and the doubts and the flu and created a whole new business plan. I'd forced everyone to believe the same thing I did, just because I wanted it so much. Because I was too stupid to see the writing on the wall.

The bookstore is gone. It has an expiration date, and always had, from the very beginning. Eleanor's face swims in front of me, her kind eyes, her sharp voice. *So what?* she'd said once, when I'd come to her upset about being called a bookish nerd in school. *Popularity fades. Smarts don't. I'm betting on you.* Turns out she lost that bet.

Cole takes another step toward me, but I back away again.

There's too much emotion running through me at the moment, more than I can handle. It burns.

"Skye..."

"You're going to tear it down," I murmur. "It'll be gone."

All of the late nights, his help, his encouragement, and in the end, it doesn't matter.

"What do you want me to say, Skye? We had an agreement."

"You helped me," I say, the blood beginning to pound in my temples. "You *helped* me with this."

He nods, but it's sad, and that's when it hits me so clearly that he did it to spend time with me, to sleep with me, and not for the business. Of course not. I already knew that, didn't I? So why does it hurt to have it confirmed? To have the illusion shatter?

I put a hand to my chest, to where my heart feels like it's breaking. "You're going to *tear it down*."

"Skye, I don't know what to do." He takes yet another step toward me, but I hold up a hand this time. I can see that it hurts him—me not letting him near. "Are you asking me to stop the demolition? That wouldn't be a sound business decision. But... just tell me what you want."

Judging from the pained look on his face, he means it, too. I could ask him not to do it. I could stand here and beg him to reconsider. He wouldn't do it for the bookstore's own sake. But he might do it for me.

What are we, exactly? Enemies, but not just that. Friends, but not just that, either. Lovers... I can't begin to think that way. And if I spent whatever capital I had with him begging... I'd never be able to show up to Between the Pages without remembering what I'd had to do to get it.

Smarts trumps being popular, Eleanor had said. I couldn't be someone who called in favors to save a business, not like this. Not the way I'd earned them with him.

"I can't," I say, backing toward the hallway. Humiliation and failure makes my cheeks burn. "You're right. I can't ask you that. I'm sorry."

"Don't. Skye—wait."

I shake my head, feeling myself unraveling and unable to stop. "I can't, not with any of it. This... it's too much."

Cole puts a hand next to me in the hallway, caging me in, his jaw clenched tight. "*Wait*. Skye, please... let me help you somehow. Let me be with you tonight."

"Why? What are we?" I fumble with the clasp of my purse. "Nothing. We're *casual*."

He frowns. "I know we agreed to that. But—"

"But what?" A laugh escapes me, though the only funny thing here is my own poor decisions. "I went into this against my better judgement. Even knowing you'd tear down the business, I did it anyway. I thought it would be an adventure. God, I can't believe I've been so stupid!"

He stiffens as if I've struck him, his hand sliding off the wall. "There is no getting around this, then?"

"That you're *tearing down* my bookstore?"

He gives a harsh nod, lips a flat line.

"No." I press the button for the elevator, the doors gayly chiming as they slide open. "No, there isn't. I can't... Cole, I can't."

"So we're over."

I don't trust my voice to speak, the taste of tears on my tongue. He's said the words, and once they're out, I can't see a way around them. We were never really *anything*, really.

I nod.

Cole's eyes shutter, and he crosses his arms over his chest, strong and sure and distant. "Well then," he says. "Thanks for a few enjoyable weeks."

I mash my fingers against the button and the elevator doors close in the nick of time as my tears break free, running hotly down my cheeks.

Sadness is a funny thing. It comes in bursts, all at once, and then disappears again, lying in wait for the perfect opportunity. Pushed away by good times or ignored when inconvenient. I'd known that Between the Pages might close for months. I had grieved Eleanor when she passed three years ago. And I'd never really expected the game with Cole to last.

And still.

All three things hit me at once, so hard that I have to reach out a hand to steady myself against the elevator wall. This morning had started with a purpose, a job, a potential future. A man who made me feel like life itself pounded in my veins, free and strong and alive.

It ended with all of those things gone. And worst of all was the feeling that all of it was somehow, someway, my fault. If I'd worked harder. If I'd known the right things to say. If I'd made different decisions.

We'd been *so* close, and instead, Between the Pages is to become dust and rubble, an impersonal glass structure rising from its wake. Maybe it'll have a hotel bar on the top floor for billionaire owners and unsuspecting young women to meet, I think bitterly, but the thought just brings on a fresh round of tears.

21

COLE

Funny how success works. I've been asked about it often in the last few years—sometimes more than once a day. In interviews. In speeches. At networking events. *Teach me something about success,* they'll say, often with a glint in their eyes. *What's the secret?*

Or, my personal favorite, *to what do you owe your success?* As if debts were involved—as if I had sacrificed to the gods.

Funnier still how public success rarely translates to private success. I could have an apartment my mother called *ostentatious*, a development company that was soon the biggest on the Western seaboard. Regular international travel and a charity organization in the works. But at the end of the day, the one person who gave me true happiness had walked out.

"So, tell me," the reporter in front of me asks, a practiced smile on his face, "what's the secret to your success?"

I don't feel particularly successful at the moment. The interview I'm giving is a necessity, according to my publicity team, to counteract Ben and Elena's smear campaign. All because I worked too much and missed what was right beneath my nose—my best friend and the woman I thought I loved. Work getting in the way of a relationship. It seems like a recurring problem in my personal life.

The reporter clears his throat. I'm taking too long to answer, clearly, my mind stuck in the past—on what happened three years ago. On what happened only one week ago in my hallway.

I lean back and cross my leg over my knee. "Well, if the answer is a secret, it's an open one. It's hard work and good luck. Being in the right place at the right time. Knocking on doors until one eventually opens." I tap my hand against my knee, contemplating a more honest answer. Skye's joking admonitions about privilege ring in my head. "And for me, I certainly had help in the beginning. My family was supportive. My friends were supportive. I graduated university without debt. I'm well aware that other entrepreneurs face difficulties I didn't have."

The reporter raises an eyebrow, jotting this down. It's an answer that will be dissected. Explained. Analyzed.

"And a helpful business partner?" he asks. Behind him, Bryan's face freezes in fury; Tyra gives me a silent shake of the head. The reporter is going off-script. We could ask for this to be struck from the record.

I meet his gaze head-on, this poor man, sent to interview someone who got three hours of sleep last night and who couldn't care less about this interview.

"Well," I say truthfully, "he was helpful until he wasn't. We wanted to pursue different directions."

The reporter nods eagerly, encouraged by my answer. "Would you say that the split was amicable, then?"

I think back to the last time I saw Ben Simmons. *Fuck you* was one of the final things I'd said, if I remember correctly. He'd been angry too. *Asshole! You always think you know better!*

"Amicably enough."

He looks through his notes, stalling for time. My tone hadn't invited follow-up questions, and he'd been briefed beforehand that questions about the article were off-limits.

But what he finally asks me turns out to be far worse.

"Porter Development will soon begin construction of a new hotel and apartment complex in East Seattle," he says, oblivious to the way my hand grows into a white-knuckled fist. "A number of old buildings will be demolished to make way for this. What's your take on the naysayers and protests that have risen up in response?"

There's only one image in my mind.

It's Skye, her beautiful eyes glittering with unshed tears. The things I'd said—the way she'd walked out—makes my body tighten with shame.

"I have nothing to say regarding that development."

The reporter's gaze travel from my eyes to my fists. "Nothing at all? Not even an official statement?"

"No. No mention of the question in the article, either. Is this interview done?"

He looks down at his notepad. "Well, if you'd like—but I have more things to touch on."

"Email any remaining questions to us. Thank you for your time." I shake the bewildered man's hand before striding out of the conference room.

Bryan follows me. "Sir?"

"That wasn't one of the pre-approved topics."

"It wasn't," he agrees. "Neither was the mention of Ben Simmons. You handled that well."

I force my voice to soften, even if the only thing I want to do is yell at him, at the reporter. At myself. "Not particularly. Let's start the development meeting early."

He nods, typing away on his phone to send the appropriate notifications. "The bookstore included in the East Seattle project just sent in their numbers, by the way. Between the Pages."

Something cold settles around my heart. "Oh?"

"They're not profitable. I'll double-check the numbers with our accounting team, but if that's the conclusion they've come to themselves, I have no doubt it's correct." There's undisguised glee in his voice. "Well done, sir. This'll make the head architects happy."

I want to punch him.

I want to punch myself.

Ten minutes later I'm seated at the head of yet another

conference table, my laptop in front of me. "Give me the latest updates," I say, though in truth, I want to walk away from this whole project. The only thing I see is Skye with pain in her eyes.

Sam, my head project manager, nods. "Given the newest information, demolition will start next Tuesday. We'll start by razing this entire area. It'll take a few days longer than usual on our projects, since we want to preserve as much of the existing pipes and sewage system as possible."

"Clever," says Gabrielle, the head architect. The two make a killer team. They designed the Legacy for me. "Although I have to say, I was enjoying testing new designs to incorporate that cute little bookstore. Oh well, now we won't have to."

Sam snorts. "Saves us a building nightmare."

Everyone around the table nods, and I find myself nodding along. It's a sound business decision. I've torn down things before. Before I'd met Skye, I wouldn't even have thought twice about this. And she's out of my life now. It shouldn't matter.

The meeting ends with a promise to reconvene next week. "I want to be there when the demolition begins," I say, shaking Sam's hand.

He shoots me a wide grin. "You can be the one to press the button, if you'd like."

Something roils in my stomach. "Thanks, but I think I'll leave that to the experts."

The rest of the day is spent on emails and meetings and phone calls. An unwelcome text from my baby sister as well, which I have no idea how to respond to.

Blair Porter: *How are things with Skye? You know I can't meet her and then hear NOTHING more about her, come on. Give me the latest updates or I'll badger you to death this weekend. That's a threat, and I expect your speedy compliance.*

I know she would. She'd badger and ask questions until I'd cave, which I always did with her.

Cole Porter: *I don't negotiate with terrorists.*

It won't hold Blair off for long, though. I know that much about my little sister. At the same time, couldn't people just *stop* asking me about Skye? Reporters, family members... I don't have any fucking answers, not for them, and not for myself.

The final straw comes in the car that evening, when Charles asks me too.

"We haven't stopped at 14 Fairfield Point for a while, sir." A delicate pause. "Or at the bookstore."

I grip the cushioned armrest and stare out of the window. "No. And we won't again."

"Ah," he says, his tone heavy with implications. I don't know if it's with censure or with approval, but regardless, it's the last thing I need. My mood blackens further. Nick will be in for a treat when I arrive, I think, and knowing him, he'll push me on it too.

He does, of course. His arm is draped around the back of the plush booth, a glass of whiskey in front of him. "You're late."

"Traffic."

He glances around the bar, at the other guests, the dark interiors. "We haven't been to Legacy for ages."

"I felt like it tonight," I say, wondering if I'm pressing my luck. I'd wanted to show myself that I could sit in this bar and not think of her.

"Well, I'm not objecting. It's one of your better developments."

"Thank you for that ringing endorsement."

He snorts, a gleam in his eyes. "What's up your ass tonight, then?"

"What isn't," I sigh, thanking the waiter when he brings my drink over.

Nick nods to the bar. A few young men in suits are lounging against it, their hair slicked back, toasting with gin and tonics. "Look at your clientele. Disgusting."

I chuckle despite myself. "That was us once upon a time, you know."

Now we always choose a secluded area of the bar, where we're mostly undisturbed. How times have changed.

Nick shakes his head. "Don't remind me. At least I never looked like one of those rich punks."

No, I think, not with his short hair and the dangerous set of his features. Even now, he's scowling. "How do you get your business partners to agree to work with you?"

"Where did that come from?"

"I realized I don't actually know." I take a sip of my whiskey, reluctantly amused. "I'd imagine you scare them off."

"I'm nice when I need to be," he says, a wolfish grin spreading across his features. "But that's unimportant. Tell me, how has your little problem progressed?"

I groan. "Don't call her my little problem."

"Well, that's what she is." He takes a sip of his own whiskey. "You never told me her name."

"And now there's no need to. It's over. And I'd greatly appreciate it if everyone just fucking *stopped* asking me about her." I run an agitated hand through my hair.

"You hit the expiration date?"

"Yes," I say. "I'm tearing down her business. It's final."

He nods, as if he understands perfectly, as if this was a conundrum men find themselves in regularly. He takes a moment, but when he speaks, his voice is low. "Are you sure the development is worth it?"

I run my hand along the table. "Are *you* really the one asking me this? *Nicholas Park?*"

"Fuck. You're right. Ignore what I said, and go after the money."

"That's what I thought."

He shakes his head at me, but it's thoughtful. "But that's *me*, Cole. Not you. And this is the first time you've been out of sorts over a woman in years."

"God, don't remind me."

"But I will, regardless." He leans over the table. "What are you doing to Ben and Elena about the article?"

"Nothing."

"Fuck nothing. What are you going to do?"

I take a sip of the whiskey and it burns down my throat. "My lawyers are looking into a potential breach of the non-disclosure agreement and slander."

"That's right. The snake." Nick shakes his head. "I never liked him."

"No, you never did." They'd been unable to be in the same room at certain points. Privately, I'd always thought they were each other's complete opposites. Nick, with a rough background and ambition and no bullshit. Ben, privilege and charm and not much else.

I know by now which friend I'd rather have; give me harsh truths over well-intentioned lies any day.

"That reminds me," I say. "What is your problem with Blair, anyway? I mentioned your name the other day and she practically recoiled. What've you done?"

Nick's features harden. "Nothing, man. Your sister and I are just different people. You know we've never been close."

"You don't have to get along. But you can at least be civil to each other," I say.

"*I* am," Nick mutters, and I don't miss the emphasis on the first word. Maybe I need to have the same conversation with her. But why? Blair is lovable. Free-spoken, perhaps, but there's no one she meets who she can't charm. Except, it seems, the man in front of me.

I shake my head and take another sip of my whiskey. It's not a conundrum I can figure out, not now, at least.

When I finally arrive home that evening, my apartment is dark and empty. There's no hallway table to toss my nonexistent key on. There are no bookshelves filled with photo albums and old yearbooks. All my old stuff is in storage, packed up by the movers. I still haven't opened a single one of those boxes.

I make my way through the empty living room—it's big

enough that my footsteps echo—and into my bedroom. Unsurprisingly, it's as empty as the rest of my apartment. The only personal touch is the books on my bedside table, piled high. I haven't touched them since Skye was here last. Somehow, I haven't been able to read, despite the sleepless nights.

I lie on my back and stare up at the ceiling. I count all the spotlights—seven of them—before familiar thoughts come creeping in, unbidden but relentless. What is Skye doing right now? How is she handling news of the demolition? Is she having trouble sleeping, too?

I shouldn't wonder. I should try to stop caring. That had been my MO for years, now. Caring gets you hurt and it makes you weak. My current predicament is the perfect example of that.

Caring for Skye has gotten me nowhere.

22

SKYE

It took grit, and perseverance, and everything she had, I write, *but in the end, the store opened. It opened its doors to a community starved for stories, and in return, its stories were read.*

I end the paragraph with a smile on my face. For the first time in months—in *years*—the writing is practically flowing out of me. Word after word, chapter after chapter, the story living in me, like it's bubbling beneath my skin. It should be difficult, considering the uncertainty in my life. I should probably not be writing at all, hunched over my desk in the evening darkness.

But ever since we got the demolition news, I haven't been able to stop.

And the best part is that my writing isn't about Cole at all. It's not even really about Between the Pages itself, but more about what the bookstore represented. About what Eleanor was to me—and to Karli—and to so many others who needed a quiet place of reflection.

When I glance at the clock, it's past midnight. I've been writing for hours again. It's funny, that. For years I thought I didn't have the words in me, and now they won't stop flowing.

I close my laptop and stow away the folder on my desk. It contains a set of printed CVs and a list of potential employers.

Brooks & King is at the top of the list, including the business card I received from the department head Edwin Taylor.

I climb into bed and try to still the spinning of my mind. Tomorrow will be another day of closing up shop. Packaging books and packing away memories. I turn over on my side, and in the stillness, my mind circles back to the one place I don't want it to go. When the words stop flowing, the thinking begins, it seems.

Cole.

He sat right there, on the other side of my bed, leaning against the headboard while I was sick. Somehow, that's the image I can't get out of my head, night after night. His sleep-deprived eyes. The murmured conversations, where my fever removed all attempts at pretense or wit. When it was just the two of us—without a game or an agreement between us.

Our casual relationship had been an adventure, and it came to an end. Just as it should've—just like all ill-considered adventures do. He'd been quick to say that it was over the last time we spoke. And since then, he hasn't contacted me, nor I him.

On my nightstand, my phone is lying innocent and quiet. Like most nights, the impulse to text him is strong. And like most nights, I fight it. Not that I'd know what to say, anyway.

I turn over on my back. "It's over," I say out loud. If I hear it enough times, maybe I'll start believing it. "He's tearing down Between the Pages."

That should be the final page of our book, the little gold lettering of a fairy tale stating *the end*. And yet… I don't know if I'm ready for that yet. For the finality of it.

The next day, Karli comes through the front door with a package of homemade cupcakes. "Look," she says, holding them up for my view. "Some carbs for comfort."

I hold up the portable speaker I brought. "I couldn't agree more."

We turn on some '90s pop and work in silence. Shelf after shelf of books get put into moving boxes, all of them clearly marked with author and genre. An entire store packed up, a legacy dismantled.

"Are you sure John is okay with this?"

Karli snorts. "No. He said just yesterday that he liked the garage as it is. But where else can we store the inventory?"

I sigh. "Nowhere. But hopefully a few bookstores will respond to my email and take some of it off our hands. If not, I already have an idea for selling them online. We should be able to recuperate most of the purchasing cost."

"Thank God," Karli says. "I might be able to sell some of the children's books to my son's school, too. They always need more books."

"That's perfect." I look down at the book in my hand, at the Art Deco font and the beautiful cover. An American classic, set in the roaring '20s.

Karli sees me pause and leans over. "Ah. Eleanor's favorite."

"Yeah." It had been a book I hated at first, mostly because I couldn't get into it. It had been assigned reading in school and nothing kills a good book more than being forced to read it. But Eleanor had helped me through it—and her commentary and insight had opened a door to reading that I'd raced through headlong. She'd set me on the path.

Maybe Karli sees my thoughts on my face, because she sinks into the old armchair. "Stop it," she says.

"Stop what?"

"What you're doing. Overthinking. Reminiscing. Beating yourself up, I'm guessing."

I reluctantly put the book into the moving box. "Maybe a little bit."

"We didn't fail her." Karli's voice is strong. "We didn't. I don't believe that for a second, Skye."

My answer takes time, because as much as I want to believe her—for both of our sakes—I'm not quite there yet. "No," I say slowly, "you might be right about that. She wouldn't be angry at us."

"Not in the least."

"But she might be disappointed. Not in us," I say hurriedly, seeing Karli's face. "But in the city, in Porter Development. In the fact that bookstores aren't as valued anymore."

"But they are," Karli says fervently. "It's just not the right time for *this* one. Everything has its time."

I reach for another stack of books. All around us, shelves are empty, the store echoing with our words. "How can you be so calm about this?"

Karli's smile is apologetic. "I know I should be angrier. But I've been angry for so long, Skye. For months and months, ever since we got the first notice."

"I get it. It gets old."

"It does," she says with a nod. "I don't have the energy for it anymore. We have to look to the future."

"Have you managed to do that, then?"

Her smile is back, but it's excited this time. "Yes. I've started looking at shopfronts for a bakery."

"Really?"

"Yes. It's early still, but… I've always wanted to try."

My smile is entirely genuine. For as long as I've known her, Karli has been a baker, her favorite section of the bookstore the recipe one. "That's amazing!"

"John is excited, too. Says he can help with website design, not to mention taste-testing," she says, laughing.

"Karli, that's perfect. You could cater. You're already well-known in this area—people love you!" My mind is racing ahead, and Karli laughs again, the glint in my eyes familiar to her.

"You're already thinking about what opening gift to get me, aren't you? We're not there yet."

"But you will be. I'm so happy for you, Karli."

She grins. "Thanks. I was afraid to mention it to you, you know."

"You were?"

"Well, maybe you'd think I was moving on too fast. Accepting the bookstore's fate." She looks around, at the beautiful old wood, at the place that has been a second home for the both of us. "Between the Pages was my grandmother's life. But it can't be mine, not any longer."

I reach over and put my hand on hers. "Oh God, Karli, I'd never think that. You're doing the right thing."

Her smile is bright. "Thanks. And so are you, by the way, focusing on your writing. Are you still going to apply to Brooks & King?"

"Yes. But I don't have a background in editing or in publishing, and I'm competing with people who do. At the same time —" I'm broken off by my phone's familiar tune. "Sorry."

Karli smiles and gets up to continue packing. Fishing my phone out of my bag, I nearly groan when I see the name on my screen. Isla.

"Hi," I say. "What's up?"

There's an annoyed sigh on the other end. "You won't believe what a day I'm having."

"Oh?"

"I overslept. Timmy was late to school, and then we had an accident on the way home."

"Are you okay?"

"Yes, yes, it wasn't a car accident. I didn't have enough gas in the tank."

"It stalled? Oh my God, Isla…"

"I *know*, it was awful. Well, Dave helped me, all is good now. But, and here's the thing, he has a car show tonight."

Ah, I think. Here it comes. "Is it out of town?"

"Yes. I'd love to go, but I know it's too late for Timmy. He has to be in bed by nine. But then I thought, Skye!"

This has to stop. "You know I love spending time with Timmy, but—"

"Perfect!"

"—I have plans tonight. I can't handle this on such short notice, not continually, Isla."

She huffs, and the sound is indignant. "You have *plans?*"

"Yeah. Even if I didn't, I'd appreciate a bit more advance notice. It's already four in the afternoon."

Isla's voice is glacial when she speaks again. "Fine. That's fine. I'll just have to figure something out."

"Yes, you will," I say, not unkindly. "I'll talk to you soon."

She hangs up. I stare at my phone for a few more moments, a smile slowly spreading across my face. Wow. That was... exhilarating.

Karli grins at me. "Well done," she says.

"With what?"

"With saying no." She unfolds another moving box with sure, practiced hands. "It's hard with family, I know. But you're getting better."

Her words echo Cole's, when he listened to my call with Isla a few weeks ago. Karli has known me forever and never asked me the reasons behind it. Cole saw our dynamic immediately. He encouraged me to stand up to her. To speak my mind.

I miss him. It's hard to admit, but it's there, every day. I miss his voice and his opinions, his teasing smile, the glint in his eyes when he sees me. I even miss his obnoxious way of thinking he's always right.

While I always said I hated him, I don't anymore. I don't hate him at all, not even when he's set to tear down this place.

And somehow, that's what hurts the most.

23

COLE

I swirl the whiskey around in my glass. It's my second of the evening, and it's only a Wednesday. "You're losing it," I say. There's no one around to listen.

On my computer in front of me, my emails seem to swim in and out of focus, and it's not because I'm drunk. I just can't seem to bring myself to care about them.

Demolition of the bookstore starts in less than fifteen hours.

Have Karli and Skye finished emptying the store? Have they taken down the memorabilia, the plants, the framed pictures? Have they stowed away all the inventory? I want to know. I want to call Skye and ask, to hear her voice on the phone. To see if she'd taken the old ratty armchair home to her already too cluttered apartment.

But I doubt she'd pick up. In the story of her and me, of Between the Pages and Porter Development, I'm the bad guy. The ones in the movies always seems to enjoy their evilness, somehow. I can't relate to that.

I could still stop it.

Sure, the plans are drawn up. The investors are happy. My building team is excited to get started, and just today, someone congratulated me on the new build.

But there's still time, if I decided to change the plans.

My team would think I'm insane. There'd be internal disagreements. Questions regarding my leadership, and perhaps even my sanity. It feels like a small price to pay. What do I have to lose?

Skye.

She might hate me for stopping the demolition for her just as much as she hates me for going ahead. Pride is an emotion both of us share. From the very beginning, she made it clear that our relationship wasn't quid pro quo. That she didn't want to *earn* anything, not that way.

If I stopped the demolition for her... While I'd never ask for anything in return, it would put her in an awkward position. If there's one thing I don't want her to feel, it's shame, especially not over anything we've done together.

I glance at the framed picture of my family on my desk. My dad is in it, a couple of years before he passed. He's tall and suit-clad, a hand on my shoulder as I graduate college. My sister is beaming beside me, braces on her teeth.

For years my dad had loved to listen to my business dealings. Wanted me to run through them so he could listen and give comments. What would he say about this one? He was always the one who instilled in me the importance of making sound financial decisions, of trusting experts. Doing things by the book.

There's never only one option, he often said. *Find the third way. That's where success lies.*

Maybe his advice isn't applicable here, but I have to try. Find the third way.

Skye had mentioned that their numbers were still up; they might be profitable in a few months' time. Incorporating their store would help appease the project's protestors, not that they were many.

Could I make the decision for the business itself, and not for Skye?

I search through the shared company drive on my laptop until I find the project. And there, in a little folder titled

"Between the Pages Financial Records," is the accounting report they submitted to my company.

I click it open. I'm immediately assailed by colorful graphics. On closer inspection, one is duplicated, the numbers just inverted. Why would their accountant do that? To make it look fancier?

I scroll through the numbers, searching for sales and inventories. Assets and debt. Instead, I fall down a financial rabbit hole.

Their numbers are confusingly displayed. It's a beautiful document, sure, if you aimed for style over substance. But the meat is sorely lacking. I parse through the pretty phrasing and the artfully created tables to scour the numbers. And that's when I find it.

The error.

At first, it's small enough that my eyes dart over it, but on the second pass it stands out like a sore thumb. It's a deliberate error, too. Their accountant has incorrectly classified a whole section of sales. Income is described as expenses.

It's embezzlement 101.

The blood begins to pound in my temples. How did my accountants not catch this? Bryan said he would run the store's numbers past our in-house financial department.

Ice sets in my stomach when I realize the reason. *Of course, Cole.* If Porter Development's accountants are worth their name, they saw it, and they didn't call it out. Why would they? We have no incentive to. Because the truth, hidden beneath this fraudulent document, is clear.

Between the Pages was profitable.

And someone submitted a forged document to our company in the hope that we'd let it slide.

Skye had succeeded. She managed to turn it around, damn it, and their accountant *and* my own damn company are trying to cheat her out of it.

My hand is nearly trembling with cold fury when I reach for the phone. Bryan is my first call.

"Sir?"

"The bookstore's numbers are falsified. Did you know?"

A delicate pause. "Sir…"

"Answer the question."

"The financial team made me aware, on the down-low, that their accounting report seemed… amateurish. Riddled with errors. I decided not to press the issue." He lets the words hang for a few moments. "Why would we, sir?"

"Because we made a business deal with them. Because I gave my word." My voice hardens. "We halt tomorrow's demolition. Nothing proceeds until our accountants have double-checked the whole thing."

Shocked silence. And then, just as I'd expected, his outraged voice. "Things are already in motion. Pausing it now will *cost* you money. Sir."

"So be it. I'm calling Sam next to let him know the exact same thing."

"Well. All right, I'll make the arrangements, too."

"I expect you to." My hand tightens around my cell phone. "I don't appreciate you deciding what information I will or will not have access to regarding my own business deals, Bryan."

"Understood."

I hang up, my anger no less sated. Bryan might have been a snake, but he's a snake I hired and promoted. I should have asked to see the numbers myself and not simply trusted.

Sam takes longer to answer, and when I glance at the time, I realize why. It's late—far too late for his boss's boss to be calling.

"Sir?"

"Sorry to bother you at this time, Sam, but it's regarding demolition tomorrow. We're going to have to halt it."

He takes it in stride, uncomplicated and competent. "Okay. Will do. Anything I need to know about?"

"Internal politics, you know the drill. We might end up keeping the structure. Possibly incorporating it."

There's silence on the other line, just like from Bryan. Sam's, at least, is just shocked—there's no dismay in his pause. "All righty. I'll let my crew know."

"Thanks."

"Don't mention it."

Running as a current beneath my skin is the need to tell Skye. She's the one who's been duped—by who, I don't know. There's no doubt in my mind where their profit has disappeared, though. That accountant of theirs has made a killing.

I grab my laptop and phone, striding for the elevator. It's late. She hates me. And yet, there's nowhere else I can be right now and nothing else I can do. I have to set this right. Having given Charles the night off, not to mention downed two whiskeys, I'm left with no other option than to hail a cab. I dial Skye's number when I'm nearly at her apartment.

There's fierce purpose in my voice when she picks up. "Skye, it's Cole. We need to talk. I'm coming over."

Her silence is absolute. And then, quiet and surprised. "*What?*"

"There's something I need to show you."

"Right now?"

"Yes. It's about the bookstore. You guys did it. You were profitable, Skye. The numbers are wrong."

Her breath is shaky, and I don't know if it's with relief or pain. "We were?"

"Yes. Let me prove it to you."

"When do you get here?"

"I'm outside now," I say, as the cab pulls onto her street.

"Good," she says, fire in her own voice. "I'll leave the door open for you."

My patience is stretched too thin to wait for change, and the cab driver grins at the obscenely large tip. I take the steps to her apartment in two. She's waiting by her front door. At first, the shock of seeing her after nearly two weeks apart drives all thoughts of embezzlement from my mind. Her thick brown hair is in a braid down her back, an oversized sweater loose on her frame. There's not a stitch of makeup on her skin. She's painfully beautiful.

"If you're joking about this," she warns, "Cole, I swear I'll—"

"I'm not."

Maybe she sees it in my eyes, or maybe she's shocked that I walk straight past her into her apartment, but for some reason Skye doesn't protest. She just locks the door behind me instead. "But the numbers didn't add up," she says. "We were told the store wasn't profitable. How…?"

"Your accountant lied." I open my laptop and pull up Between the Pages' documents, sitting down at her kitchen table. She takes a seat next to me. The scent of her shampoo, as floral as ever, washes over me.

"How?"

"Look." I point at my screen, at the error, at the numbers that don't add up. "She didn't try to hide it particularly well." My voice grows hard. "I'm guessing she gambled that neither you or Karli would figure it out, and what's more, that Porter Development would let it slide."

Skye's voice is shaky. "Could it be a mistake? It's not… it *can't* be deliberate."

"It's a hundred percent deliberate." I'm harsh, but this is too important, and I'm too angry on Skye's behalf. "She must have funneled your profit into her own accounts."

"But… I've known her since college!"

"Yes, but that means nothing, really," I say, thinking of Ben. "I'm sorry."

Her hazel eyes are blazing. "So we're profitable?"

"The numbers sure seem so, yes. But I'll make sure my accountants run a thorough check on it." *And* give me the correct information this time, I think.

Skye gets out of her chair, energy running through her body, and starts to pace in front of me. In her pajama shorts and slippers, she's a glorious sight.

"I *can't* believe this. I was the one who recommended her!"

"You had no way of knowing."

"But I should've. We should've double-checked the numbers." She wraps her arms around herself. "Damn it, if only I knew how bookkeeping works."

I close my laptop. "You know now."

"If we're profitable…" she says, eyes boring into mine. There's hope there, and confusion, and anger. All rolled into one.

"I've called off the demolition."

Her eyes widen. "You have?"

"Of course. You made a deal with me, Skye, and I'm going to honor it."

"We did it," she whispers faintly. Her voice is dreamy. "We actually turned it around. The store is saved."

"You did it."

"I *knew* it! We had so many more customers. Our sale was working. Damn Chloe." She sits down next to me again, her hand landing atop mine gently. "Karli and I need to take legal action against her, don't we?"

I nod, wondering if I could grasp her hand in mine, or if that would be pushing it. "Yes. What she did was illegal."

Skye gazes off into the distance, her face set in a mask of determination I recognize well. "I'm going to make sure the store gets every cent back."

"I have no doubt about that."

"Thank you, Cole," she says, her hand tightening around mine. "You didn't have to bring this to me. I appreciate that, you know."

"I was already considering halting the demolition." The admission spills out of me of its own accord, her nearness and warmth like a blanket of comfort.

Skye's mouth drops open in surprise. *"Why?"*

"Because I couldn't stand the idea of you hating me," I say. My gaze travels across her face, noting the surprise in her eyes, the tendrils of hair escaping her loose braid. "But that's a discussion for a different day. What are you going to do now?"

"I need to call Karli," she says. "And I have to see Chloe. Our accountant," she adds, seeing the confusion on my face.

"You want to confront her?"

"Yes. I have to know, to hear her say it."

"It might make things harder for you, and not easier," I

caution. Confronting Ben hadn't helped me in the least, especially not hearing him admit to what he'd done.

Her eyes soften. "You're right. But I have to. I'll... I'll invite myself over tomorrow evening."

"Anything you need, Skye." I reluctantly pull my hand out from underneath hers. It's late, and she has much to think about. She needs to call Karli. To process this. As much as I want to stay, it would be pushing things.

Skye reaches out to put a hand on my sleeve. "Wait. What happens next?"

And damn it, but I can't help myself. I reach out and push a lock of her hair back behind her ears. Skye doesn't seem to be breathing, looking up at me. "Invite Karli to my office the day after tomorrow," I say. "We'll meet with my accountants and lawyers. Go over the bookkeeping in detail and work out a strategy for the bookstore going forward."

Skye's breath is shaky, and then she's hugging me, her head against my neck. Slowly, I wrap my arms around her. She's so warm. The scent of her hair is in my nostrils, the curve of her waist beneath my hands.

I don't want to let her go.

"Thank you," she murmurs. "I don't know what to say. Thank you."

I touch my lips to her ear, unable to resist. "There's no need to thank me, Skye. You did all of this yourself."

My tone is warm. I wonder if she hears the truth, all the things I find myself wanting to say, and unable to bring myself to. Not yet.

"Not the plants," she says, a smile in her voice.

She's still in my arms. "Okay, so maybe I helped a little. But I'm the one who should apologize."

She pulls away and I let her go reluctantly. There's a smile on her lips. "I think we both should, but..."

"That's for another day. I understand." I take a step back, releasing her hand. "Call Karli. I'll talk to you tomorrow."

"Okay." She wraps her arms around herself again, the long

sleeves covering her hands, and watches me as I open her front door. Despite the subject matter, despite the confusion between us, the look in her eyes makes my chest tighten with emotion. "Thanks, Porter."

There's a smile in my voice. "You're welcome, Holland."

24

SKYE

I square my shoulders. Despite my calm assurance to Karli that *yes, I can do this, don't worry,* anxiety runs through my veins. And right behind it, guilt. I had recommended Chloe. She'd been hired on my suggestion, and then she'd screwed us over.

I press the intercom to Chloe's apartment. "I'm downstairs."

"Come on up!" Her cheery voice makes my stomach drop even lower. If Cole is right—if her mistake isn't a mistake at all but deliberate embezzlement—she's still willing to have dinner with me. Just imagining it makes me feel nauseous.

My phone feels like a box of dynamite in my pocket. It's recording all sound, anything we say saved for posterity. That's the second reason I'm here tonight. To get an admission on tape.

Chloe opens the door to her apartment with a smile, her hair in a high ponytail. "I'm so glad you took me up on the offer of dinner."

Does she mean that? Twenty-four hours ago I wouldn't have doubted her for a second. Now, I can't *not.*

"Thanks for having me. Wow, whatever you're cooking smells good."

"Pasta carbonara. It's a simple enough recipe."

I follow her through the living room—a plush couch, a large TV—into a big kitchen. "Well," I say, "that's still a huge step up.

Do you remember in college? We'd make Pop-Tarts in the toaster in our room."

Chloe laughs, stirring a pot of boiling pasta. "Yes. Vanilla for me, chocolate fudge for you."

"Those were the times." I lean against the counter, wondering where we went wrong for this to have happened. Sure, we'd drifted apart, but there was a time when we'd shared both our days and nights together.

She offers me a glass of wine, her smile still in place. My palms feel sweaty around the glass. Dinner had been a pretext to get invited, to ensure I got answers face-to-face, to avoid being a dodged phone call. But how do you bring it up? *This wine is divine. Also, did you steal money from our business?*

"So," Chloe says, "how has the job hunting been going? After the bookstore closed?"

I clear my throat. "So far so good. I have a few applications going out this week."

"That's great, that you're staying on top of it. And please, let me know if I can do anything to help." There's a beautiful display of compassion in her eyes. "I'm truly sorry about the way it ended."

My wine tastes sour. "Thank you."

She turns back to the pasta. "I tried everything I could."

"Did you?" I say. "How nice." I put my glass down and wipe my hands on my dress. If I'd ever harbored a long-lost dream of becoming a spy, this little attempt would put an end to it. I'm awful at it. Nerves are making my throat feel tight. "Where's your bathroom?"

"Down the hall and to the right."

"Thanks. I'll be right back."

I shake my head at myself as I walk swiftly from the kitchen. Just confront her, Skye. How hard can it be? Cole's words come back to me, the ones regarding my sister. *You never seem to have a problem standing up to me. Do the same to her.*

The fire is there, inside me, burning at a comfortable distance. All I need to know is if it was deliberate. And if it was...

Absent-minded as I am, I open the wrong door to the bathroom. It's her walk-in closet. And it's filled top to bottom with handbags, with shoes, with belts. Beautifully displayed bags in a myriad of colors, both brands I recognize and ones I've never seen before. Designer handbags has never been my thing, but even I know that the collection in her closet is worth thousands of dollars.

My mind makes the assumptions lightning fast. The fire in me erupts and burns, righteous and fierce. I shut the closet with a bang and stride back into the kitchen.

"Chloe."

"Yes?"

"We found an accounting error in your bookkeeping." Maybe I should have phrased it differently, maybe I should have been smoother, but suspicion and anger are like a cloud around my mind.

Chloe gives a wan smile. "Is there? I triple-checked, Skye, but if you want to point it out to me I'd be happy to look it over. Just send it to me tomorrow, okay?"

"No, it's not that kind of error." My hand isn't sweaty now; it's clenched into a fist at my side. "I've been informed that it's a big one. The kind you'd know about while you're making it."

Chloe puts down her phone. "Skye, what are you saying?"

"Have you been embezzling from the bookstore?"

"*What?*" She blinks at me, once, twice, but the outrage looks superficial. Her eyes are too impassive.

"Why would you do that?" I demand. "Why would you *need* to? Chloe!"

Her affronted mask crumbles, her mouth turning down in a frown. "Damn it. You were never supposed to figure it out. You weren't supposed to be told!"

"To be told?" I'm shaking, I'm so angry. "How could you? That's Karli's *livelihood*. It's my job. And for what? So you could buy more designer bags?"

She shakes her head angrily, but it's not in denial. "You have your books, you always did. I like something different. God, you were always so judgmental!"

"For judging you about committing a *crime?*"

"The business was over, Skye. Neither you nor Karli was willing to see the writing on the wall. The store was going to close. All I did was give it a little nudge."

"Are you serious? We had a deal; we could stay if we were profitable. And we were, until you tried to hide it. How the hell could you?"

Her smile becomes an ugly thing. "If you thought Porter Development was ever going to honor that little deal, then you're a fool."

I want to shake her, I want to slap her. I take a deep breath. "Give back the money. Every single cent, Chloe."

"I don't have it."

"You spent it all?"

"So what if I did?" Her eyes narrow, a nasty expression in them. It's a side of her I haven't seen for years, and never this pronounced. "Demolition began today. I know the timeline, Skye. Where would you get the support? Who would help you? I'm pretty sure Porter Development saw my error, but why would they care? They're getting exactly what they wanted."

I can't believe what I'm hearing. I take a step back, wanting out of her presence. "If you think you've won here, you've got another thing coming."

"Do I? I'm sorry, Skye. It wasn't personal. It was just business."

"*You bitch.*" Chloe blinks at me, like she can't believe I went there. Frankly, I can't either, a part of me observing myself as from a distance. The other part—the part in control—has no time for niceties. "You destroy someone's business and you say *it's not personal?* Absolutely unbelievable. And you're the fool if you think either Karli or I are going to take this lying down."

I walk through her living room, grabbing my jacket off the chair where I'd thrown it.

"Good luck!" she calls. "Porter Development is knocking!"

My skin feels hot, my blood boiling close to the surface. What I do next surprises even myself. On a peg next to her front door is a crossbody purse. The designer label on it is one of the few I recognize. So I reach out and snatch it, holding it close to my chest as I race out of her front door and out onto the sidewalk.

The large Jeep is waiting for me, and so is the driver. I jump into the passenger seat. "Oh my God."

"Did it go well?"

I glance at the front door. There's no sight of her, not yet at least. "Yes. Go, go, drive!"

Cole turns the key to the ignition. "I've never been a getaway driver before."

"It's never too late to learn." I slump against the seat, my breath coming fast. "She did it. She admitted to it. I can't... I'm so angry."

His hand twitches on the steering wheel. "You have every right to be. Did you record her saying it?"

I double-check my phone and turn off the recording function. "Yes. Yes, and she admitted it outright."

"Excellent."

"She said she didn't have a cent of it left. And that Porter Development was going to bury us."

Cole's mouth tightens. "Well, I have it on good authority that Porter Development will do no such thing."

I close my eyes, breathing through my nose. "I'm on such a high right now. Wow. Do you know what she said? *It wasn't personal!*"

Cole shakes his head, and this time, he reaches over to put a hand on my knee. "She's unbelievable. I'm so sorry, Skye."

"I'm not. I'm determined. I'm going to get the money back, somehow, someway."

"I have no doubt about that."

"Oh, and look!"

He glances over at the handbag in my hands. "What's that?"

"I took it. She had a whole closet full of them. She must have used the money she stole from us. And... oh my God," I say, the reality of our encounter hitting us. "I stole her handbag."

Cole's laughter is freeing—large and deep and strong. He turns the car around with his left hand, his right grasping mine in his. "You're ridiculous."

"I committed a crime, too." I look down at the design, tightening my fingers around his. "These probably go for quite a lot of money. I'm going to hold it ransom until she pays us back what we're owed."

His voice is warm. "Sounds perfectly reasonable."

"You're laughing at me," I say, and then my own anger drains out, bubbling into shocked laughter. "I can't believe I did that."

"I can," Cole says, his voice warm and strong. "You're a formidable opponent."

His profile is strong, illuminated by the late evening light streaming in through the car window. Tonight's the first time I've seen him drive himself, without Charles. "Thank you for being my getaway driver."

His gaze softens, flickering over to me. "I couldn't let you be reckless without me."

"There's something you should know about tomorrow, by the way."

He squeezes my hand once before withdrawing, placing both hands on the wheel. From this angle, the backs of his hands are wide, the fingers long, his tan forearms on display. Funny how such a mundane task as driving can make a man look irresistible.

"About the meeting?"

"Yes."

"Well?" he prompts. "If you're trying to build suspense here, consider me on the edge of my seat."

"Karli knows about you and me."

His gaze on me is concerned. "She does? How?"

"Timmy. He was bragging about his idol and she overheard."

Cole's lips curve into a fond smile. "How did she take it? Will I face an execution squad tomorrow?"

"She didn't take it well at first. I had a bit of explaining to do."

He nods, turning onto the highway to avoid the evening traffic in the city. My gaze drinks him up greedily, relishing in watching him when he can't watch me. Two weeks without any interaction had been two weeks too many. I'd missed the width of his shoulders and the depth of his mind.

"I imagine the explaining was difficult," he says dryly.

I chuckle. "Yes. I think that's what convinced her, though. That I couldn't explain it myself. I've never been able to, you know."

He gives a deep *humming* sound, and once again, things are unsaid between us. About what we are. Where we're going. If our relationship is best kept as a fond memory.

I know what I want. It's there, hiding in the back of my mind, a fragile hope. Screaming at Chloe has made it clearer than ever, paradoxically, that I liked who I was around him—who he'd helped me become. The bravery he'd helped me find.

I want to be something more than enemies. More than casual, too, and definitely more than friends. I just have to gather the courage to tell him that.

There's a wry smile in Cole's voice when he pulls up outside my apartment, the glint in his eyes speaking of his own hidden thoughts. "We're here."

"So we are."

His gaze caresses my face, my cheek, my lips. "I'm proud of you for standing up to your friend like that."

"Thank you."

"A simple thank you? I was sure I'd be chewed out for that."

"I'm not *always* awful," I say, wetting my lips.

His smile is a curve of possibility. "Oh, I know that, Skye."

The silence between us is warm, and heady, and I want him to come up. I want to say all kinds of things, some more sappy and outlandish than I'm sure he thinks me capable of.

But then he nods at my door. "Take your contraband and go inside, Skye, before I push my luck."

"Maybe I want you to."

He closes his eyes with a dark exhale. "We're doing it right this time. That's my mantra, anyway. And that includes settling things with your business *first*. We're not mixing the two again."

I give a shaky nod. "That sounds like a plan, Porter."

"I'm trying to have one this time around."

His eyes are still closed, head leaning against the headrest, the picture of masculine restraint. So I press a soft kiss to his cheek.

His eyes fly open, but I'm out of his car and on the sidewalk before there's a sound of protest.

"Until tomorrow," I say.

His gaze lingers, watching as I find the keys to my apartment. The voice that reaches me through the open window is soft. "Can't wait."

25

COLE

"We've run the numbers," Tyra says. "Between the Pages *was* profitable. Not by a huge margin, that's true. But it was."

Karli visibly slumps in the chair she's in, like hearing it from one of my staff makes it real—real in a way it hadn't been before. Next to her, Skye shoots me a look that's equal parts triumph and pride. What Chloe admitted is true.

I tap my knuckles on the table. "This means, ladies, that Between the Pages will be incorporated in the upcoming Porter Development build, per our agreement. Congratulations," I say. "You managed to turn it around."

Karli releases a shaky sigh. "I can hardly believe this. You'll really keep the bookstore?"

"Yes," I say warmly. "You won the bet. Besides, having seen how much the store increased its sales these past two months has made us reconsider. It could be an interesting business venture."

Skye clears her throat. "And the renovations will begin right away?"

"Yes. My design team drew up two different alternatives for the new hotel, depending on the outcome of this. Kassandra?"

My head designer gives Karli and Skye a huge smile. "Between us," she says conspiratorially, "I was always hoping for Between the Pages to stay. It's not Mr. Porter's usual style, but I think a more Old World-feel to this development could be a fantastic thing. It would diversify the brand." She pushes over some sketches, the ones she'd shown me before Skye and Karli arrived.

The theme of the bookstore will set the theme for the entire hotel. There's nothing minimalist about it. No hard lines or brutalist glass. Kassandra's vision is dark wood, chandeliers, a speakeasy-themed bar in the back.

It takes me a minute to see the brilliance.

Porter Hotels are known for their sleekness, their elegance. It's a concept we share with many other chains. But this design... well, it's unique. If it's received well, it could launch a new line of hotels for us.

Skye inspects one of the images. "The bookstore would be a part of the ground floor?"

"Yes, on the corner. We'd essentially build around you. Tricky, but not impossible."

Her smile widens as she looks through the sketches. "When did you prepare all this?"

"Weeks ago," Kassandra replies. "We had both options ready, depending on the outcome of your two-month business agreement."

And that's when Skye's gaze meets mine, her hazel eyes wide and warm, and I know exactly what she's thinking. That this was in the pipeline from the beginning—that we were always going to honor our agreement. I knew she'd doubted that, and no words of mine could've set that fear to rest like Kassandra's just did.

I can't say anything to Skye here, not with these people around. So I nod instead, a smile playing on my lips. She looks away with a grin of her own.

That's right, I think. *We're not over, you and I.*

We're just getting started.

I approach Karli and Skye as soon as the meeting is over, letting the rest of my team filter out behind us. I ignore the curious glances they throw my way and focus on Karli. "Mrs. Stiller, I'd like to apologize on behalf of my company."

Her eyes widen. "What for?"

"For accepting your initial bookkeeping reports, despite their obvious errors. We should have been more vigilant."

"Oh. Thank you, but that's okay. We're the ones who should have double-checked." Karli straightens her blazer, a hint of nerves in her voice. "If you feel the need to apologize, then I definitely feel the need to say thank you."

"Thank me?"

She meets my gaze. "Yes. I know that it would have been easier for you to accept the false numbers and ignore our initial agreement. But you didn't. Thank you for that."

My gaze drifts from her to Skye, both of them looking up at me with an emotion I'd never expected to see from them. Gratitude. I reach up and rub my neck. "We made an agreement," I say simply, "and I always adhere to mine. That reminds me of something—are you in contact with a lawyer for dealing with Chloe's embezzlement?"

Karli sighs. "No. Skye and I haven't even spoken about it yet, but we'll find one."

"I've already made a shortlist of possible firms," Skye adds.

I want to smile. Of course she has. "I'd like to offer our in-house lawyers. As Between the Pages is now a member of Porter Development, you're free to use them."

Karli's mouth opens. "We couldn't do that."

"Of course you can." I stride to the door of the conference room, holding it open for them both. "I keep them on retainer. Might as well get some use out of them."

Skye mouths a silent *thank you* behind Karli's back, her hand brushing against mine as she walks past. I escort them to the elevator and the lobby beyond, the need for Skye burning inside

245

my chest. To talk about *us*, about the things we haven't said. To ask her if she's willing to turn the page.

Out on the curb, Karli extends a hand to me. "Thank you for this, Mr. Porter," she says. "We won't forget it."

"It's been my pleasure," I say, and find that I mean it. "I've visited the bookstore several times these past few months. Your grandmother created a beautiful place, Mrs. Stiller. I'm glad it's still standing."

Her smile deepens, from civil and professional to something real. "I think we have Skye to thank for that, too," she says warmly.

Skye's cheeks flush at the comment, but her smile is warm, too. She extends a hand to me. "Thank you, Cole. We should get going."

"Actually, Skye, I was wondering if you'd join me for an early dinner."

There it is. Let her take it or leave it—she'd told me Karli already knew about us. For a breathless moment, my words hang in the air between us.

Karli's the one who breaks the silence. "I'll see you later," she says to Skye, voice conspiratorial.

And then it's just Skye and me left.

"That was bold," she tells me, but her voice is teasing. For the first time in weeks, there's no censure in her eyes—no hidden dislike, no argument with herself.

"I'm a bold kind of guy," I say. "Come on. Let's get some food."

She falls into easy step beside me. In her patterned dress and trim blazer, she looks professionally artsy. Like a writer—like a bookstore owner. It makes me want her even more.

"Did your staff really like the change of style for your new hotel?" she asks. "That wasn't staged?"

I smile, despite myself. "Knew you'd ask that. Honestly, yes, some really did. Some didn't, but they'll come around. The new style has charm."

"It's very different from your usual style."

"My usual *charmless* style?"

Her eyes dance, caught in her own words and completely unrepentant. "Yes."

I laugh, wrapping my arm around her shoulders out of habit. She doesn't shrug it off. "Well, the Amena was a necessity. I'm not opposed to comfortable, homey living."

"Like my place."

"Like yours, all twelve square feet of it."

She elbows me softly. "So, we're having dinner, huh?"

"Yes. I figured it was time to have that conversation we've been putting off for days."

"The one you wouldn't let us have until the business deal was settled." She looks up at me. A lock of hair has escaped from her bun and it curls gently around her face. "I'd like that."

The soft, shy smile on her face is my undoing. Skye has been a firecracker since the start—strong-willed and strong of opinion—but I've always known there's vulnerability behind that facade. She's letting me see it.

My words spill out of me of their own accord. "I demanded an answer from you about us, the evening you came to my apartment. When you'd just been told the store wasn't profitable." I tuck the lock of hair behind her ear, the back of my hand lingering on her cheek. "I shouldn't have done that."

"It's okay."

"No. Pushing you away was the easier option, but it wasn't the right one."

"I did the same thing," she says softly. "Keeping you at arm's length, because the alternative would have been more than I could bear."

"Oh?"

"Yes. To actually *like* my enemy… unthinkable. And I'm sorry for saying I hate you so often. I don't, actually. I'm sure you've already figured that out."

My smile is entirely genuine, my thoughts running away from me. "I kinda liked that."

Skye's teeth dig into her bottom lip. "Well, I can still say it, every now and then. As long as you know I don't mean it."

"That's a deal."

Her gaze shifts from mine to the building behind us. Her voice is teasing when she speaks. "*This* is where we're having dinner?"

Our leisurely stroll has taken us to the Amena, located just a stone's throw from my work. As ever, convenience had been king when I chose it. "That was not part of the original plan," I say. "But if you want to stay in, perhaps order takeout..."

Skye's eyes glimmer in the evening sunset. "Restaurants are overrated anyway," she says. Heat claws up my spine at her low voice, at the feel of her hand in mine. We walk through the familiar marble lobby and into my private elevator. Her skin feels hot against mine as the doors open, revealing my hallway and the living room beckoning beyond.

"I hate this place," I say.

The laughter that spills out of her is surprised. "What? Where did that come from?"

"You've made me reevaluate things," I say. "I bought it after Elena, and I've barely spent any time here. It's like one giant hotel suite."

Skye reaches up to lace her fingers behind my neck. Behind her, the floor-to-ceiling windows offer me a view of the burning evening sky, the setting sun blazing across Seattle. It's a beautiful view, but this Skye is prettier.

"If only you had more fridge magnets," she teases. "You'd feel right at home, then."

"Oh yes," I say. My hands close around her waist, pulling her flush against my body. "I need tons and tons of them."

"I'll go shopping for some tomorrow for you."

"How generous of you." I tip her head back, our lips a hairsbreadth apart. "I can't believe I survived two weeks without kissing you," I murmur.

She rises up on her tiptoes. "Never again."

I kiss her. My intention was to go soft, to kiss her gently, to ease back into this. But Skye has never been the one to follow my lead. Her soft lips open for me and draw me in, the warmth of her mouth intoxicating.

She sighs against me, her body melting into mine, and I lose myself in the feeling of Skye. My hands flatten against her back and push her firmly against me. Her breasts are soft against my chest, her fingers winding their way into my hair, tugging and pulling.

"I'm sorry," I murmur, my lips finding their way down her neck, her cheek.

"So am I." Her body, as if moving by its own accord, twines itself around mine. My hand fists her dress, pulling it up, my fingers finding the soft skin of her thigh. I hike her leg around my hip.

This has always been an area Skye and I have excelled in.

I lift her up and she laughs, her hair tickling my cheek. "Where are we going?"

I sink onto the couch with her in my arms, her legs neatly on either side of me. "Not far," I say. "You're so beautiful."

She reaches up to undo her ponytail. "Oh?"

"Yes. It was the first thing I thought when I saw you in the hotel bar, and I'll never stop thinking it." My hands run up her thighs, sneaking under the hem of her dress. Her skin is like silk.

"We should go back some time," she says. "Maybe I'll try to pick *you* up this time."

My smile is crooked. "I'd be willing, baby."

A shudder runs through her as my hands continue upwards, finding her hips, soft and warm under my touch. The perfect handhold. She smells like warm skin and woman and Skye, and my whole body tightens at the overwhelming need that sweeps through me.

She puts her hands on my chest. "Wait. Cole, if we do this again, I can't do casual," she says. "I'm sorry, but I just don't think I'm that kind of person."

I smile against her collarbone. "I know that."

"You do?"

"Yes." I say, my fingers tracing the curve of her spine under her dress. "I don't think we were ever truly casual. We were just very good at convincing ourselves that we were."

Skye smiles, and with her flushed skin and the joy in her eyes, she's breathtaking. "So what does that mean? Are we dating now?"

"Yes," I say, squeezing her hips for emphasis. "Exclusively, too."

"Oh, really?"

"Yes. There's no way I'm sharing you."

Her laughter is breathless. "Good, because I'm definitely not sharing you."

Excitement and need and joy pounds through me, all in one heady mix. Her lips are on mine and her body is warm under my hands and for a few long moments there's no thought. I need her—and she wants the same thing, tugging at my shirt, kissing my shoulders. I pull her dress clean off and feast on her skin.

Undoing her bra takes a few seconds and then her breasts are in my hands, the perfect weight, her nipples growing taut beneath my thumbs.

"Cole," she murmurs and rolls her hips against me. "*Two weeks.*"

My hands are lightning quick, undoing my belt, pushing her panties to the side, groaning at the wetness already there. "Skye, fucking hell, baby."

She rises up on her knees and then sinks back down, both of us groaning as I slide inside. It's hot and fierce and quick, over as soon as it began. Skye collapses against me with a soft sigh.

"I don't ever want to move," she murmurs, head against my shoulder.

I close my eyes in pleasure. For the first time in weeks, I'm perfectly at peace. "Me neither."

She gives a breathless snort. "Well, at least we don't have to hate each other to have great sex. Good to know."

"That was never the secret to our sex."

"No?"

"No." I lean in closer, letting my teeth graze her earlobe. "Even when you hated me, and even when you drove me mad, we were always clearly meant to be together."

Her fingers slide into the hair at the nape of my neck. "Cole Porter's a romantic," she says softly. "Who knew?"

"You do." I tighten my arms around her. "Besides, I'd rather be hated by you than loved by anyone else."

Skye draws back to meet my eyes. There's emotion in her gaze, more than I've ever seen before, and it strikes me speechless. She smooths her fingers down my cheek. "Well," she says softly, "you'll just have to get used to being loved by me instead."

"Sounds difficult," I say, catching her lips with my own.

"It's a proper challenge." There's laughter and happiness in her voice, breathless in between kisses. "But you love a challenge."

I kiss her back. "I do. And you just happen to be my favorite one."

26

SKYE

Two months later

I wake up to sunlight and an empty bed. Groaning, I roll over, but Cole's side is cold. He's been up for a while already. "Damn it," I murmur into his pillow. "You're too disciplined for your own good."

I contemplate staying in bed and falling back asleep. Despite the sun streaming in through the window, it's early still, not to mention it's a Saturday.

Rolling over, I find myself face to face with the pile of books on his bedside table. There's a few new additions, courtesy of me. I smile at the one on the top. He's going to love that one—it's a fast-paced psychological thriller.

Reluctantly, I get out of bed and pull on one of the fluffy robes from the cupboard in his giant bathroom. When I'd asked if anyone else had used them, he'd looked surprised. *I have bathrobes?* He hadn't been joking when he said he spent very few waking hours in this apartment.

As expected, he's not in the living room or in the kitchen. The door to his home office is ajar, but it's empty. There's only one place he can be.

"Fine," I say, heading into his bedroom again, to the drawer he's dedicated to me. "You win. I'll join you."

Fifteen minutes later, I walk into the Amena's indoor pool, the scent of chlorine faint but unmistakable. There's only one person in the water. I wrap my towel firmly around myself and sit down on one of the poolside benches.

I've watched him swim half a dozen times now, but it's still a thrill. He cleaves through the water like it's silk. Arms and shoulders emerge out of the turquoise water, his forward crawl the fastest of his swimming styles. When he reaches the end, he flips underwater and pushes off from the wall, shooting like a lightning bolt.

Seeing him like this, it's not hard to understand why his body is shaped the way it is. Strong, lean muscle mass. Wide shoulders and a muscled back. Powerful legs. I watch him swim shamelessly.

Cole spots me during one of his turns, and without pause, he changes direction. He pulls himself out of the pool right next to me.

"No," I warn, watching him advance. "No, no, Cole, stop!"

He shakes his hair at me like a dog, cold drops of water hitting my skin. I try to dance away but he catches me around the waist. Laughing, he tugs at my towel. "Here for your lesson?"

"Yes, but now I've changed my mind."

"Oh no you haven't. Come on, coward. Get in." His skin is wet and droplets cling to his eyelashes, his hair sleek on his head. It's impossible to feign anger at him when he's grinning like that, so handsome it hurts.

"One day I'll snap, you know. I'll never swim with you again."

"Sure you won't." He slides into the water next to me and rolls his eyes as I frown at the temperature. It's only bad for the first minute, and yet, every time is a struggle.

Under the surface, his hands close around my waist. "I'm glad you finally woke up."

"You could have woken me when you left, you know. I wouldn't have minded."

"You were sleeping so soundly." He glances down, a wicked spark in his eyes. "Wow. You really do find the water cold, don't you?"

"Yes, I—" He flicks one of my hardened nipples and I gasp. "Not here!"

"We're alone," he says, bending to kiss my cheek. "We're always alone at this hour."

I wrap my arms around his neck and press my chest to his—no more access. He carries me through the water, his body strong and hard against mine. "You insist on doing this on weekend mornings too, huh?"

"I was in the water two hours later than usual today," he muses. "Because of you."

I rest my head against his shoulder. "That's okay. You're not swimming for competitions or tryouts anymore. You're allowed to relax."

His hands tighten around my thighs, moving us gradually into the deeper section. "Discipline is everything," he says. "My father taught me that. Manners maketh man, they say, but that's wrong. It's habits."

He tips my head back and kisses me, soft, searching, gentle. His lips taste clean and warm. "And you're destroying mine, Skye."

My smile is crooked. "I'm not going to apologize for that, you know."

"I'd never ask you to."

I kiss him again, and he stops walking, my body molding to his. Sweetness turns to heat, softness to pressure, and by the time I break away I'm breathing heavily.

So is Cole, his eyes dark.

I clear my throat. "Guess what?"

"You've abandoned your swimming lesson? That's all right. Your instructor agrees."

I laugh. "No. I've decided to turn the novella about the bookstore into a full-length novel."

"You have?"

"Yes. It has all the right ingredients." I lean back, dipping my hair into the water. "Even if no one wants to read it."

"False modesty is a sin, you know."

I smile up at the vaulted ceiling and float in the water, supported by his arms. "You're right. I'll stop."

"Brooks & King wants the first chapters next week, right?"

"Yes." Hearing him say it sends shivers down my arms, even though it's been weeks since I'd received the phone call. They'd loved my query letter and said they'd looked forward to reading the finished product.

"I wrote an article too," I say.

"You did?"

"Yes. About the renovation of Between the Pages, and about Eleanor. If I can make it interesting enough, maybe I can build some hype for the reopening."

Cole laughs and the sound makes me smile. "Baby, the opening is *months* away. We just broke ground on the hotel!"

"So I'm just a tiny bit excited," I say teasingly. "Is that a crime?"

He wiggles his fingers, tickling my sides, and I struggle fruitlessly to break free. "Cole!"

"No, it's not a crime." He kisses me swiftly before releasing me, pulling away with a leisurely backstroke. "Blair texted earlier. She wants us three to go out to dinner tonight. She says she still hasn't met you properly."

"I've met her three times!"

"Yes, but apparently meeting someone properly has to include dinner. Who knew?"

I swim after him. "Of course I want to go. Your sister is awesome."

"That's what I thought you'd say," Cole says morosely. "I've been replaced."

I splash him, and he looks at me accusingly. "Terrorist."

"Vandal," I counter.

"*Vandal?*"

"Yes. Did you think I wouldn't notice the rip in my panties last night? They were brand new, too. All lace."

His smile is wolfish. "I have no regrets."

"Brute," I say. "Never stop."

"I won't."

I swim after him, the temperature of the water perfect now. "I don't have any going-out clothes here at yours. I'll have to stop by mine before we meet up with her."

Cole dives clean under the surface and I watch as he clears the distance between us easily, strong arms working.

He emerges right in front of me. "Just move in with me already," he says. "You're here practically every night. It's going to happen, you know. It's only a matter of time."

"You'd go insane," I tease. "There'd be hair ties everywhere. Can you imagine?" It's not the first time he's suggested moving in together, always jokingly, and I've always responded in turn. We've only been dating properly for two months, after all.

"For you, I'd endure endless hair ties."

"How chivalrous." I turn on my back, floating in the water. "Maybe you should invite Nick along tonight. They like each other, don't they?"

"Absolutely not."

"No?"

"They hate each other," Cole says happily. "I've tried to get them to see eye-to-eye for a decade, and trust me, it's not going to happen."

I frown at him. *Hate* is not the feeling I'd picked up the one time I'd seen them interact. "Are you sure?"

"Yes. Now come on, baby. You're stalling." Cole grabs his swim goggles from the edge of the pool. "Do you want these?"

"Yes." I swim after him, mentally steeling myself. Cole's been teaching me how to forward crawl, and though I'd felt clumsy in the beginning, I'm improving with every practice. I doubt I'll ever have his powerful grace doing it, but I'm willing to try.

Cole smiles at me as he puts my goggles on. "Give me at least ten laps before we go to brunch."

"Fifteen," I say.

He grins and pushes off the edge of the pool. "Fifteen, then. Have I ever told you how much I love your competitive nature?"

"Yes. You've also cursed it, pretty frequently." Like when I protested about the obscene amounts of money he spends on me. Dinners, excursions, a few beautiful dresses…

Cole winks at me. "Whatever I say, don't stop. I love it."

My insides warm. I love *it*, he'd said, but my mind is already racing ahead. To the day we'll say those three little words to each other. I know we're not there yet, but it's been dancing on the tip of my tongue for days, the feeling overwhelming. It won't be long.

"Come on now," he says. "I want to see you swim."

So I push off and follow him across the deep.

EPILOGUE

Cole, a year and a half later

Skye smiles and pushes back her hair, accepting the huge bouquet given to her. "Thank you," she says, though I'm too far away to hear the words. I'm familiar enough with her lips to read them without effort.

She's wearing the floral dress I'd bought her. I'd seen it walking by a high-end store and picked it up without much fuss —simply because I wanted to see it on her. I'd known the silken fabric would look amazing on her, and I'd been right. It shines in the low bookstore lighting.

Skye had argued against the purchase, of course, as she so often does. *You can't spend this kind of money on me, Cole.*

It's taken me a lot of effort to meet those arguments with logic and understanding. Now, nearly two years into our relationship, she's much better at accepting it. I have more money than I would need if I lived a hundred lifetimes. A nice restaurant for dinner makes the both of us happy; a beautiful gift is something I enjoy getting for her. The point of working so hard, after all, has always been to one day enjoy the fruits of that labor. And there's no one I want to enjoy it with more than her.

Karli breaks me out of my musings, stopping at my side. "She's earned this," she says, both of us watching as someone asks Skye to sign a book. The pride in her voice echoes mine.

"She certainly has," I say warmly.

"The renovation of Between the Pages turned out beautifully," she says softly. "I never doubted you, nor Skye. And still… this is better than my wildest dreams." She sweeps an arm out at the expanded space. More little nooks and crannies have been added. Nearly every section has been enlarged. And yet, the original structure and the old-fashioned charm is intact. The old spiral staircase remains, and in the corner stands a ratty armchair. Antique beams have been installed, and books surround us like trees in a forest.

"I'm glad you approve," I say smoothly. "And you know you're welcome to take back the operational role if you ever want it."

Karli gives a little laugh. "Thank you. I appreciate it, but I doubt that. I'm enjoying my new job too much."

"Good," I say. "Because you're about to get busy."

"I am?"

"My company regularly has meetings and events where we need baked goods. I gave the name of your new bakery to my head of planning. Expect a call this week."

Karli's eyes widen. "Cole, I couldn't ask that of you. It's too much."

"You're not asking, I'm offering. Besides," I say with a wink, "Skye has brought me some of your cupcakes. I'm doing my own employees a favor here."

Karli swallows. "Thanks."

"Don't mention it."

"No, I have to. And thank you for this," she says in a low voice. "For the bookstore, for Skye… for making her happy. For all of it."

"I won't say you're welcome to that," I say firmly. "Not when it's so clearly benefitted me too."

"Right," Karli notes. "The hotel."

But that's not what I'd meant at all. "No, although that too. I meant Skye."

"You're good for each other," she says. "Will you excuse me for a moment? I want to check on the caterers. I *think* I just saw a tray of unpowdered beignets being served…"

I can't help smiling. "Of course, go ahead."

"Thanks…" She's already heading off, pushing through the throngs of customers. Above us, the Skye Hotel stretches ten stories tall. Between the Pages set the tone for the decor, all dark tones and Old European furniture. It's comfort and culture all rolled into one.

Skye had protested at first. *You can't name the hotel after me!* But it was a stellar name, and I loved seeing it on all my documents. And after I'd proposed it to my team… well, it took on a life of its own. Soon, I couldn't change it even if I wanted to—and I certainly didn't.

I turn back to watch her talk to a customer, happiness clear in her features. This is a day she's earned. Becoming co-owner of the newly re-opened Between the Pages has done her good.

So has the release of her debut novel.

Maybe she feels me looking at her, or maybe her eyes roam of their own accord… but she sees me standing in the wings.

A smile lights up her face. It's a private one, meant just for me, and it's filled with intimacy. I watch as she excuses herself and a few seconds later she's in my arms. "You're here."

"Of course I am."

She glances back at the line, at the crowd. "Can you believe this?"

"Yes," I say. "It's a fantastic book, Skye. *They* see it. That's what they're here for."

"Not to mention Brooks & King pulled out all the stops for this launch party," she says archly, but her eyes dance. "I can't believe I'm having a book reading of my own."

"Are you nervous?"

"Yes. I'd have to be dead not to be."

I kiss her, reassuring, warm. "You're going to knock them dead, baby."

Her hands flex around my shoulders. In the dim light, her engagement ring glitters. "Thank you."

"And as soon as you're done you'll be drinking champagne, a celebrated author, basking in people's congratulations."

She rolls her eyes. "Just what I wrote the book for."

"Sarcasm is the lowest form of wit, they say." I bend down further, my lips against her ear. "But I love it when you use it."

I can feel Skye's smile against my skin. "I hate you," she says.

"Yes, that's it."

She leans into my side and I wrap my arm around her waist, pulling her into my body. "I'm so proud of you. Now go out there and kick ass."

And she does. I stand in the back, watching as she takes a seat on the impromptu stage. Edwin Taylor clears his throat into the mic, and the crowd quiets. "We're here today to listen to Skye Holland, our newest author, read an excerpt from her debut novel. But first—what inspired you to write this novel?"

Skye's answer is lengthy, and personal, and I watch several people dab at their eyes. Eleanor's dream became her dream, and with it, the bookstore. Her eyes flicker to Karli in the front row.

She reads a passage from the book to rapt silence. It's an excerpt I've heard many times before—she's been practicing this reading with me as her audience—and still... I want to burst with pride.

She accomplished her dream, and I know it's only the beginning.

I join in on the feverish applause as she finishes up. Her smile, shy and proud at the same time, makes me ache inside. Hard to believe she's all mine, sometimes.

"Cole!" Timmy pushes his way through the crowd to me. "There you are!"

I pull him in for a half-hug. "Man, you get taller every time I see you."

He straightens a bit. "I know. I'm getting faster, too. Yesterday at practice I managed to get *two* home runs."

"Really?"

"Yeah. I had to tell you."

"That's impressive." I put a hand on his shoulder and he beams up at me. Two years with Skye has also meant two years with her family, and while Isla and I still don't see eye to eye, Timmy is mine to the bone.

"We're still going to the game on Saturday, right? You and me?"

"Wouldn't miss it for the world," I say. Timmy and I go to most games by ourselves now. Skye joins occasionally, but she's just as happy to send us off for what she calls "guy time." I don't mind at all. In fact, I'm currently in talks with the team to organize a meet-and-greet with the players for Timmy's birthday.

Isla joins her son and shoots me a polite smile. She shares Skye's brown hair and hazel eyes, but she wears the features so differently that they hardly look related. "This is beautiful, what you've done for Skye," she says.

"Thanks," I respond, "but she wrote the book by herself. Got it published herself, too."

Isla smiles, but there's a glint in her eye that tells me she's not convinced. I swallow my anger and look for Skye in the crowd again. She's glowing. As the months have gone on, she's learned to tune out her older sister's negative energy. As for myself, I only grow more and more incensed by it.

"Oh, I'm sure," Isla says. "She's worked very hard. But then again, having you as a boyfriend certainly can't hurt."

She says it with a wink, but there's nothing humorous about the implication. As Skye's success has bloomed, Isla's little comments have grown in rancor. "Fiancé," I correct. "And if I've given anything, it's only been moral support."

Isla snorts good-naturedly, but it doesn't fool me. She's not convinced. I leave her behind in search of my fiancée, finding her halfway through her first glass of champagne and with a beautiful flush of excitement on her cheeks. I slide an arm around her waist. "The reading went so well."

"It did, didn't it?" In her heels and her sleek dress, she's somehow professional and irresistible at the same time. It reminds me of how she'd looked at Legacy, the first time I'd seen her. Mysterious and alluring. "I've signed so many books, too. Do you want your own copy?" she asks, eyes glittering. "Who should I make it out to?"

"Dear stud," I say.

"Oh, of course. I can't believe I even needed to ask."

"I forgive you," I say. "I'll accept 'to my future husband,' too."

"I like the sound of that." She stands on her tiptoes, pressing a soft kiss to my lips. "Should we head to dinner soon? I don't want to keep Blair and your mom waiting."

"We can go now," I say. "Do you feel finished here?"

"I do. I'm not sure how much more attention I can take." Her voice is playful, but the sentiment is genuine. Being the center of attention—having a function revolve entirely around you—is tiring as hell. I'd know.

I take her hand in mine. "Then come on, baby. Let's get out of here."

We make our way out of Between the Pages and the Skye Hotel, out to where Charles is waiting with the car. I open the door for her and she slides into the backseat. Charles gives her a warm hello, shooting me an excited smile. He's in on the surprise.

"I've gained a whole new appreciation for you tonight," Skye says.

"You have?"

"Yes. For handling all those press conferences and interviews without breaking a sweat."

"Well, I've had a fair bit of practice." Reaching over, I put a hand on her knee. "And I hope you're not completely worn out. We're making a surprise stop before dinner. I have something to show you."

"You do?" Her eyes instantly alight with mischief, a smile on her lips. I press a kiss to her temple. Two years in, and those eyes still get me going.

"Just something to celebrate my author wife."

"Author fiancée," she corrects. "We're not married yet."

"Because *someone* can't decide on a venue."

She tugs at my arm, mock outrage in her voice. "Try finding a place that will fit two hundred people and still feel intimate."

"I would be happy eloping," I say. "I've said that since the beginning."

Skye rolls her eyes at me, scooting over until she can rest a hand on my thigh. "You say that, but then I ask you about guests, and you rattle off a list a mile long. I know what you're doing, you know."

"What am I doing?"

"Using our wedding as a chance to network. It's like you're giving out favors to people, because you know they'll appreciate being invited, and they'll inevitably be more positive to your developments because of it."

I open my mouth to argue, but what she's saying is too spot on. Skye grins in triumph. "See? And I don't object, but that means I'm inviting a dozen authors and half the publishers in Seattle."

I wrap an arm around her. "Have I told you lately that I love you?"

"No," she lies. "Tell me again."

I murmur it against her ear. "I love you."

"I love you too. Will you please tell me where we're going now?"

"Good try, but no."

"Torturing someone with suspense isn't a very loving thing to do."

I laugh, my hand tightening around her waist. "You're not the least bit tortured."

"Perhaps I'm just good at keeping it all inside."

Her hair smells like flowers underneath my lips. "You did well tonight. I'm so proud of you. The bookstore. The *book*. The reading. You're born for this, baby."

She's quiet for a few moments before she murmurs "thank you" into my neck. It's muffled with emotion, and *this*, this right here is what I love the most with Skye. It's always real between us. Every word, every touch. Not once have I had to wonder if she cares about me, and I've done my best to make sure she never wonders it about me.

Trust. Communication. Love.

All the things I never had in previous relationships. Experiencing it with Skye now, it's obvious how false my last one had been. To believe I'd ever missed Elena!

"You know," I say, "If I were to meet Ben now, I'd shake his hand in thanks."

She turns to look up at me. "You would?"

"Without hesitation," I say. "He helped pave my way to you."

Skye's mouth drops open slightly, her gaze locked on mine. She's speechless. I'd smile at the sight if I wasn't knocked over by the emotion in her eyes.

"Oh, Cole," she murmurs. "I love you so much."

I clear my throat and look past her, at the driveway we're turning onto. The large gate swings open on our approach. It diffuses the moment, and I'm glad of that, because this conversation has drifted into territory I'd rather not have Charles exploring with us.

"We're here," I say softly.

Charles parks the car in front of a large porch. The house is three stories tall, the facade white brick and ivy. Skye climbs out of the car before I can open her door, eyes wide. Artfully placed lights illuminate the beautiful brick inlays. "What's this?"

"It's a house," I say.

"I can see that, silly. Who lives here?"

"No one, currently. What do you think?"

"It's beautiful. There's so much charm." She runs her hand through the little pealing fountain in the center of the driveway. "There are lights on inside. Are you sure no one lives here?"

"Positive." I take her hand in mine and pull her along up the stairs. "Do you want to look inside?"

"Can we? Cole, what is this place really?"

"It's a suggestion." I open the front door wide for her. Charles had prepped the place before, and there are lanterns everywhere, all filled with burning candles. The lights line the double staircases. They illuminate a large living room. Even devoid of furniture, it's easy to picture the place filled with life and love.

Skye walks ahead of me. Her silk dress shimmers in the candlelight, her hair a waterfall down her back. "Oh my God. It's magnificent."

I put my hands in my pockets and follow her as she explores the bottom floor. "It's spacious," I say. "Has a great view, too."

She stops dead in the living room. "Oh, look at this fireplace. It's massive."

"There's two, actually. The master bedroom has one as well."

"Oh, and look at all these built-in bookshelves!"

"Let me show you the best part." Grabbing her hand in mine again, I lead her onto the back porch. It opens up onto a wide lawn and beyond it, the million-dollar view over Puget Sound.

"Oh my God, Cole."

"Beautiful, right?"

"Yes." I wrap my arms around her waist, resting my head atop hers. For a few moments, both of us stand in silence, taking in the view. "I've bought it," I say finally. "What do you think?"

"I think you're insane."

"Good insane, or bad insane?"

"A bit of both."

I run my hand over her hip. "It's okay if you don't like it. We can find someplace else. I can rent it out or sell it."

"Don't you dare sell it," she says. "Oh Cole, it's too much."

I tug her firmly against me. "Of course it's not. We're getting *married*, Skye. We need a house together. One filled with knickknacks and books and all the refrigerator magnets you like."

"No minimalism?"

"Nope. I've left that behind."

"And no fake fruit?"

I snort. "None at all."

"Good." She relaxes against me, her hand on top of mine. "And maybe a few kids one day?"

The tentative hope in her voice makes me smile. Before her, children had felt so distant. As had buying a house. But here with her, in this place, with my ring on her finger... I can't wait. "Yes," I say. "As many as you want."

"Good. We need drawings, you know, for all the refrigerator magnets."

"Right, of course. What else are kids for?"

Her sigh is one of pure happiness. "And so they lived happily ever after for the rest of their days..."

I laugh, turning her around in my arms so I can see her eyes. They blaze with joy. "Are you narrating our life?"

"Perhaps. You're marrying a writer, you know."

"Oh, I know." I tip her head back to close the distance between us. "And I am very glad you came to Legacy that night to do research."

Her words are a soft whisper against my lips. "Not as happy as I am."

"Oh? Want to bet?"

"Sure, but you know what happens when you make deals with me."

My smile is wide. "You win, I know. But somehow I like that even more than myself winning. Funny, that."

"Love," she says softly. "It's called love. And that's a wager we both won."

Want more Cole and Skye?

I couldn't quite let them go... so I wrote a 7500-word bonus story that takes place the week leading up to their wedding!

Join my newsletter to receive the story for free. Warning: contains lots of banter, fluff and steam. There is a bathtub involved.

THE STORY CONTINUES

Billion Dollar Beast follows Blair as she reluctantly agrees to work for Nick, her brother's best friend and the man who's disliked her for years.

At least she hates him right back.

He has the worst reputation in the city, not to mention he's made his opinions about her perfectly clear.

Working together will be difficult, sure. But Blair never expected it to be so passionate…

Grab **Billion Dollar Beast** now or read on for the first chapter!

CHAPTER 1
BLAIR

I'm at a wedding out of state when I'm confronted with my worst enemy. I spot him before he spots me: across the crowded reception hall, wearing a suit disdainfully, like he wants to shrug it off and transform into the brute he is inside.

Enemy might be too tame a word. *Nightmare* is a much better description. For a people-pleaser like me, he's a personal affront. I've tried to make him my friend for near on a decade and I've failed for just as long.

He takes a sip of his brandy and sweeps a dark gaze over the guests. I'll be noticed any second now. How had I not known he'd been invited to this wedding?

"Is that Nicholas Park?" Maddie asks at my side, speaking his name with obvious relish. I wish I could say no. I want to tell her that his reputation isn't deserved, that he's not that special when you've seen him drunk and disheveled.

But that would be lying.

"Yes," I say, feeling like I'm confirming something far more than just his name. Because even drunk and disheveled, he's absolutely magnificent.

"Aren't you two friends?"

"He's my *brother's* friend."

Maddie's laughter is a bit too high-pitched. "Well, that's even better! You have to introduce me, Blair."

"I don't think so."

"Why not?" Her voice drops. "Is what they say of him true, then? Is it better to stay away?"

"I wouldn't know," I say, though I do. It's definitely better to stay away. I've been trying to for the better part of a decade, but like a bad rash, he keeps returning, and there are no over-the-counter remedies in sight.

"I've heard that he once burned down a club he owned, just to get the insurance money." Maddie's voice is vibrating with delight at the idea of Nick committing fraud. "I had no idea he'd be here today. Did you know he was invited?"

"No," I say honestly. "I had absolutely no idea. I can't imagine he knows either the bride *or* the groom."

I reach up to run a hand through my hair and glance casually around the room. Nick is leisurely strolling through the throng of people with his glass in hand. Despite his suit, he looks out of place amongst the mingling guests in brightly colored dresses and dark tuxes—like a fox in a hen house. Who'd left the gate unlocked?

"Introduce me, Blair," Maddie urges again. "Come on."

And before I can protest, her hand is on my arm and I'm pulled forward on my heels. They dip into the grass with every step I take.

Nick sees us approach, his eyes flitting past Maddie to bore into mine.

Dark, so dark, and not a hint of amusement in them. His lips grow thinner, the rough cut of his jawline working once. So he hadn't expected to see me here, either.

"Blair," he says. The gravel in his voice is no surprise to me, but it still makes my stomach tight with nerves.

"Nick."

Beside me, Maddie preens. I clear my throat. "This is Madeleine Bishop. She's a friend from college. We both know the bride."

She extends her hand and Nick gives it a brief shake, face impassive.

"A pleasure," she says smoothly. It's her flirting voice—I recognize it from our partying days.

Nick doesn't acknowledge it. He nods to the bar behind us instead. "The groom was on the thirty under thirty list in *Forbes*, but can't shell for an open bar?"

Maddie laughs, like he's being unbelievably clever. I cross my arms over my chest. "So you know the groom?"

"That's not what I said."

"So you're here on the bride's invitation?"

His eyes flit back to mine. "Wouldn't you like to know?" he asks. "But I think I'll keep you guessing. Ladies, it's been a pleasure."

And then he strides off toward the bar without a second glance. Beside me, Maddie turns to me with incredulous eyes. "*Wow,*" she breathes. "You weren't kidding. You two really aren't friends."

"That's what I said," I say tersely, running a hand over my hair again. It shouldn't be a sore subject. It's been years, after all, since my big brother befriended Nicholas Park. And still, his dislike of me stings like salt in a never-closing wound.

Maddie takes the hint. "Let's ignore him altogether," she says. "They're dividing guests into teams. Come on, let's join."

I take another sip of my champagne and give her a bright smile. We're at a wedding. We're here to celebrate love and life and happiness. The sun is shining. It shouldn't be difficult to put Nicholas Park out of my mind.

"Let's," I say.

But as it turns out, that's absolutely *impossible* to do when he refuses to stay out of sight. I'm standing in line for the cornhole toss when a shadow stalks in beside me. Like an electric current sliding over my skin, I know who it is before he speaks.

"Blair Porter, Seattle's top socialite, playing outdoor games."

I roll my neck and pretend to ignore the jab. I fail. "It's a time-honored sport. Besides, as a guest of the wedding party, you're supposed to attend all the wedding festivities."

"And I suppose you think I haven't?"

I squeeze my lips tight to prevent my words from spilling out. I manage restraint for a proud five seconds. "I hadn't seen you at any of the pre-ceremony events."

"Well, I've never been good at following rules."

"Why were you invited, anyway? Who do you really know here?"

He raises a dark eyebrow. "Such skepticism, Blair. Don't you think I have friends?" The mocking tone in his voice makes it clear that the question is rhetorical. I answer it regardless.

"Other than my brother? No."

He steps up beside me. Somewhere from the corner of my eye, I see Maddie slink back in line, abandoning me to my new partner. Damn.

Nick doesn't answer my question. "This is a wedding to be seen at," he says smoothly. "Have you seen how many photographers they've hired? Why do you think *you* were invited?"

My stomach churns at the question. Becca and I had been friends in college... Sure, we hadn't spoken much since, but I hadn't thought twice about accepting the invitation to her wedding.

"You're saying I'm a trophy guest." I speak the words harshly, like they don't offend me.

Nick raises an eyebrow. The sharp sunlight throws his rough features into relief. "Tell me Cole wasn't invited as well."

Bending down to pick up a corn-bag, I weigh it in my hand, refusing to answer his taunt.

Nick's voice is satisfied. "He was, then. But he didn't come."

"He couldn't," I say, hating how defensive the words sound. At the time, it didn't seem odd that Becca had invited my billionaire big brother. I'd thought it a kindness. How had I been so stupid?

If Nick sees my realization, he doesn't acknowledge it. He

unbuttons the clasp of his gray suit jacket instead, a smirk on his lips. He must be aware of the way the other guests are watching him. Watching us.

"Is that why you were invited too? For the press and prestige?"

Nick's chuckle isn't amused. He understands the words as I'd meant them—having him attend an event made it noteworthy, but not always in a particularly good way. If my brother is seen as a powerful businessman, Nick is the unscrupulous one.

"We're up," he says instead, voice like crushed glass. "Don't miss."

And of course I do. Despite my aim, there's no scoring after his words. The opposing teams cheers, high-fiving each other.

When I turn to Nick, his lip is curled. "I told you not to."

"I didn't know I needed advice."

"It couldn't hurt."

I grit my teeth against the annoyance that rises up inside me. I'm a happy person. I like to smile and converse and make people happy. It's what I'm good at, damn it. And somehow Nicholas Park *always* makes me forget that.

No longer. I give him a blinding smile. Judging by the faint widening of his eyes, it wasn't what he'd been expecting.

"Here, why don't *you* throw the next one."

He accepts the corn-bag I hand him with suspicious eyes. "I see," he says. And that's all he says, even as he lines himself up, focusing on the cornhole. Tall and muscular, with wide shoulders, he's an imposing figure. Always has been.

He throws. It flies in an arc through the air and lands solidly in the hole. I don't look him in the eyes—I turn away instead, but I don't head to the back of the line.

Nick follows me towards the bar.

"What are you doing?"

"I'm participating in the wedding activities. I was recently told that I wasn't being a good guest."

"Why are you really here?"

His gaze fastens on something in the distance. I'm left staring up at the column of his throat, the rough-hewn features that have held me captive for ages.

"Nick, I—"

"Shh."

"Did you just shush me?"

He looks down at me, speculation in his gaze. His words come quickly. "Pretend you like me for fifteen minutes."

I blink at him. "Fifteen minutes?"

"I know it's a rather long time frame," he grinds out, "but yes, fifteen minutes."

"No one's that good an actress," I mutter. He rolls his eyes at my words.

And then Nick does the most amazing thing. He puts a hand on my low back, like it belongs there, as if he touches me all the time—as if this isn't the first time we've touched since we shook hands eight years ago.

He bends down. "Look up at me," he instructs. "Laugh as if you enjoy talking to me."

"Why?" I hiss back.

Brief hesitation. "I'll owe you one."

"Whatever I want?"

Longer hesitation this time. "Within reason, yes."

I turn on my biggest smile, then. The one that stretches wide and reaches my eyes. It's my killer mingling smile, the one I only pull out when I really need to pack a punch. "Fifteen minutes," I say, batting my eyelashes. "Start the timer."

Nick blinks once. Twice. Then he gives a subtle nod to a few men standing not too far from us, drinks in hand.

"See the one with glasses?"

"Yes."

His hand drifts higher, flattening against my back. The touch is warm even through the fabric of my dress. "I'm going to talk to him, and I want you by my side as I do."

"Pretending to like you."

"Yes."

"Why?"

"Need to know basis, honey," he says sweetly. The endearment sounds mocking from him.

"All right, sugar muffin," I respond just as tartly. "Fourteen minutes left."

He grits his teeth audibly at that.

The men look up as we approach, their conversation abruptly dying.

"Mr. Park," the man in glasses says. His tone is cold. "I didn't know you'd be here."

"Last-minute invite," Nick says, an odd tone in his voice. Is that… gentleness? He must be trying to win points here somehow. "This is Blair Porter."

I extend a hand, still smiling widely. "A pleasure to meet you all."

They introduce themselves. "I've met your brother a few times," the man in glasses—Mr. Adams—says. "Lovely guy."

I resist the urge to glance at Nick. So that's why I'm here, smiling at him. He's using me in all of my trophy invitedness. "Yes, he is," I say, leaning into Nick's side. "Despite being friends with this one."

They laugh at my joke and Nick is forced to join in. The pressure of his hand on my back increases in a not so subtle warning to behave. *Idiot*, I think. *I just made you look more likeable.*

"That's right," Nick says. "We've known each other for what, eight years now, Blair?"

"Something like that," I say.

The shorter of the three men smiles at me. "I hope you'll stay long enough to meet my wife. She's around here somewhere, and she reads every style interview you give."

"That's lovely," I say warmly. "I'd love to meet her."

Nick clears his throat and I tear my gaze away to look up at him expectantly, forcing friendliness into my gaze.

"Enjoying the time away from Seattle?" Nick's question is

open-ended, but his entire body language is focused on Mr. Adams. *Subtle,* I think, wondering how Nick would react to my hand on his back in warning.

"I am, yes," Mr. Adams says. "Some time away can be good. Clears the head."

Nick nods gravely. "Lends itself to making excellent decisions."

"This is not the place to discuss business," Mr. Adams retorts. The two men at his side both look away, clearly uncomfortable with the turn of conversation. Nick is tense beside me.

This won't do.

I put a hand on his arm affectionately, looking over at Mr. Adams with a smile. "Even at a wedding," I say, making my voice light. "Can you believe it? It's impossible to get this guy to relax!"

Nick sighs. "About as impossible as you walking past a store without purchasing anything."

"Well, we all have our vices," I tease, my wide smile still in place. "I'm sorry we bothered you."

"Not at all," Mr. Adams says. "It was a pleasure to meet you, Miss Porter."

"Likewise."

The three men stroll on, leaving Nick and I to revel in our peaceful, friendly bliss. I hit his arm.

"What the hell was that for?"

"You call me a trophy guest, someone invited here for appearance's sake, and then you use me in just the same way?"

There's no remorse or denial in Nick's eyes. Just sly calculation. "You did well."

"I was coerced."

"No, you weren't. Now I owe you one." He speaks the words with obvious distaste.

I put my hands on my hips. "So you're what? Trying to take over his company? Buy out his board? Tank his stocks?"

Nick narrows his eyes at me. "You don't need to know," he says, articulating every word.

I flick my hair over my shoulder and feel a faint sense of triumph as his eyes track the movement. "Well, that was the first and last time you use my name to boost your reputation."

"Trust me, it's *definitely* the last time." He takes a sip of his drink and mutters something that sounds an awful lot like *not worth it*.

I shake my head at him and start to head back to the festivities, to people who actually enjoy having me around.

"Running back to your sycophant friends?" he throws after me.

"Don't you have a hostile takeover to plan?"

His crooked grin is wolfish. "Good idea," he says. "I heard a few of the bridesmaids are single…"

"Oh, screw you."

"Are you offering? I don't think your fifteen minutes are entirely up yet."

"You wish," I hiss, retreating across the lawn before he has a chance to answer. How much easier my life would be if my brother hadn't decided to become best friends with the least friendly man on the planet. Infuriating, maddening, and absolutely impossible to ignore.

I remember the first time I'd seen him. It had been nearly a decade ago, when he'd stalked into the restaurant together with my brother for dinner. I'd had no advance warning that my brother's friend would be joining us. That was Cole's way, sometimes, especially in those days—he did what pleased him, like a bulldozer or a rocket. You could either stand in his way and get crushed, or adapt to his speed. Over the years, I've gotten very good at adapting.

Nick had worn their college jersey, ironically, like it was beneath him. I'd never seen a man who moved like he did—he walked like a street fighter.

He'd joined our table with a perfunctory nod to me.

"This is Nicholas Park," my brother had said, flipping open the menu. "We're seniors together."

"A pleasure to meet you," I said, extending a hand. He'd looked at it once before he shook it. I remember that clearly—his brief hesitation.

That's when I'd felt the scars on the inside of his palm. Faint, but raised, and unmistakable. The surprise in my gaze must have been easy for him to read. He'd withdrawn his hand and opened his menu.

And that had been that. I'd been too intimidated—too impressed, to be honest—to speak much during that dinner. The next time Cole and I were alone, I'd peppered him with questions about Nick. I'd done it with an air of impetuousness, and he'd rolled his eyes at his annoying little sister and all her questions. He'd never realized that my inquiries came from a place of burning curiosity and genuine interest.

Because handsome was far too tame a word for Nicholas Park. There was a slight crook to his nose that gave his face character; his black hair was cut too short to be fashionable. And yet, the olive tone to his skin, the dark of his eyes, the wildness in his jaw…

I'd been struck.

And then he'd struck me.

Oh, not like that, of course. But his verbal spear had found its mark just the same. That damn party and that damn poker game. Even recalling it eight years later, it makes my cheeks burn with indignity. Anger. The way he'd turned me down with a tone of voice that was so cold it burned.

He'd been playing poker. The room was smoke-filled, the air heavy, the tension around the table high. I'd walked straight in. It had been foolish—I can admit that much in retrospect. I barely knew anyone at the table; Walker was the older brother of one of my childhood friends, and our fathers worked together. But the rest were strangers.

Apart from Nick.

He'd seen me when I'd walked in. His eyes had met mine for a few seconds and then he'd refocused on his cards like I was nothing at all. There hadn't even been a hint of recognition in his eyes.

That should have been a sign, really. But I'd had two and a half glasses of wine and I was heady with nerves and excitement. Nick was here at this party, without my brother in tow. We'd already been introduced. I was his best friend's little sister.

It was time he saw me as something other than that.

So I planned on joining the game with a couple of hundred bucks to my name. It was a lot, and I was reluctant to risk it, but my reluctance was worn thin by the memory of Nick's sharp-edged jaw.

I was brave-verging-on-stupid.

I stopped next to Nick, almost leaning on his chair. He didn't acknowledge me.

"Good game?" I asked.

"Can't tell until it's over," he'd responded. A few of the guys around the table had smiled at that, like the answer was obvious, like I'd been a fool for asking.

That didn't dissuade twenty-one-year-old me. "Deal me in? I have the cash."

At that, Nick had actually put down his cards. The other guys were looking at me then. Some with interest in their eyes—one of them ran his gaze up my form in a way that was nothing short of lewd.

Nick met my gaze. The eyes gave me no quarter, offered no mercy. They were dark like coal and just as fiery.

"This isn't a game for little girls," he said. "Run back to your friends now."

Maybe it would have been okay if he'd said it as a joke. If there had been a teasing note to his voice, a bit of irony. Perhaps even anger—I'd know what to do with that. But the cold civility in his tone shocked me to my core. It was a dismissal. I wasn't used to being dismissed.

That was the first time I'd reached out to Nick in the hopes of being friends, and it was the first time he rejected me out of hand.

But it wouldn't be the last.

———

Read on in Billion Dollar Beast.

OTHER BOOKS BY OLIVIA
LISTED IN READING ORDER

New York Billionaires Series

Think Outside the Boss
Tristan and Freddie

Saved by the Boss
Anthony and Summer

Say Yes to the Boss
Victor and Cecilia

A Ticking Time Boss
Carter and Audrey

Seattle Billionaires Series

Billion Dollar Enemy
Cole and Skye

Billion Dollar Beast
Nick and Blair

Billion Dollar Catch
Ethan and Bella

Billion Dollar Fiancé
Liam and Maddie

Brothers of Paradise Series

Rogue
Lily and Hayden

Ice Cold Boss
Faye and Henry

Red Hot Rebel
Ivy and Rhys

Small Town Hero
Jamie and Parker

Standalones

Arrogant Boss
Julian and Emily

Look But Don't Touch
Grant and Ada

The Billionaire Scrooge Next Door
Adam and Holly

ABOUT OLIVIA

Olivia loves billionaire heroes despite never having met one in person. Taking matters into her own hands, she creates them on the page instead. Stern, charming, cold or brooding, so far she's never met a (fictional) billionaire she didn't like.

Her favorite things include wide-shouldered heroes, late-night conversations, too-expensive wine and romances that lift you up.

Smart and sexy romance—those are her lead themes!

Join her newsletter for updates and bonus content.
www.oliviahayle.com.
Connect with Olivia

- facebook.com/authoroliviahayle
- instagram.com/oliviahayle
- goodreads.com/oliviahayle
- amazon.com/author/oliviahayle
- bookbub.com/profile/olivia-hayle